Also by Greg Barron

**HarperCollins** Publishers Australia

Rotten Gods
Savage Tide
Lethal Sky
Voodoo Dawn (short fiction)

**Stories of Oz** Publishing

The Hammer of Ramenskoye (short fiction)
Camp Leichhardt
Galloping Jones and Other True Stories from Australia's History
Whistler's Bones

# Red Jack
## and the
# Ragged
# Thirteen

by Greg Barron

First edition published 2019
by Stories of Oz Publishing
PO Box K57
Haymarket NSW 1240

ABN: 0920230558
facebook.com/storiesofoz
ozbookstore.com

ISBN: 978-0-6480627-7-6
Proof reading: Robert Barron
Cover design: James Barron
Cover photo: Catriona Martin
Typeset in Garamond by Stories of Oz
Printed and bound in Australia by IngramSpark
Red Jack motif by Indo the Artist

Dedicated to the memory of

Steve Flockton

This is the life you would

have lived, if you'd had the chance.

# Prologue: The Legend of Red Jack

They called her Red Jack, for her hair was as bright as an outback sunset, hanging to her waist from beneath a stained cattleman's hat. On her jet-black stallion, Mephistopheles, she roved the north, riding into towns and setting up camp, knocking up a rough set of yards where she would break horses, bring rested mounts back into work, and even train racehorses. A month or two later, she'd load her packhorses and move on.

Stockmen from Hughenden to Cloncurry, awed by her abilities in the saddle, whispered of how, as a young woman, flames set by an arsonist had consumed her house. Legend had it that her husband of three years and their two children were inside – babes she had birthed and hugged and nursed and loved through fever and colic.

When they brought out the blackened, charred bodies, so the story went, Red Jack collapsed to the ground. Two men carried her to her mother's house. For six weeks, they said, she lay cold and silent. Not once did she speak, her skin growing paler than white.

Then, one morning, Red Jack rose from her bed. She saddled Mephistopheles, and loaded two packhorses with every practical thing she owned. That day she commenced her wandering, breaking horses and hearts all the way; countless men bewildered by her beauty, skill and the folklore that followed as she passed through.

The legend of the house fire was the most common story, but front-bar chat had it that Red Jack's real name was Hannah, and that she hailed from the Darling Downs. Was it true? No one knew for sure. She was polite but would say nothing of herself. Neither confirm nor deny. One rumour held that Red Jack's husband had not died in a fire, but rather of gunshot wounds just a week after the wedding. Some reckoned it was an accident. Some said that Red Jack shot him. Others said that her wandering across Queensland and the Northern Territory was a manhunt for her husband's killer, and that when she found him she would tear his beating heart from his chest.

Whispers followed Red Jack wherever she went. Some called her Australia's greatest horse breaker. But to those who knew her, her cold beauty was so ethereal that she was no mortal woman, but a legend who walked the earth.

# Chapter 1: The Man at the Waterhole

Not far from where the Mataranka Pub stands today, upstream from the Bitter Springs, the Roper River broadens into a waterhole. Giant paperbarks crowd the banks, the spaces between pierced with blades of sun-lit pandanus. Archer fish dart here and there in the green water, and cormorants hunt deep, surfacing amongst the snags.

Back in the pioneering days this was a popular place to hobble out the plant and unroll a swag. There was a store nearby that doubled as a grog shanty. For those inclined to fish, black bream and catfish were plentiful – easy to catch and good tucker.

One afternoon, in the year 1885, Tom Nugent rode up fast from the south. He wasn't easily rattled as a rule, but he'd stumbled on a gang of ten horsemen back along the track, and wanted to steer clear of them. They were as heavily armed as any police patrol, and looked twice as dangerous. He urged his gelding into a trot, keeping that pace up, all the way to his planned night's camp.

Reaching the waterhole, Tom reined the gelding to a halt on the river sand. White men called this place Abraham's Billabong, after a labourer who'd worked on the Overland Telegraph line. It had Jangman and Mangarrayi names before that, of course, but Abraham's Billabong was the name Tom Nugent knew.

First he watered his pack horses and spares, then his gelding, leading him, with a loose grip on the bridle, to the lily-fringed edge of the hole. Tom's hands were gentle and caring, his soft words soothing. He was in his late thirties, tall and sun-browned, all muscle and sinew after a thousand-mile ride.

Tom was born in Maitland, in the Hunter Valley of New South Wales, baptised as Thomas Brian Nugent. His father James was, at that time, licensee of the Gordon Arms Hotel in Lochinvar. Tom, as a child, had wanted to be like the rough men who washed the dust from their throats at the pub, though he never quite understood why there was always so much dust to wash away, even when it rained.

When Tom was fourteen, already working on local cattle stations, his father went bankrupt, turning bitter with it. Just before Christmas 1867, James Nugent was charged with threatening to kill his wife. He probably would have done it, too, if nineteen-year-old Tom hadn't stood in his way.

Yet, the Hunter Valley was too small a canvas for a wild young man like Tom. At the age of twenty-two he rode north, seeking adventure in Queensland, in the days when the west of that state was just opening up.

Tom worked his way up to head stockman at Carandotta Station on the Georgina River. He was known for his horse-manship and calmness of manner when faced with anything from a rush to an angry piker, or even a rum-crazed ringer.

Cattle magnate John Costello hired Tom to establish Lake Nash station on the Territory/Queensland border. Tom droved the first herd of seven hundred breeders there from Carrawal in 1879. He could have stayed on as manager, but he was a drifter at heart.

He met up with the infamous Harry Readford, who had once stolen two thousand head of cattle and driven them to South Australia, inspiring the Captain Starlight character in Rolf

Boldrewood's novel, Robbery Under Arms. Tom and Harry joined forces for a cattle duffing jaunt or two, and remained the best of mates through thick and thin.

In fact, Tom and Harry Readford had shared this latest journey north together. With them on the trip was a lad from around Moree, who had run away from home. The lad and Readford himself had, just five days earlier, left Tom and headed for Brunette Downs on the Barkly.

Tom told Harry, on the day they parted. 'I've a hankering to join the Hall's Creek rush, before all the sparkle is panned from the gullies. No doubt I'll be back before long, with the arse out of my pants and ready for stock work.'

'No doubt,' agreed Harry. 'But if you do ride back this way, loaded down with gold, give me a shout and I'll help you spend it.'

Leading his gelding up from the water, Tom unsaddled, hobbled and night-belled him, letting him loose with the packs. He collected sticks for a fire and established his campsite on the waterhole's southern bank.

Thinking of the wild ten horsemen he had seen – men who may well be heading this way – he considered fetching his revolver, or squirt as stockmen called them, from his saddle bag before settling down. Yet, Tom wasn't in the habit of using guns on any man, black or white, so he decided against it.

With a small mug of whisky close at hand, Tom sat on a paperbark root near the fire and opened a volume of poetry written by an Australian called Henry Kendall. His favourite verse was called Song of the Cattle Hunters. He'd read it a hundred times or more, but it still quickened his pulse and warmed his heart.

> Down the ridges we fly, with a loud ringing cry,
> Down the ridges and gullies we go,
> And the cattle we hunt they are racing in front,
> With a roar like the thunder of waves ...

Tom was softly reading the words aloud, the stub of a cigar between the corners of his lips, when he heard the sound of hoofbeats. It was one man, riding fast, the rhythm changing where the waterhole sand began.

Down came a horseman, one of the biggest men Tom had ever seen. Twenty stone if he was an ounce, riding a stallion that matched him in stature. The whiskers of the rider's beard curled like a coir mat over his face from ear to ear and chest to nostrils. He carried a black Colt revolver in a holster at his waist, reining in when he saw Tom, towering over him, his mount's black chest like a cliff of veined muscle.

Tom recognised the bulky man as one of the ten riders he had seen earlier. Knowing instinctively that showing any weakness or fear would be a mistake, he barely moved, just flicked his eyes up from the pages of his book to the grizzled face of the rider.

'Good afternoon,' Tom said. 'You must be new to the bush. Riding up on a man's camp like that isn't the way things are done.'

The rider shrugged. 'I'm no new-chum. I just don't much care about the way things are done. I have my own ways and they work well enough.'

Tom took a handy twig from the fire and used the smouldering end to resuscitate his cigar, puffing with his lips until it was drawing well. 'You could at least tell me who the hell I'm talking to.'

'My name's Alexander McDonald, but men call me Sandy Myrtle. You might have heard of me?'

Tom thought for a moment, then shook his head. 'No. Can't say that I have.'

The rider scowled. 'In any case, my mates are back a ways, and I've come ahead to scout out a place to camp.'

'Plenty of space for it. Take your pick.'

Sandy Myrtle grunted. 'Well, a polite way of saying this

doesn't spring to mind, so please, your Lordship, excuse me if this is not the way things are done. Put simply, I'd be grateful if you moved on. My mates and I don't care for the company of strangers, especially not ones with smart mouths.'

Tom blinked, surprised. He stood up and crossed his arms over his chest, still holding the book. 'So,' he said softly, 'What if I've already made up my mind to stay here for as long as I damn well like?'

'That,' said the big stranger, 'will be a problem.'

## Chapter 2: The Eleven

Still in the saddle, Sandy Myrtle peered down at the stranger camped on the waterhole. 'I'll give you five minutes to piss off,' he said, then dragged a silver pocket watch from a recess in the flowing caftan he wore in place of a shirt. He lifted the face to one eye, and squinted. 'When the five minutes is up I swear I'll stick that book down your throat and kick your arse so hard that they'll have to pick you off the telegraph line yonder.'

The stranger didn't so much as blink, and Sandy had to credit the man with some guts. He crossed his arms to wait out the five minutes, wondering if he'd have to fight to enforce the eviction. The prospect didn't bother him much. Sandy was an uncommonly big man, at least the twenty stone Tom Nugent had estimated. Some of it was muscle, and some of it, he liked to joke, was muscle lying fallow.

Back in his youth he'd been as thin as the next lad. The weight came later. The fourth child of Scottish immigrants, he was born in Myponga, South Australia. His father took a liking to the sturdy 'wee lad', and bestowed on him his own name, Alexander MacDonald. Within an hour it had been shortened to Sandy.

Blessed with a capable brain, Sandy worked on the land from an early age, and was a natural leader. He was running Myrtle Springs Station at Farina, near the railway line to Oodnadatta, when he decided to chuck it all in. The horse he was riding now, the station owner's part-Percheron stallion called Jonathan James, had, he told anyone who would listen, 'followed' him as he headed north.

Thus mounted, Sandy rode a zigzag course into the Territory, drawn to prospectors' camps and desert shanties, farm huts and telegraph stations, living hard, playing poker and whist, racing horses and skylarking at every opportunity. He found a niche in the brand-new settlement of Stuart (later Alice Springs), taking a genuine interest in the Arrernte and Luritja women around the town. He was charmed by their old ways; the culture. Rare amongst bushmen in that part of the world, he was soon able to make himself understood in two or three Indigenous tongues, many of the words learned from the women he lived with at various times.

Sandy left Stuart with a bunch of mates, after they'd worn out their welcome. They'd been forcibly ejected from a race meeting, after one too many dud cheques and drunken fights. Word of a rich gold rush at Hall's Creek had just hit town.

'Nuggets as big as footballs,' someone said. 'An' just lying there ready to be picked up.'

Sandy and his mates hadn't been able to load their packs fast enough. Another three men, also headed for Hall's Creek, had joined them at the Elsey.

Now, Sandy divided his attention between watching the minute hand move closer to the time limit, and studying the stranger, who showed no inclination to move, his eyes flicking evenly over the words in his book.

The sounds of horsemen came from a distance, quickly closing on the waterhole. Tom's eyes flickered up. Hoofbeats; pintpots clicking on saddle dees; and laughing conversation.

'Right,' announced Sandy. 'Time's up.' He gripped his horse's mane with his left hand preparatory to dismounting. 'And do you hear those horsemen coming? If you're not afraid of me – and you should be – there are ten of us here now. You'd do well to piss off out of here as fast as that bony little neddy will carry you.'

Tom Nugent closed his book with a snap. 'Well now,' he cried, springing to his feet. 'I can take an insult, but once you start on my horse, that's when I get shirty.'

The first man in the main party came up alongside Sandy Myrtle. It was Tommy the Rag, a bean-pole of a lad with a stockwhip looped around his shoulder like a rope. His quick mind summed up the situation at a glance. 'What are you gonna do, mister? Fight all ten of us?'

A third man nosed up on a delicate grey. He was also of slim build, but with wiry muscles, and broad shoulders. His dress was flash: a snake skin belt tight around his trim waist; tooled leather boots and a red shirt. A silk kerchief was tied loosely around his throat. 'Fighting?' he said. 'There'll be none of that. This man here is our mate, Tom Nugent.'

Sandy's forehead furrowed like a ploughed field, 'You know this deadbeat?'

'Know him? Tom is like a brother to me. Not only that, but he's mates with Harry Readford, if that means anything to you. Tom has as solid a reputation as any man on the tracks.' The speaker slid off his horse with more than usual style and extended a hand to Tom. 'G'day there old mate. Haven't seen you since we split up at the Macarthur.'

Tom smiled as they clasped hands. 'Hey Larrikin, good to see you mate. And who's this riding up? Well if it isn't Fitz. You sly bastards. I saw you mob this morning and gave you a wide berth. If I'd recognised you two I'd have ridden straight in.'

'Fitz and I met up with Sandy Myrtle here and his crew at the Elsey, and we're all heading for the Kimberley rush to try our hand, so we decided to ride together. Look, here's Bob Anderson too.'

'Hi there Bob,' said Tom, 'it's good to see you again.' Bob was only recently arrived from Abernathy, Scotland, and still serving his apprenticeship, but was a likeable young bloke. His nickname was 'The Foot Runner' due to an uncommon turn of speed.

While the newcomers dismounted, there was a rush for saddle bags to take out pipes and tobacco pouches, pack the former with the latter, and drop live coals from Tom's fire in the bowls to light them.

Sandy came down off Jonathan James with astounding grace for such a big man. 'Mates with the great Harry Readford? Well why didn't you say so? You're welcome sir. I figured you were just a drifter heading for the goldfields. As Larrikin just explained, our lot met up with their lot down the track a ways and joined forces.'

Sandy and Tom shook hands, and by then all ten of the riders had come up. They were like a whirlwind visited on that waterhole: unsaddling horses, hobbling others, removing packs, hunting firewood, and peeing behind trees while others stripped off and plunged into the waterhole. The stock boys started to arrive; a lean Bularnu teen from the Georgina River country, others from the Gulf. Most came in on horseback, black chests glossy as they went about camp chores.

'Any 'gators here?' someone shouted.

'Swim for a bit and we'll find out,' shouted another. 'I'll stand guard with my carbine.'

That, to Tom's surprise, was exactly what they did. The air was soon filled with the sound of splashing men, drops of water flinging rainbows in the afternoon sun. Someone fired a round from a Snider rifle into the waterhole just to 'let the scaly bastards know that we mean business.' It sounded like a cannon shot, and birds took to the wing from all around.

Once camp had been pitched, the lure of the nearby shanty and its grog was too much. Sandy Myrtle cupped his hands over his mouth and bellowed. 'Get ready, you lads. Directly we're going to walk up to the store. I don't know if any of you has a thirst for whisky that can compare to mine, but that's where I'm heading.' Sandy looked across at Tom, who had relit his cigar, looking at all the activity with a bemused expression on his face. 'If you feel like company you might want to join us? It'll be a good chance for a chin-wag. It sounds like we're all pointing our noses for the Kimberley Rush.'

'So it does, and I'll be glad of a peg or two. I'll pull on my boots and join you.'

Eleven men gathered on the banks of the waterhole, buckling on gun belts and emptying sand out of their boots. Some had bathed in their underwear, and the wetness showed through their dungarees.

As they walked together through the scrub towards the store, full of that shared energy a group of men get when heading off for a drinking spree, Sandy Myrtle slapped Tom Nugent on the back with the power of a thunderclap. 'I'm sorry we got off to a bad start. I hope we can put it behind us.'

'Of course we can,' said Tom. 'I'm not a man to bear a grudge.'

'In that case I think some introductions are in order,' said Sandy, calling the gang to a halt. 'Now you already know Larrikin, Bob Anderson and Fitz. You also met this skinny little streak of shit, Tommy the Rag.'

'I did,' agreed Tom.

'Well here's the blokes who've ridden up along the 'line' from the Centre with me. First up, Jack Woods, but we have a few Jacks so we call him 'New England Jack.' Tom's eyes met a scrawny character who looked like he hadn't touched soap or water in months, if not years. Still, he had the twinkle of fun in his eye and the look of a man who lived life to the full.

'Here's the brothers,' Sandy went on. 'Wonoka Jack and George Brown. South Australians like me. They call themselves escaped farmers, but no one's quite sure what they're escaping to.' The elder of the two wore a dirty-brown bowler hat, and they were both missing a tooth or two.

'Good to meet you,' said Tom.

'This fine young man over here is Jack Dalley,' Sandy went on. 'And this is Hughie Campbell.' Tom sized up the latter. He was a big bastard, uncommonly muscular and handsome with it. 'He was a seaman on a ship anchored off Port Augusta when he decided he liked the look of bonny South Australia and took a dive overboard.'

'Call me Scotty,' said Hugh, in a deep, smooth brogue. 'These rude bastards all do.'

Sandy Myrtle grinned at Tom. 'Eleven of us in all, that's a drinking party and no mistake.'

'Enough talk,' growled Jack Dalley. 'Let's go raise some hell.'

They walked in a line towards the shanty.

# Chapter 3: Jimmy Woodford's Horse

For the first time in two long weeks, Jimmy Woodford knew that his journey's end was nigh. Two weeks of scarcely a solid hour of sleep. Half starved. Near perishing for water at times. Tracking the mongrel bastards who stole his horse.

Now, at last, he was so close to the thieves he could almost smell them. His breath quickened as he walked faster, though his dungarees hung loose around each leg, and his shirt flapped against bony arms.

The trouble had started at the Daly Waters Telegraph Station. Jimmy's mare had developed a case of colic. At first he'd ignored her restless pawing, but when she started dropping abruptly and trying to roll, he was forced to rest and examine her. Normally a beautiful horse – a blend of sweet nature and high spirits – she became irritable and sweaty – nostrils dilating with each laboured breath.

With any other horse Jimmy might have sold her and moved on, but she had been a parting gift from his parents, and her bloodlines were second to none in South Australia. He elected to stop with her while she recovered. Sandy Myrtle and the rest of the boys went on without him.

The recovery from colic took less than a week, but she remained poor, and instead of following the telegraph line north, Jimmy elected to veer east until he struck the Strangways River, guided by a Wilingula boy he had 'borrowed' for a few shillings from a fellow traveller.

One night he was camped on a waterhole called Paddy's Lagoon. There were two other white men there, taking a smuggler's route from the Gulf. They did not offer their names, but one in particular worried Jimmy. He was swarthy of skin, with eyes like the devil. With just three of them on the waterhole, however, bush etiquette declared that it would be impolite not to share their campfire.

As usual Jimmy hobbled out his mare and set the boy to watch her, patting the glossy black skin between the lad's shoulder blades and giving him a stick of Barrett's tobacco to keep him happy. The other white men had a cask of 'rum', and Jimmy had always had a weakness for the stuff. This was sly grog: a witch's brew of brandy and fermented sugars, poisoned with wood alcohol. After a few hours of yarning and gambling, followed by singing, shouting drunkenness, Jimmy fell asleep where he sat.

When he woke in the morning the two men had gone. They'd left Jimmy's old bedroll. Still hidden in its recesses, he found with relief, were some coins, a note or two and some questionable cheques. They had left his cracked and hard boots. The Wilingula boy they had either taken, or chased off.

But it was the theft of Jimmy's mare that brought a succession of pitiful tears rolling down his cheeks. Apart from his strong connection to her, he was at the mercy of the much talked about and feared inhabitants of this area, on a little travelled route, with no horse.

Jimmy was nothing if not persistent. He wanted his horse back, and he vowed that he would get her. He did not need a tracker. With a plant of four or five horses, including packs, the thieves had left a trail any fool could follow. Besides, they were lazy bastards. They rode hard for one morning, figured they were well ahead of one man on foot, then relaxed, stopping for a dinner camp that lasted most of the afternoon. Jimmy could see the marks where they had lain down in the shade.

Days of trailing the two thieves and their plant from waterhole to waterhole followed. Slowly Jimmy gained on them, the trail seeming fresher each morning.

Leaving the Strangways they headed for the harsh country around Mount Mueller. There Jimmy found the carcass of a beast they had killed, taking just the backstraps and the rump. Jimmy had eaten well for the first time in days. He had no Vestas, so he chewed the meat raw, blood running down his cheeks and beard.

From here they headed west, crossed Elsey Creek, bypassed the homestead, then dawdled along a rough track that shadowed the south bank of the Roper River. The heat grew worse, pulsing off the river pandanus in humid waves.

At the limit of his physical strength, Jimmy saw the shanty ahead. The building itself looked new; more civilised than most of the structures he had sampled grog in from Stuart and up along the line. It had sawn panels on the walls, and a wide verandah strewn with tables. The roof was clad with paperbark sheets. A dressed bullock hung from a cross pole at some rough yards nearby.

There were tents and campers under every tree, with horses tied or hobbled here and there. Noise and argument. The clink of harness and the sound of crows cawing in the trees. Groups of Yangman sat at smoky fires with fish spears leaning on trees and children running. The ground had been beaten to dust from hooves and boots.

Jimmy heard his mare before he had her in sight. At the familiar nicker he turned and saw her looking at him, one of a half-dozen horses tethered by halter leads under a woollybutt tree. He broke into a stumbling run towards her. She had been hard used, bones hanging out of her chest like roof battens. Her coat was dull and dusty, and her eyes rimmed with dried fluids.

Jimmy was surprised by the strength of his mingled concern and pleasure at seeing her. He stroked her neck and let her nuzzle close. Hand resting behind her ears, he glared at the tables under the shade of the shanty's verandah.

The two thieving bastards were there, lounging with glasses of spirits close to hand. Jimmy would have recognised them anywhere. He felt anger surge in him. Retribution was at hand. He was going to take what was his. A skelter of gear was stacked around the tree branches. Swags, hobbles, and three saddles laying on boughs. One of these was Jimmy's own, made by a saddle maker at Keith, and paid for as a lad through months of labour, knocking up split rail fences for local cockies at sixpence a panel.

Jimmy did not hurry. The men were intent on their drinks, and he nursed his anger coldly. His mare was the first priority. He delved in the stolen gear and found a brush. Starting at her neck, running down the barrel to her hindquarters, he brushed her all over, talking all the while, frowning at small nicks and cuts, vowing to use some of his limited funds to purchase some iodine to treat them.

'Don't worry girl, I'll fix you up and find you some good grass. You an' me are alright now. I'm going to punish the bastards who done this to you then we're going to get you good as gold.'

When the body was done, he worked through her tail, then dropped to one knee, lifting her off front leg with a firm grip. He shook his head sadly as he examined the foot, anger tugging at his lips. She had been cold-shoed badly. And the frog was black and smelled bad. This, unfortunately, would have to wait.

Standing, Jimmy tacked her up, then arranged his gear on the Ds and saddle bags. Untying the halter lead, he walked her over towards the shanty. Men, black and white, jealous of their patch of shade, stared as he went past. There was no mistaking the grim expression on his face.

He walked to the shanty and stopped near the two thieves, gripping the mare's bridle loosely in his right hand. The mongrel bastards were so brazen they did not try to run, but Jimmy did not fail to note the cut-down Snider carbine that lay on the table in front of the meanest-looking of the pair. Still, Jimmy was far beyond fear, or even reason.

'You're the bastards who stole my mare,' he shouted, spit flying from his lips with the force of his anger.

The mean one took a clay pipe from his mouth, rested it on the table, then turned and spat on the ground. 'That's not right. I won her off you at cards when you was drunk.' The speaker turned to his mate. 'It's true all right, isn't it Carmody?'

His mate said nothing, just stared with black eyes.

'You stole her, you swine,' Jimmy hissed, 'and I'll have satisfaction. Get out here and take what's coming to you.'

The horse thief lifted the carbine and pointed at Jimmy. 'Satisfaction, eh? How about you turn around and walk away from here, without your horse, and without a hole in your damn gut.'

Jimmy stared, lips twisting with hatred and indecision. The .577 calibre mouth in the Snider's muzzle glared at him. 'I'm taking my horse and be damned to you.'

The thief levered back the hammer on the carbine. 'Last chance Jimmy. I swear to God I won't let you take what's rightfully mine.'

Jimmy heard a shout, turned and looked down the track, and saw eleven men walking in a line along the track. Even at a distance, one, in particular, was unmistakable, mainly because of his massive bulk. It was Jimmy's mate, Sandy Myrtle himself, and there also was Wonoka Jack, George Brown and Jack Dalley there beside him.

'No, you piece of scum,' said Jimmy. 'I'll take my horse, and damn you for the cowardly horse thief you are.'

The gunman turned his head and saw the men coming. 'I tell you again, Jimmy, you're not taking that mare. One thing you should know is that I never make an idle promise.'

The eleven men were coming up to the shanty now, forming up in a silent row. 'These men are my mates,' cried Jimmy. 'How are you going to stop me taking my horse now?'

'Like this,' said the thief.

The carbine boomed, and a gust of black powder smoke burst from the muzzle. The sound of the discharge numbed every ear around that shanty. The heavy slug struck Jimmy's mare in the middle of her forehead and she fell like a bag of bones into the dust.

At first there was silence. Even the crows ceased their cawing.

Then a commotion developed out on the road. A hushed whisper rolled through the crowd. Something else was happening. A rare and unusual rider was coming. And with smoke still curling from the barrel of a carbine, they turned to watch her come up along the track.

It was a woman riding astride like a man, in moleskins and chequered shirt, with three laden pack horses behind her. Her stallion was even more impressive than the legend had promised.

'Jesus Christ, it's Red Jack,' someone whispered. 'And Mephistopheles.'

Red Jack's long red hair was in plaits, hanging from the sides of her hat. As she passed her eyes did not seem to rise from the ground, stonily avoiding eye contact with one and all. The stock of a rifle extended from her saddle. A woman in a man's world. Not as a curiosity, as part of it. No one there doubted that she was a force to be reckoned with.

Hugh Campbell broke the silence, his eyes glazed with admiration. 'My Lord, is that really Red Jack. I canna believe she's so bonny!'

And as she came up to them, the hooves of her horse raised a puff of dust with each footfall. It seemed that she would keep going past the dead mare, for the stallion smelled death and became skittish. When she came alongside, however, Red Jack reined in and looked at the pitiful body with its protruding bones and arched neck.

Now Red Jack looked from one to the other of the men gathered there, until her eyes settled on the man with the smoking gun.

'You're a mongrel dog, Maori Jack Reid,' she said. 'It's time someone hung you from a damned tree.'

Red Jack rode on, but at a distance of some hundred paces she stopped again. Her shoulders relaxed as if she had been holding her breath. Then, with a touch of her heels against her stallion's flanks she continued on her journey into the west.

# Chapter 4: The Hanging of Maori Jack

om Nugent had packed a lifetime of experience into his thirty-seven years, but he'd never seen Red Jack in the flesh, and had never watched a man murder a horse. Today, at this Roper River shanty, he'd seen both those things. Each was troubling in different ways.

Most of the crowd were still in shock, but Tom knew that Jimmy Woodford would not take the killing of his horse lying down. Sure enough, Jimmy stood slowly from the limp and bloody body of his mare, and then, with a barging run that sent chairs and tables crashing, he went for Maori Jack.

'You'll die for that, you cur,' Jimmy cried.

Tom was ready, and with a lunge he grabbed the struggling man's shirt around the bony chest, holding him easily. 'Steady on, lad.'

'Let me go. That mongrel shot my horse!' This was Jimmy's last despairing shout before he broke down, wailing like a child. His face was soon a mess: tears ran from his eyes, and jelly-like snot, streaked with dirt from the track, hung from his nose and clotted in his beard.

'Just calm down,' said Tom. 'Let me handle it.'

Slowly the struggles subsided, and Tom released the now

limp body into a chair. Jimmy blew his nose on his shirt and waited expectantly.

Tom glared at the gunman, 'That was a low act, Maori Reid. No real man would kill a horse.'

'Ar, and if it's not that esteemed gentleman, Tom Nugent. Keeping poor company these days Tom.'

Big Sandy Myrtle turned on Tom. 'Is this character a mate of yours?'

'Mates? Never!' muttered Tom. 'But I know him, yes, I met him down at the Macarthur River. His real name is John Reid. Some men call him 'Black Jack Reid.' Mostly he's known as 'Maori,' for you can see by the swarthy shade of his skin, and the deep black of his hair and beard, that the noble threads of New Zealand's proud and true race are woven through him. The man sitting next to him is his brother-in-law, known as Carmody.' Tom raised his voice as he went on. 'Listen now my friends, and I'll tell you the nature of a man who would kill a horse in cold blood.' After a long stare at the body of the mare, still bleeding into the dust, Tom explained: 'Maori Jack Reid was a seaman, who escaped his country just ahead of the Royal Navy, who caught and hanged many of the officers of his last ship there, an infamous brigantine called the *Carl*. This cruel man was crew on a blackbirder in the South Sea Islands, kidnapping labourers for the sugar plantations of Queensland.'

'That's a low trade indeed,' added Sandy Myrtle. And every man on that shanty's verandah was spellbound.

Maori Reid betrayed a smile in one corner of those whiskered lips, as if enjoying hearing the recount of his own misdeeds. 'Go on, Tom, I'm flattered that you made the effort to learn of my past.'

'Oh it was no effort,' said Tom. 'It was the man sitting next to you, your brother-in-law Carmody who told me much of this when last we met, at that outpost they now call Borroloola. The remainder I read in the newspapers during the trial of your captains.'

Maori Reid fixed on Carmody a look that clearly said, I'll deal with you later. But Tom was not finished.

'Now I must share,' he said, 'the trick used by Maori Reid and his shipmates to capture their human prey. They would anchor in a bay of some South Sea island and invite the locals aboard, promising them gifts laid out in the hold. As soon as the trusting crowd went below to look, the hatches would slam shut, and the ship would sail for Queensland, where their captives would be sold at auction.

'The young women suffered most, for Maori and his mates would abuse them violently while their interest lasted. Afterwards they would throw them overboard. The difficult or untameable men would likewise feed the ravenous sharks of those remote waters. Yes, my friends,' added Tom, 'this is the resumé of a man who would shoot a horse then smile. Shall I go on?'

Taking the grim silence of the crowd as encouragement Tom finished the story, 'On the final voyage of this blood-thirsty vessel *Carl*, the heavily armed Royal Navy ship HMS *Cossack* espied and chased them. Maori Jack and his mates were determined not to be caught with their living cargo.' Tom dropped his voice to a whisper, 'Those bastards shot every man, woman and child, and weighted them down to the bottom of the sea: a slaughter that churns the gut. The hangman took vengeance on the Carl's officers, but this man here escaped. He ran to Queensland where his ill-gotten funds bought and outfitted a schooner. Now, styling himself as a sea captain, Maori filled her holds with goods in Burketown, and sailed her up the Roper, then the Macarthur, making a fortune on cheap whisky, weevilled flour and flimsy wares.' Tom raised his forefinger. 'Maori made only one mistake. He never paid a cent of customs duty, bringing goods from the colony of Queensland to the Territory, and he was caught red-handed by Alfred Searcy, the sub-inspector of customs.'

For the first time Maori Reid reacted. 'That officious bastard, Searcy. It's he who's ruined me, impounded my vessel and arrested my dear wife Henrietta. Now I am ruined. Why should I not be bitter?'

Tom glared at Maori. 'Killing this horse was the last straw. Red Jack was right. It's time someone hung you from a tree.'

Maori's eyes darted like those of a snake about to strike. He raised his carbine.

'Don't bother,' Tom warned. 'We all know that Snider rifles carry but a single round. You spent yours on that horse. Soon you might regret making that choice.' He turned to the rest of the eleven who, with the addition of Jimmy Woodford, had now become twelve. 'Get him, boys, while I fetch a rope.'

While Maori Reid kicked and spat, throwing curses to the wind, they carried him from the verandah and towards a tall, spreading kurrajong tree. Everyone helped in one way or another: Bob Anderson, New England Jack, Sandy Myrtle, Jack Dalley, Scotty, Wonoka Jack and his brother George. Tommy the Rag ran alongside yelling encouragement and cracking his stockwhip. Fitz and Larrikin grabbed Carmody and brought him along, each holding an arm.

Tom Nugent found a dozen men camping around that shanty who were willing to lend a rope for the enterprise. He ignored various plaited greenhides, and selected a stout length of hemp.

Imprisoned under that handy bough, seeing Tom walking towards him with a rope, Maori Reid showed fear for the first time. 'You can't hang me. You have no right. This ain't no court of law.'

Larrikin pointed to Carmody, whose face had turned the same shade as his yellow hair. 'What about this one? Does he hang as well?'

Tom shook his head. 'No, Carmody's not bad, just too weak to stand up to this mongrel. Let him go.' With those words Tom stepped forward with the rope and threw it over a suitable bough. On the other end he tied a hangman's slip-knot while

Maori swallowed so that his adam's apple bobbed like a rowboat on a heavy sea.

'You can't. You won't,' he muttered.

Holding the noose in his hands, Tom glared down at the prisoner. 'John Ward Reid, known variously as 'Maori' and 'Black Jack,' you are charged with stealing a horse, the property of James Woodford, then feloniously slaying the said horse instead of returning it to him. You are also charged with other acts of bastardry too numerous to mention. How do you plead?'

Maori Reid made a determined bid for freedom, but New England Jack stopped him cold with a two-handed thrust that sent him flying. 'That means guilty, I reckon, Tom.'

At the last minute, rather than fitting the noose around the prisoner's neck, Tom kneeled near Maori's feet, snugging the loop around his ankles. Once they saw this the men understood Tom's joke. This was not to be a death-by-hanging, but a grand amusement.

'Now lads, pull,' Tom cried.

The mood changed in an instant, from heavy and expectant to a wave of laughter, as the rope tightened and Maori Reid went upside-down into the air, shouting with discomfort. They pulled until his head was dangling a yard off the ground, then tied the rope off on a neighbouring tree.

'You bastards, it hurts,' Maori shouted, his face reddening quickly. A leather purse fell from the folds of his shirt, hanging from a string. Tom used his knife to cut it free.

Jimmy Woodford was smiling now, and Tom called him over.

'Now how much was your mare worth, do you reckon?' Tom asked. 'Don't hold back, there's a goodly sum in here.'

Jimmy cocked his head to one side and scratched his beard. 'She were a good horse. I'd say twenty-five pound.'

'Don't you touch my money,' wailed Maori Reid.

Tom handed a roll of notes to Jimmy. 'Here's thirty pound in notes, for your pain and trouble. You'll be able to buy a decent nag for that.'

Sandy Myrtle came across. 'Thanks Tom. Jimmy's a good mate.' He called out to Tommy the Rag. 'Hey Tommy, would you take Woodford back to camp and get a feed into him? He's had a hard road.'

'What about my horse?' Jimmy cried. 'I can't just leave her there, dead and all.'

'Leave that to us,' Tom said. 'We'll get her buried good and proper.'

Tom was true to his word, offering twenty shillings from Maori Reid's purse to a couple of travelling Irishmen. They were to dig a hole away from the shanty, drag the mare's body up with a team and bury her.

'Now,' Tom said to the others. 'Let's go have some fun.' He looked at the upside-down Maori Reid. 'You can watch from here,' he said.

A rain of curses flew from that unfortunate, some of which even Tom hadn't heard before.

As they walked towards the shanty Tom fell in beside Carmody and gave him the purse. 'You can pass the remainder back to Maori later, if you feel inclined. There's still a useful sum inside.'

'Thanks Tom, you're a fair man.'

As they reached the dusty shade of the shanty's verandah Tom stopped and lowered his voice. 'Tell me, Carmody, it wasn't like Maori Reid said, was it? He didn't win that horse at cards did he?'

'Afraid so. Jimmy Woodford was so drunk he didn't know what he was doing. Maori won the horse, then the saddle and everything else fair and square. Jimmy must have forgotten it all when he waked.'

'Why didn't you say something earlier?'

'Maori's my brother in law but he's a bastard. And it's a dog act to fleece a drunk man like that anyhow. It's nice to see someone stand up to him. I was pretty sure you weren't really going to hang him.'

Tom laughed. 'No, but that's the best fun I've had in ages.'

Carmody went on, 'So are you going to cut Maori down?'

Tom clapped the other man on the shoulder. 'Maybe later, first I'm going to drink my fill with grog and share a few yarns with mates new and old.'

# Chapter 5: The Shanty

S andy Myrtle fronted the bar, standing like a giant with his hair almost brushing the cypress rafters. He pulled his chequebook from his pocket, borrowed a pen and inkpot, then scribbled a figure.

'Here boy, let me know when this runs out. Whiskies for me and the Scotsmen, then rums all round for the rest of the lads.'

The shanty keeper looked like he'd just stepped off the steamer from 'down south.' He was around twenty years old, neatly dressed in a long-sleeved shirt and tight button-up vest, sweat dampening his armpits from the heat. He picked up the cheque as if it were a poisonous spider, holding it close to his spectacles. Clearing his throat, he turned to the Jangman teenager who was sweeping the floor. 'Hey you, where's Mr Kirwan?'

'Mister Kirwan go shoot ducks down the river, *Mulaka*.'

'Go find him, quick and tell him to come here.' The young shanty keeper turned back to Sandy. 'Might I ask if this cheque is valid ... we have a policy of—'

'Of course it's bloody valid. Hurry up man. We're thirsty.'

'I know, it's just that ... the more experienced man is not here at present, I've sent for him but—'

Sandy slammed both massive hands down on the bar and

leaned on them, eyes glowing like slow-burning campfires. 'Now listen, laddie. If there's one thing that makes me very, very angry it's having my character questioned, especially by a pup whose balls have scarcely dropped.'

'I beg your pardon sir,' huffed the shanty keeper. 'Well I mean to say that I am very new at this, and my much more experienced colleague will be here shortly.'

Again the hands came down, this time striking like a cannon shot. 'Just fill up those glasses and hurry up about it, or I'll come over there and do it myself.'

Meanwhile, Tom and the rest of the men spread out on the verandah. The table-tops were slabs of cypress, fresh from the saw-pit. The chairs were sawn sections of woollybutt trunk, but even this was luxury to bushmen who had been so long on the tracks. Tom seated himself with Fitz and Larrikin, his best mates from the crew. Scotty occupied the end chair, a glazed expression on his handsome face.

Tom looked around. The shanty was brand-new and businesslike. On his last visit it was quite the opposite, being run by an old soak called McPhee. It was now owned by the firm of Armstrong and Bryden, who also operated the store at Roper Bar.

'I heard this place burned down just a few weeks ago,' said Tom. 'They've done a mighty job in rebuilding it so fast.'

'When Matt Kirwan is around,' said Fitz. 'Things happen.'

'They do indeed,' said Tom. 'Anyway, it's good to see you bastards. I knew you were planning on heading for Hall's Creek, but wasn't sure if we'd meet up.'

Fitz smiled his usual grin. 'Oh we knew where you were headed. There seemed no doubt we'd hear of your shenanigans sooner or later. Though mind you, we had some troubles of our own on the way over.'

'Like what?' Tom asked.

Larrikin took over, his smiling blue eyes lively in his fore-head while his strong hands remained constantly busy, tearing a dry gum leaf up into tiny squares. 'Maori Reid was right about one thing ... that mongrel Alfred Searcy. He's out of control. We had a run-in with him and another 'pink' by the name of O'Donohue.'

Tom crinkled his eyes. 'Wait a minute. Alf Searcy's a police-man? Since when? Last I saw he was a customs inspector, and a jumped-up excuse for a man at that.'

'He *was* a customs inspector,' Larrikin explained, 'but In-spector Foelsche up in Palmerston was short-handed so draft-ed him into the force. Anyway, we were headed out of Roper Bar, maybe ten mile out, travelling with a bunch of prospec-tors, when Searcy and O'Donohue tricked us into having a pipe with them. Searcy recognised us from the Macarthur River, I'm guessing.'

The first round of drinks arrived on a tray from the young shanty keeper, shooting disapproving glances as he went.

'What's your name, sonny?' Tom asked mildly.

'George Bowen, sir.'

'Straight off the boat by the look of you.'

'Pretty much, sir.'

'Well keep the rum flowing and we'll have no quarrel.'

At that the shanty keeper emptied the tray and went back inside for another.

Larrikin took a swig of his drink, then patted his gut. 'Hell that feels good. Anyhow, to go on with the story, half way through our pipes O'Donohue pulled a revolver and forced us to ride back into Roper Bar police station to see if there were any charges against us.'

Tom's face hardened. 'So you weren't under suspicion of anything, Searcy and his mate just didn't like the look of you?'

'That's right. They said we looked like a mob of ruffians and marched us in. Donegan at the Roper is a decent bloke and let us go, but not before every drifter on the Roper had laughed themselves silly at our expense.'

Tom shook his head slowly. 'That doesn't sit well with me. Searcy and this O'Donohue mongrel had no right to do that.'

Larrikin shrugged. 'No harm done. Not really. Come on Tom. It's not like you can do anything about it.'

'Maybe there is. Maybe there isn't.' Tom turned to look at Scotty, who was drinking his whisky at a rapid rate, but still hadn't said a word, staring into space. 'Now what's wrong with you? I can't recall ever seeing a Scotsman lost for words.'

'I just canna get the sight o' Red Jack out of my head. How can a woman be so beautiful?'

Tom rested his tumbler on his bottom lip and spoke into it reflectively. 'Aye gentleman, we were very lucky to see Red Jack the Wanderer. She can ride better than any of you flash bastards, and break anything on four legs in a week.'

'Bonniest face I ever seen,' Scotty breathed. 'May our paths cross again.'

'Don't go down that road,' warned Tom. 'Red Jack leaves heartbreak in her wake.'

Matt Kirwan came in from the river, a Purdey breech-loading shotgun hanging, open, over his back. A couple of lean but muscled boys carried, in each hand, two or three still-bleeding ducks tied together by the feet.

Kirwan's timing was good – young George had just accepted the third cheque from Tom Nugent's party. This one was made out to some illegible recipient in Alice Springs. Apart from bearing the marks of several owners, none of whom had used soap on their hands in many a long week, it was partially torn, and hardly legible.

The conversation shushed while the youngster took Matt Kirwan inside for a hurried conversation. Kirwan walked outside presently, red in the face and obviously angry. 'No more of your worthless cheques, you bastards.'

Tom Nugent stood, 'Well if it isn't good old Matt Kirwan. Nice to see you.'

'It's not in the slightest bit good to see you. If you lot don't have cash you won't get another drink here this afternoon.'

Tom liked Matt. He'd been running the Hay and Company store at the Roper Landing for some years. Kirwan was afraid of no one, could fight bare-knuckle with the best of them and did not tolerate fools. Fortunately, the campers from the water-hole had enough cash between them to keep the drinks flowing.

Darkness fell, and one of the Irishmen who had disposed of Jimmy's dead horse retrieved a concertina from his camp, and played old-country jigs so lively that the tapping of feet filled the night. Larrikin Jim, as always, was the first to get to his feet. And Yangman women came in from the fringes. Music was universal.

Matt Kirwan had mail to distribute. Most of these letters were secreted away, to be treasured later. There was one from Fitz's lady friend, down in Brisbane. This he opened immediately, wafting the scent of perfume far and wide across the verandah. Fitz sat by himself for an hour, nursing his drink, reading and rereading each sentence, a wistful expression on his face.

Other men came through that night, some travelling in the darkness, some Tom knew from cattle work. One was Charlie Gaunt, with hollowed eyes and sadness evident in his heavy tread. He paused only to buy provisions and to down a quick rum before riding off into the night.

Jimmy Woodford and Tommy the Rag returned from camp. Jimmy seemed as ready for a glass of grog as ever. He announced his arrival by shouting the bar with his new-found riches, courtesy of Maori Jack Reid.

'Hey Matt,' Tom shouted, during a lull in the music. 'We haven't had beef in Gawd knows how many days. How about you make a start on that beef carcass you've got hanging out there at the yards?'

Kirwan stood with his arms folded across his chest. 'That meat's all spoken for, and beef is in short supply because of redwater fever.'

'That's a bit rough, Matt,' said Tom. 'We're hungry, and we've got money to pay for it.'

'I told you, and I can't speak any more plain,' called Kirwan. 'There's no beef for you. And what's more, I've had enough of you lot. That's last drinks. I'll sell bottles if you want to take grog back to your camp, but you can get out of my store, every bloody one of you.'

While the others downed last drinks and organised the purchase of take-away bottles, Tom went out in the dark with Carmody to cut down Maori Jack. At first he thought Maori might be dead, for he knew that his guts would be lying heavy on his lungs after all this time inverted.

A movement of the eyes showed that Maori was a long way from dead. Still alert. Still dangerous. Tom released the knot that held him suspended and lowered the horse-killer down to a slumped mess in the dust. He carefully removed the noose.

Maori did not get up straight away, but sat, shaking his head, massaging his ankles and glaring like a brown snake at Tom. 'I should kill you for that,' he said.

'Keep your mouth shut. Now listen, I put your carbine with the rest of your gear, and your boy has packed everything ready. Time for you to get on your horse, and ride away.'

Maori's eyes fell on Carmody, hanging back in the darkness. 'What about you, Carmody? You ain't gonna desert me now, are you brother?'

'I'm going to ride with these blokes now, sorry Maori.' Carmody gave him the purse, then walked back across the dust to the others.

'Don't come near us again,' Tom warned. 'You have a dark heart, and I want nothing to do with you.'

'I can hurt you,' hissed Maori Jack.

'How?'

'I know about something – or should I say someone – down Borroloola way.'

Tom tried to hide the fear that crossed his face unbidden. 'You can't hurt anyone if I kill you now,' he said.

'You're no killer, Tom. You're not like me.'

'You don't know the first thing about me. Get out of here. Ride away and don't come back.'

'So be it then,' Maori said softly. 'But don't say I didn't warn you.'

Tom watched as Maori Reid limped across to his camp, where the boy waited with two saddled horses and laden packs.

Finally, with the beat of horses driven hard, thudding away into the distance, Tom let out his breath and walked off towards the twelve men who were waiting for him outside the shanty, bottles of rum and whisky in their hands.

# Chapter 6: The Bitter Springs

It was a two-mile ride to the thermal pools known as Bitter Springs, but no one considered the time wasted. Leaving the stock boys in charge of the camp, the thirteen men rode in double file down the moon-lit track, swigging from bottles and skylarking as they went.

With their horses tied to paperbark trees, they stripped off boots and clothes, then staggered on tender white feet for the pools. The water was clear as air, surrounded by sprays of fan-like livistona fronds, reeds and pandanus. The stench of flying-fox sat heavily in the air, and stars glittered through the spaces between the trees. One by one the group splashed or slid into the steaming water.

'The Yangman grill those damn fruit bats an' eat them,' said Larrikin, surfacing with his hair slicked back like the fur of a rat. 'Buggered if I know how they can stand the stink.'

'You'd eat them too, if you were hungry enough,' Fitz said.

Bob Anderson made a noise through his nose. 'I've nar been that hungry, and by God's grace I ne'er will be.'

Sandy Myrtle, wearing just an oversized pair of underpants, busied himself making a fire on the bank. Finally, when dancing flames flickered across the water surface, he lowered his elephantine body into the water. 'That's hot,' he sighed.

'Whoops,' Tommy the Rag cackled. 'Damn water level just rose by a yard.'

The others laughed while the big man tried to catch his scrawny tormentor, then grew exhausted and gave up. 'Watch your mouth, you little turd. I'm too drunk to tolerate your foolery.' Sandy sank back down into the water until it lapped against the whiskers that followed the double curves of his chin.

Tom Nugent found himself a patch against an underwater rock, smoking a cigar in damp fingers. Entertainment was provided by George Brown, sneaking up behind his brother, Wonoka Jack, holding a mess of rotting vegetable matter he had gathered from the edge of the pool. With a hoot of glee George slapped the sulphurous mess on his victim's head. Wonoka Jack reacted with a shriek, ran a few paces, then realised the trick and turned to retaliate.

The high-jinks went on for a moment or two, then they all settled down to luxuriate in the hot water, thirteen of them in a circle.

'Ah this is guid,' said Scotty. 'An' must surely be why I left jeelit bleddy Scotland.'

'Aye,' said Bob Anderson. 'I would nar have dreamed there could be a place as braw an' bonny as this in all tha warld. Where aboots in the auld country be tha from, Mr Campbell, eh?'

The older man sized up his countryman. Bob was tall and skinny, with a long face. 'I'm an Argyll man, but a long taim past. I'm near thir'y now, and was scarce fi'teen when I bairded me first tub – a windjammer she were. But dinny call me mister. Scotty will go jes' as guid.'

'I'll call you Scotty then,' said Bob. 'I'm as like a Perthshire man meself; from Abernethy as a bairn, though me da were a tailor and we moved with his work; down Edinburgh way for a time. I would have tarried, but me and the laird I was working for had a wee disagreement.'

'Can you damn Scotsmen stop your jawin' and pass that bottle?' someone called, and around it went. When it was empty someone climbed out of the pool and dripped their way over to a saddle bag for more.

Tom Nugent was watching the twelve men in turn. They're not, he decided, really bad apples, just misfits like himself, spat out by polite society and united by a love of the Australian bush. Usually he liked travelling solo, but the idea of lively and entertaining company suddenly appealed.

'Since we're heading to the rush at Hall's Creek we should all ride together,' Tom said at length. 'I think I can safely say that there'll be plenty of fun to be had.'

'No one will argue with that,' said Sandy Myrtle. 'And I reckon I speak for all of us, Tom, when I say that we'd be pleased if you'd agree to be our captain. Thirteen of us rough bastards raising Cain from here all the way to the Kimberley. What a grand adventure!'

'I'd be honoured to lead you,' said Tom. 'But if we're going to be mates we'll do it right. That means we stand shoulder to shoulder through thick and thin. We never shirk the things that need to be done. And if we do fight amongst ourselves we solve it, man to man, with our fists.'

There was a muttering of agreement. 'It's settled then,' said Tom. 'From now on, we're thirteen. An insult to one is an insult to all. '

'Now here's an idea,' said Sandy Myrtle. 'On our way up from the Centre we were camped at Milner's Lagoon when Nat Buchanan and one of his sons rode up. They stopped to shoot the breeze, and before he rode off, old Bluey said: "That's a ragged bunch you're riding with, Sandy." We had a good belly laugh about it at the time, but what say we call our gang the Ragged Thirteen?'

There was silence for a moment, and it was New England Jack Woods who spoke first. 'That's a grand idea.'

43

'The Ragged Thirteen it is then,' said Tom. 'And we don't take a slight from anybody. That starts with Matt Kirwan and his damn beef carcass we saw hanging there tonight. The first thing we do is take the meat he should have let us buy for good money earlier.'

A rash of smiles broke out at this, but Tom wasn't yet finished. 'Then I say we should deal with those two traps, Searcy and O'Donohue. As soon as they hear that we call ourselves the Ragged Thirteen they'll start boasting about how they bested us all at the Roper. Searcy has his head so far up his own arse he hasn't seen daylight for years. Time he got taught a lesson.'

'Too late for that,' said Fitz. 'They would have left the Roper by now. They're heading down to the Macarthur where Commissioner Foelsche has posted them. That's why Donegan has taken up position at Roper Bar – he's been relieved.'

Tom grinned, 'If I can't ride faster than a couple of "pinks" and be on them in a day or two I'll hang up my spurs. Besides, Alf Searcy can't travel in a straight line to save his life. The bastard fancies himself as a naturalist, always poking around trying to figure out why grass is green and why mountains are high and valleys low.' He paused. 'I want to travel light, three horsemen altogether, and we'll live off the land. No packs to slow us down. We do what needs to be done, and meet up again near the Katherine.'

Tom didn't say that there was another reason for the trip. Business that, since Maori Jack's threats, needed attending to in Borroloola.

'So who's to go with you?' Sandy Myrtle asked.

'I dunno. Care to volunteer, anyone?' Tom asked.

Fitz nodded grimly. 'I'd love a chance to get back at Searcy and that other dog O'Donohue.'

'Fair enough,' said Tom. 'You're in.'

Larrikin grimaced, 'My mare's just coming into season and, well, I was talking with Wonoka Jack here back at the shanty …

I'm hoping to join her with his chestnut stallion. I think I'll stay with the group.'

'That makes sense.'

'I'll tag along if you'll 'ave me,' said Jack Dalley. 'I 'aven't seen the Gulf Country yet and I've a mind to. If the diggings are as rich at Hall's Creek as we 'ope, this might be me only chance.' He paused. 'I don't want to sound like I've got tickets on meself but I won't slow you down any.'

'I'll vouch for that,' Sandy Myrtle said. 'Jack's got an arse made of glue, an' I haven't seen him come unstuck yet.'

'That settles it then,' Tom said. 'Me, Fitz and Jack Dalley will go do what needs to be done.'

'Take me too, please, Mr Nugent,' said Tommy the Rag.

'Why would he take you?' Sandy Myrtle blasted out. 'A stripling with a smart mouth? He'd sooner take a dingo pup than you.'

Tommy hovered closer in the water to Tom, the earnestness of his face lit by reflected ripples in the firelight. 'You want to travel light, Mr Nugent? I can kill game. Bush Turkeys without firing a shot. You never saw a man like me with a stockwhip in his hands. Snakes … goannas … whatever you can think of don't stand a chance.'

'That's true,' offered Jimmy Woodford. 'Tommy's bloody amazing with that whip.'

'Why would you want to come along so much?' Tom asked.

Tommy's eyes shone. 'Because one day I want to be a real bushman, like Harry Readford,' his voice trailed off, 'and like you.'

'Can you stick to a saddle for fifty hard miles from sunrise to sundown, and all night if you have to?'

'I can. My oath Mr Nugent. I'll prove it to you, just give me a chance, I swear.'

'Alright,' Tom drawled. 'We leave at first light and if the blue-wing jackass howls and you're not yet out of your swag

I'll not wait for you. What's more, if you let me down on the track you'll need more than a stockwhip to stop what's coming to you.'

The lad's face split into a grin. 'You won't regret this, Mister Tom.'

'You'd bloody better hope not. Now, first things first. I'll not ride on an empty belly. Put the stoppers in those bottles, boys, and we'll wallow here until we sober up. Mister bloody Kirwan is about to find out that the Ragged Thirteen don't take no for an answer.'

# Chapter 7: The Beef Raid

**M**att Kirwan was no fool. He'd left a guard on the bullock carcass that hung from a chain in the yards beside the store. The guard was a young Jangman helper. White men called him Billy, though he already had a name, that they did not choose to learn.

Billy heard the Thirteen coming from a distance, walking through the scrub towards him. He was frozen with indecision, trying to guess their intentions. Should he shout and wake his white employers? Kirwan would be furious if he was disturbed for no reason. Yet wouldn't he be still angrier if someone stole the beef without being warned? Wracked by indecision, Billy stayed where he was, squatting in the dust, every sense alert.

Thirteen men advanced out of the trees. Thirteen of the big, rowdy men who had been at the store earlier. Billy now saw their faces and the knives they carried. He was certain they were after the beef. No one, not even Mister Kirwan, could stop so many. There was no doubt in Billy's mind whose fault this would be.

Whatever happened, trouble was coming. Serious trouble. Billy's overwhelming impulse was to get away from this place as fast as possible. He sprang up, vaulted a rail, then sprinted into the horse paddock, where George Bowen's grey was passing the night in peace. Billy vaulted onto the startled animal's back. He galloped away, pausing only to open the gate, and did not turn back.

By that stage the Thirteen had reached the hanging carcass. Carmody's nimble fingers were at the chain that held it suspended, lowering it to working height, where men and knives were waiting.

All the men knew how to butcher, but New England Jack Woods was an enthusiast, with a folding leather satchel of tools. These included a hatchet that he used to cleave through joint and rib. With razor-sharp knives he carved out huge chunks of meat; back straps and tenderloins; rumps and rounds, sirloins, briskets and ribs.

The noise of Billy's flight on horseback, and of hatchet strokes on bone, were not lost on the occupants of the donga that stood behind the store.

The door burst open, 'What the hell is going on out there?' came Kirwan's screech. He stormed out, wearing just a pair of trousers. His bare torso was heavy with muscle, and his face red with fury. He carried his shotgun in his hands as he approached them. When he pointed it skywards and fired a round, flame leapt from the barrel in the darkness. Even New England Jack paused in his work.

'You bastards have got a hide,' Kirwan shouted. 'Thieving scum – that's what you are.'

Tom walked out to meet him. 'Call us what you like, Matt, but you refused our fair offer to pay for the meat. That offer still stands. Take our money and we can all get some sleep. Just send down to the Elsey for a new bullock to replace that one tomorrow and everyone is happy.'

Many of the campers, wakened by the shotgun blast, gathered 'round, ashen faced and quiet, watching as Matt Kirwan leaned the shotgun against a handy tree and began to limber up.

'Choose your man, Mr Nugent,' he snarled. 'I'll fight him one on one. If I win you can pay me for damage and loss, as well as returning the meat. If I lose you can ride off with the beef and never darken this little corner of the Territory again.'

Scotty raised his right arm. He was the biggest man apart from Sandy Myrtle. 'I'll do it. Let me take the rude bastard on.'

Sandy Myrtle moved to his side. 'Good one, Scotty, I'll pick up for you.'

It only remained to find a second for Kirwan. Bowen was hanging back near the donga, pale and shaken. No one expected him to come forward. Tom Nugent volunteered himself. 'I wouldn't like to see a man fight without someone watching his back.'

As the two men faced off, Tommy the Rag took up the role of bookmaker. 'I'll hold your bets fellers. Even money, pick your winner.'

The growing crowd studied the boxers' physiques, and asked pointed questions.

'Hey Matt, I heard you've had a few bouts of fever, how long ago?'

'Let's see you shadow box, Scotty.'

'Kirwan's lean and hard, but look at those biceps on the Scot, for fuck's sake, if he gets a clean punch in …'

'If is the word,' opined Fitz. 'I've seen Kirwan fight before, and he can move, I'm telling you.'

Finally, with all bets in, the fighters squared up. Kirwan went at the Scotsman hard, battering in with a jab, cross, hook and a cross. Scotty, however, was tough, with a strong neck and shoulders, and knew how to protect his face. He withstood the initial flurry and delivered a couple of probing jabs, then a right cross that thumped into Kirwan's solar plexus.

There was a sigh from the men watching, but Kirwan was back on the attack in an instant. For the space of ten minutes or more the sparring continued: flying fists, ducking heads, rolling shoulders and dancing feet, with both fighters tapping wells of blood on the other man's face.

A break in the routine came with Scotty almost tripping on a tree root. Distracted, he caught a solid right hook in the temple, a blow that would have seen most men tumbling to the ground. Instead be floundered forward and pushed Kirwan with both hands in the chest, sending him sprawling.

The storekeeper sprang back to his feet, shook the blood and sweat from his head and took his stance. But his concentration faltered, whether from the dark, or having been recently wakened from sleep. He let in a beauty from Scotty, a magnificent straight right, that took him on the mouth. His legs folded and down he went.

'That'll do,' Tom said, going to the storekeeper's side. 'Throw in the towel, Matt, you've proved your point.'

Scotty stepped back, grinning, but Matt Kirwan struggled to his feet and growled through bloody lips. 'No way, I'll bring the bastard down yet.' With that he tore into his unprepared opponent with a flurry of body blows. It didn't take long for Scotty to respond, however, and another powerful right landed on Kirwan's nose, sending a spray of blood and the storekeeper flying.

Groggy but determined, Kirwan again tried to get back up, though his legs, seemingly, would not support his weight.

'Stop him, Sandy,' drawled Tom.

The big man pushed Kirwan down. 'The fight's over, Matt. Scotty's murdering you.'

'Like hell he is, let me up. I'll fix the bastard.'

Sandy sat on the struggling man, who wheezed and carried on, struggling like a madman. 'Let me up you fat lump. I can't breathe.'

'Not until you agree that the fight's over.'

'No way. It's not over until I say it's over.'

Sandy grabbed Kirwan's arm and twisted it, and there was a shriek of pain. 'Alright, for fuck's sake, just get off me.'

When Sandy stood up, Matt Kirwan's arm was hanging at a crooked angle from the elbow. 'You broke my arm, you idiot.'

'Sorry mate. I didn't mean to.'

Kirwan stood, breathing like a bull, unsuccessfully trying to wipe the blood from his face on his good forearm. 'Don't dare come back this way again, you lot, or I'll fill your hides with buckshot.'

Tom tipped his hat. 'You're game Matt, and I admire that. But if we want to come back this way, then we will. And don't ever say no to us again.'

The two men stared at each other until finally, Matt Kirwan turned and walked towards the donga, a defeated slump to his shoulders.

Tom, Fitz, Jack Dalley and Tommy the Rag rode off, down towards the Gulf, just as the first white and yellow glow of piccaninny dawn was showing on the eastern horizon. The air smelled fresh and full of promise, scented with the spice of adventure.

Fitz yawned, for none of them had slept a wink. Tom's face took on a serious frown.

'Bear up you blokes. We've fifty miles to cover before we throw our swags tonight.'

# Chapter 8: Searcy and O'Donohue

Alfred Searcy loved a good camp, and the Hodgson River crossing was a first-rate site, with flat shelves of dark rock, waist-high waterfalls, and fish to be had in the deep pools below.

With a suitable rock as a seat, Alfred lit his pipe and sighed contentedly. He considered himself a true bushman: the kind of gentleman adventurer that was destined to bring civilisation and the rule of law to South Australia's vast and wild Northern Territory.

Alfred had, to be sure, enjoyed an adventurous life. As a lad, working as a seaman on a schooner off the Jenimber Islands, he had taken a dinghy on a solo fishing trip. When a storm blew up without warning, he was blown onto land and wrecked. He joined forces with a gang of Malays, and the ordeal that followed included the murder of most of his companions, and a second shipwreck, onto the Northern Territory coast. He lived with a ragtag assortment of indigenous hunters, trepangers, and buffalo hunters before finally making good his own rescue.

Back in the more civilised world of Palmerston, he had taken up the position of sub-collector of customs, extracting duty on goods arriving into the Territory from abroad, and attempting to levy taxes from the Macassars, who were intent on stripping Top End waters of bêche-de-mer. In the process of this work, Alfred had been kidnapped by Chinese smugglers. He had faced down Malay captains, brumby hunters, and even the infamous Maori Jack Reid, of whose arrest he was most proud.

He'd seen things that his family, back in Adelaide, would scarcely have believed: fleets of Macassar dredging canoes coming down before the wind in Bowen Straits, their triangular matting sails billowing full. He'd seen proas at anchor off gorgeous northern beaches fringed with sand and tropical forest. Horsemen in full cry at the Victoria River, droving cattle across the ford at sunset. He'd seen men's throats cut, and held a prospector down while a doctor sawed off his leg below the knee.

When the opportunity came to join the police force, Alfred had willingly taken up the challenge. He suspected that this might be his true calling; pacifying the lawless elements of the north. His first posting was to be Borroloola. His partner was an Irishman called O'Donohue, who stood a solid six feet in height. Fearless and fond of swinging his fists, Alfred's new companion was also enamoured of soft and lovely Irish ballads, sung in a fair voice and lilting accent.

Since leaving Palmerston on horseback, bound for the Gulf, the pair had already enjoyed a number of adventures. O'Donohue had won over a crowd at Adelaide River, riding a bush buckjumper to a standstill. Alfred had been alone when facing a 'bank robbery' at Burrundie, and a barrage of bullets from a disgruntled ruffian near the Elsey.

Further down the track the two of them had apprehended a clutch of rascals and marched them in to the Roper Bar police station. Even now Searcy laughed at the memory. Under the waving barrel of O'Donohue's revolver, Alfred had cut the buttons and suspenders from the miscreants' trousers, so that they were too busy protecting their modesty to fight back.

Then, at Roper Bar, the two lawmen had seen an amazing

sight: the travelling horsebreaker called Red Jack, her magnificent red hair spilling out from her hat, leading a string of horses no less beautiful than herself into town. None were so impressive as the stallion she rode, Mephistopheles.

Red Jack had paused to fill her packs with rations from the Armstrong and Company store. And Alfred was certain that she had nodded in his direction, though O'Donohue wasn't so sure. Either way, it was an event to remember. Most of the little township had turned up to watch her ride out of town, into the west, destination unknown, the famous wanderer dwindling into a haze of dust and red sunset.

And finally, now with a black trooper called Jimmy, seconded by order of the Superintendent, at Roper Bar, they had reached the Hodgson without further incident. The three of them had just finished an evening meal of black bream from the pool, picking the white chunks from the backbone, and charcoal flavoured skin, when a traveller rode down the track from the north, leading two packs.

The three horses splashed white water to the knees as they trotted across the ford. Seeing the established camp the new man dismounted and came in on foot.

'Evening you fellows,' he called. 'The name's Joe Jefferies, riding down to take up a position on Costello's Valley of Springs Station.'

Alfred stood, lifting his pipe from his lips as he did so. 'Searcy and O'Donohue here. We're policemen heading down to the Macarthur. You're welcome to our fire and campsite. A fine one it is too.'

'I don't mind if I do,' said the stranger. 'A cheery blaze and some new mates to yarn with is always welcome.' After seeing to his horses, he dug in his packs. There was the clink of glass and a bottle of rum appeared in his hands.

'Ye are welcome indeed,' grinned O'Donohue.

While Jimmy whittled away at a stick with his pen knife, the white men drank from tin cups.

'Have you heard the news?' asked the traveller. 'I dare say that being lawmen, you'll be interested.'

'What news?'

'There's a new gang on the loose. They call themselves the Ragged Thirteen. Just two nights ago they held up the store at Abraham's Billabong, stole a cart load of beef and broke Matt Kirwan's arm.'

Searcy narrowed his eyes. 'Who are these men?'

'Their captain is a bloke called Tom Nugent, but I reckon I know a couple of the bastards, Jim Fitzgerald and Larrikin Smith for a start.'

O'Donohue almost choked on his rum. 'Now let me get this from ye straight. Those dunderheads we took in at the Roper have jined up with some other ruffians and are calling themselves the Ragged Thirteen?'

'I don't know what happened at the Roper but I guess that's about it,' said the stranger.

'Well blow me down,' said Searcy. 'Should we ride back up and apprehend them?'

'I'm game,' said O'Donohue, 'but not yet, I'm thinkin'. Best we wait and see if we hear anything else. Besides ...' he swept his right hand in an arc towards the still distant Macarthur River. 'I'll wager there's many a lawless ruffian ahead that'd smile to see us ride away.'

'You're right,' said Alfred. 'The Ragged Thirteen can wait. But they'd better not get too far out of hand, or they'll be risking more than their trousers.'

# Chapter 9: The King River

While Tom Nugent, Jack Dalley, Fitz and Tommy the Rag headed for the Gulf, the rest of the Thirteen struck camp and rode the track in a north-westerly direction, towards the Katherine. With the stockboys droving a plant of near forty horses they moved slowly, often with the Overland Telegraph Line in sight, six or eight miles from breakfast to dinner camp, then the same again in the afternoon, depending on distractions along the way.

After a couple of days there was no longer any difference between the South Australian mob and the Queenslanders. They were all mates now. They shared a sense of fun, and a love of the bush and its dangers.

One morning, New England Jack tried to slip on his right boot. Finding the task difficult, he looked inside to find that a brown snake had taken up residence where his foot was supposed to go. With a shout of surprise Jack threw the boot underhand, watching it spin into the air. The surprised reptile extracted itself, fell to the ground, and slithered under Sandy Myrtle's swag. Sandy, who was sitting on it at the time, did not appreciate the visitor.

The incident brought on a spate of raucous laughter, jokes,

and even a line of verse or two. Before an hour or two had passed, however, the agile minds of the bushmen had moved on to other topics. There was always something new on the track up to Katherine; bucking horses, a 'dropped' bullock that 'accidentally' ran into a .577 Snider bullet, and best of all, Larrikin's attempts to cover his mare with Wonoka Jack's stallion.

The poor animal had gotten the shit kicked out of him by the stubbornly resistant mare the first few times the act had been attempted. These eagerly anticipated 'breedin' sessions,' saw the gang fetching drinks and laying bets before watching the poor stallion, his dark penis hanging erect, finish up with a couple of hoof prints across his face. That wasn't the worst of it, for Sandy Myrtle's huge mount, Jonathan James, was also taking an interest. Several times he interrupted proceedings, keen to fight for the right to cover the mare.

'I'll shoot that bastard of yours if he tries it again,' promised Jack.

'You'd better shoot me first,' warned Sandy. 'For I love that animal like a brother.'

'Well, for pity's sake, keep him out of it.'

Finally, camped on the King River, the mare gave up fighting. Fitz held her by a long halter, while Wonoka Jack brought up the stallion. This time she let him rub the underside of his neck against her shoulder, then draw deeply of the oestrous scent from under her tail. He mounted her at last, finding the place he needed with exploratory thrusts. The jokes ran free as he deposited forcefully, then slumped onto her back when he was done.

They stayed three hot and humid days on the King. The nights were not so bad. Many of the stockboys were not boys at all, but women. There was a great pretence about this. Everyone knew but no one spoke about it. Some of these relationships were full blown love affairs with tiffs and sulks. Others more one-sided. The women's stories varied. Never mentioned aloud.

Most have been lost in tearful silence.

On the third night the riders from the Gulf returned. Horses and men alike were thin and dusty from hard riding. Fitz removed a bandage to show off a wound on the muscle of his upper arm, an ugly, burned channel along the surface of the flesh. His shirt sleeve was dark with dried blood.

'A real bullet graze,' declared Tommy the Rag, proud to bear the news. 'He might'a come a cropper, if the aim'd been true.'

Larrikin examined the wound critically. 'By crikey! It was made by a bullet. You're a lucky devil, Fitz.'

Stranger still, and a source of mystery, was the fact that Tom Nugent was not alone in the saddle. Riding with him was an Aboriginal lad just a few years old. Dismounting first, Tom lifted the lad from the saddle and deposited him on the ground, where he stared with deep brown eyes at the white men, belly rounded and hair in lank curls. Even the stockboys gathered around to look.

'He's a bit young to be of much use,' declared Carmody. 'Where did he come from?'

Tom unfastened the girth and lifted his saddle down, arms taut with muscle. 'Unlike your brother-in-law, I don't measure people by how much good they can do me. Someone grab a chunk of damper, poor lad will be famished.'

Sandy Myrtle's face was twisted with curiosity. 'Can you tell us what the hell went on down there?'

'All in good time,' Tom said. 'Tucker first, then a good mug of rum, and I'll tell the yarn from start to finish.'

# Chapter 10: What Happened in the Gulf

After a feast of salt beef and johnny-cakes, Tom Nugent stoked the fire and took pride of place on a stump. Jack Dalley, Tommy the Rag, and Fitz took their places nearby.

'Gather 'round and hear the yarn you blokes,' Tom called. 'There's been deeds done in the name of the Ragged Thirteen.'

There was no need to ask twice. The men were aching to hear the story, pouring tots of rum and finding spots around the campfire.

And there, with a crackling blaze, the sighing of casuarinas and the clink of hobble chains as a background, Tom began to speak, drawing on all his skills as a bush raconteur: descriptive words, searching glances, and expansive gestures.

'We rode day and night, and didn't spare the spur. We struck the Hodgson at Minyerri waterhole, but scarcely stopped to wet our lips. Young Tommy killed a fat goanna with that whip of his, and we ate the bastard raw. Here's a tip, boys, a lump of meat wedged between the saddle pad and a horse's flank cures from sweat and heat. Tasty enough for a man in a hurry.

'Finally, with dawn blooming in the east, we rested. Men and horses slept like dead things 'til the flies roused us in swarms of millions. On we went. Even the wild spearmen of the Alawa people let us pass, for we moved too fast for them to gather in strength.

'Reaching the Hodgson crossing, we found the place where Searcy and O'Donohue and a third white man had camped. They had a smart Ngalakan tracker with them so we knew we'd have our work cut out. But as I've said before, Searcy likes to ride at snail's pace, a-looking under rocks and writing in his journal at every turn.' Tom grinned fiercely. 'We caught them up by nightfall, seeing their tents along a creek. We camped dry that night, and waited for our chance.'

'Waking after midnight, we surrounded their camp in the dark, and lured their tracker away. While Searcy and O'Donohue snored and drooled on their pillows, we unhobbled their horses and took them away. For good measure we went back and stole their undershorts, trousers and shirts, for the bludgers had left them hanging on a rope beside the creek. When it was done we rode like the clappers of hell for the Tablelands.'

Tom paused for an outbreak of laughter. Sandy Myrtle clutched at his heavy chest and shook like a wagon with a loose wheel. 'Oh you funny bastards, I wished I could'a seen their faces.'

Waiting until the noise died down, Tom slapped his right fist into his open left hand like a pistol shot. 'And oh, they chased us hard. They ran on foot, half dressed, to some desperate little cattle camp, and borrowed mounts. They came after us determined. They made us work, and we were near dead with lack of sleep by then.'

George Brown couldn't help but interject. 'Is that when Fitz copped that slug?'

Tom raised a hand. 'That's right, they managed to close up with us one morning, and Searcy sent down a hail of lead with that Winchester of his. Thought Fitz was a goner for a tick, but then he fired back with his Snider and I knew he was still with us. Bear with me, though, there's more to tell. We weren't finished with the bastards yet.'

'Each day we rode hard, leaving cheeky little signs behind. Jack Dalley blazed a tree and carved a fair image of Searcy with his pants down on the trunk. We rode them ragged, made them spitting angry, then sold their nags to a bunch of Chinese prospectors half-way to Anthony's Lagoon on the Barkly track.'

Wonoka Jack shook his head, incredulous. 'Now tell us about the boy you brought back. Where did he come from?'

'Well,' said Tom, then stopped to heave a deep long sigh. The fast rhythm of the tale fell away into a slow and thoughtful plod. 'Years ago I come upon a mob of fallen blacks down near the Macarthur. Bloodied and dead, cartridge cases scattered around the spinifex like seashells. I heard they'd speared a drover, and had paid for the crime in blood. There, wandering around the corpses, was a lad – just a toddler really – starving and near dead.' He pointed towards the boy, sitting with the stockboys. 'That's him there. I took him to some Yanyuwa women I regarded highly. They housed and nurtured him. As far as I was concerned, that's where he would have stayed, with just a visit and some assistance from yours truly now and again. But then, just days ago, Maori Jack Reid – Carmody here's brother-in-law – made it known that he knew the boy meant a lot to me, and that he might get at him to hurt me. Such a diabolical threat I couldn't abide, so we rode down to fetch him. Here he is, and amongst a good mob of his own people, with the Territory as his classroom.'

'Here, here,' said Sandy Myrtle, beginning to clap. The others joined in.

'Thanks, mate, but here's a word of warning. I fear that Searcy and O'Donohue will not let us get away so easily this time. As I said, they have a handy Ngalakan man as a guide, and he'll see our trail like a paved road.'

Tom had scarcely got the last word out of his mouth when

a bullet struck a pintpot someone had left sitting close to the flames, followed by the bellowing report of a heavy rifle. The pintpot jumped of its own volition, and sparks and embers flew like fireworks. The Thirteen scattered for cover and reached for their weapons. Actions closed and cartridges slammed home.

Out of the darkness came a ringing laugh. The stockboys cowered in fear, and even Tom felt the prickle of unease in the hairs along his spine.

'That's just a taste,' came a voice, 'just be sure that I could 'a killed any one of you bastards if I'd'a really tried.'

# Chapter 11: Jack Comes Back

Their ears were still ringing from the gunshot, scattered embers glowing all around the camp, when Carmody raised his head warily. 'Hey Tom,' he hissed, eyes glowing white in a face shiny with sweat. 'That sounds like Maori Jack out there.'

'So it does,' said Tom. 'I'd know that devil's voice anywhere.' Standing, holding his carbine at his hip, aiming vaguely out into the scrub, Tom called. 'If that's you, Maori, you're not welcome here.'

The reply came from the darkness towards the river bed. 'Be that as it may, I'm here. Put your guns down boys. I'm coming in.'

Tom spat back, 'You walk in with a loaded weapon and I'll shoot you down.'

'I'm unloading,' said Maori Jack. They heard the click of a Martini-Henry action, then; 'My rifle's in the scabbard now. I'll walk my horse in, real slow.'

In he came, spurs jingling as he walked, and though the breeze took the campfire smoke in his direction, Maori Jack never coughed or hid his eyes. He kept his hands visible, so no one would misinterpret a movement and open fire.

There was nothing good about the New Zealander's presence. They all felt it. Even the night birds stopped their calls and the drone of insects stilled to a whisper.

Nice and slow, Maori Jack fastened his horse to a tree just behind the camp, then came in and squatted at the fire, warming his hands like he belonged there. Though he must have realised that thirteen gun barrels were trained on him right then, his whiskered face showed no fear.

'You've got a hide coming here,' cried Jimmy Woodford. 'You mongrel horse killer.'

Maori swivelled his head, spat at the ground, then levelled two black eyes on Jimmy. 'Why boy, is this here your property?'

'No, but …'

'Then shut your mouth, or I'll do worse than kill a useless nag.' No one spoke back, nor did so much as a twig break.

Tom growled with displeasure. 'Mind your threats, you dog. Or next time we hang you it'll be the right way up. By the neck.'

Maori Jack ignored the comment and looked around the camp, scowling at each of the Thirteen, then the stock boys until his eyes picked out the young Yanyuwa boy Tom had brought back from the Gulf.

'Aha,' growled Maori, 'so there he is.' Looking at Tom, he continued; 'We both rode to Borroloola on the same errand. Unfortunately, I was waylaid at the Roper by a card game that seemed never to end. You beat me to him. Come here boy.'

The child walked closer, eyes wide and fearful. Maori Jack reached out, holding his fingers like pliers, using them to tug at the boy's chin.

'What's the lad's name, Tom?'

'Haven't thought up one for him yet.'

'He'd have a blackfella name though?'

'Yeah, but he's too young to remember it.'

Maori removed his thumb and forefinger from the child's chin, and watched him scamper back to the company of the stock boys. Then he turned his attention to Tom.

'I was angry, I admit, at what you and these other bastards done to me at Abraham's Billabong. But the way you fixed up Searcy and O'Donohue has gladdened my heart. You made fools of them, good and proper. Every man from here to the Queensland border is laughing about it.'

Fitz, who was not afraid of anybody, said, 'We didn't do that for you, Maori Jack Reid. We did it for us. Now why don't you get on your horse and leave us in peace.'

'Well maybe I will, in a minute. But I guess I should tell you that Searcy and O'Donohue are riding this way, right on your trail, with the aim of arresting you lot for horse thievery. Here's my offer, as a sign of friendship. I'll wait for the bastards at some lonely place, and nail them both. I'll bury them deep, where no one will ever know, just as a favour.'

There was not a sound in the camp. As if no one dared breathe.

'But that's not all,' continued Maori. 'Just twenty miles ahead, on the Katherine, is Jim Cashman's store. I hear that a dray-load of brand-new goods has just arrived. While I deal with Searcy and O'Donohue, you can knock over the store. Fill your pack saddles for the long ride to Hall's Creek, and give yourselves an alibi for the death of two policemen into the bargain.'

'Get out of here,' drawled Tom. 'We're already planning on knocking over Cashman's store, but I won't have anything to do with shooting Searcy and O'Donohue in cold blood.'

Maori Jack threw back his head and laughed. 'You've set yourselves up as a gang. What have you done so far? Nicked some beef and broke a man's arm. Big fucking deal. It's time to prove yourselves.' He paused for a moment, looking at each of the Thirteen in turn. 'Prove yourselves.'

Not far away, the Yanyuwa boy shivered with fear. He was afraid of the sly looking stranger with the demonic eyes.

He fingered the stone knife he carried in his bundle of rags. He had a feeling that one day soon, he would need to use it.

# Chapter 12: Katherine Town

The last leg of the journey to the Katherine covered mile after mile of flat woodland. Tommy the Rag entertained himself by flicking his stockwhip at the tops of termite mounds along the way, and Bob Anderson sang as he rode, old Scottish songs, that strangely seemed not out of place in the Territory.

The weather was steaming hot, however, and most of the others rode in a silence, half asleep and swigging from waterbags, horses and men alike dark with sweat.

In the flat scrub just shy of the river, they stumbled on a round-yard made of cypress posts and rails lashed together with greenhide strips. A neat canvas tent sat alongside. Camp ovens were embedded in the coals of a smoking fire and washing hung from a line.

Working a colt in the yard was the red headed woman, Red Jack. Even through the scrub, for they didn't dare ride too close, the Thirteen could see the grace of her movements and the concentration in her eyes.

'There she is again,' Tom said. 'What a trip this is turning out to be.'

Not wanting to disturb her, the Thirteen rode on to the river, intersecting it downstream from the township. The green channel lay deep between high clay banks, fringed with a lush growth of pandanus and stately paperbarks. By unspoken agreement they rode on past a colony of flying foxes and stopped to pitch camp on the high bank, where a dry season blaze had left a sharp stubble and green pick coming through for the horses.

'Where the hell is Scotty?' asked New England Jack.

'I'll ride back and find him,' said Tom, with a knowing smile.

Retracing their steps, Tom found the big Scot with his horse hitched to a black wattle tree, and Campbell himself leaning on the round-yard rails, watching Red Jack break the colt.

'Hey there, Scotty,' said Tom. 'I thought I might find you back here.'

'Ah but it's bleddy poetry,' the Scotsman replied, 'watchin' 'er work.'

Tom nodded slowly. 'True enough. I've seen a lot of horse breakers, but few have her touch.'

'I suppose you wan' me tae gae up now.'

'It'll be dark before long. We've got plans to make.'

Scotty untied his horse and mounted up, following Tom as he rode off. It seemed to them that Red Jack turned and looked as they went, and they tipped their hats to her as they rode off towards the river.

'Don't be getting obsessed with that woman,' Tom warned.

Scotty wouldn't look him in the eye. 'I'm tryin' Mister Nugent, but a man is only flesh an' blood.'

Just before dusk, while Sandy Myrtle and the Brown brothers forded the river and rode off towards Springvale Station in search of a 'lost' bullock that might be shot and butchered for meat, Tom took Larrikin, Bob Anderson and one of the stockboys into town. The main purpose was to case out Jim Cashman's store, but they had pennies for a rum or two jingling in their pockets.

'Now, if anyone asks,' said Tom, 'my last name is Holmes, not Nugent.'

'And I'm Bill,' Larrikin said. 'That's my real name, but no one knows me by it.' He turned to Bob. 'You're so fresh off the boat no one will know you anyway.'

The Katherine township was a straggling, untidy little outpost; situated on the south bank of the river, at a crossing place named after a prospector called John B Knott. The river's edge was busy with men fishing, drinking, bathing or washing clothes. Above the water a dirt track that served as a main strip wound through the scrub. There was a pub called the Sportsman's Arms, owned by a man called Barney Murphy, a couple of stores, and bough-sheds, shanties and tent camps over a few blocks.

The telegraph and police stations were located a few hundred yards away, almost invisible with all the trees, huts, and pandanus clumps. Tom looked warily in that direction. Traps would make their work more dangerous.

Seeing a handy clearing, with old fireplaces marked by scorched stones lying abandoned in the shade, Tom suggested they stop. 'Pull up here, boys, and we'll wander around on foot.'

While the stockboy, a wizened character of about fifty years called Blind Joe, guarded the horses, the three white men packed their pipes and strolled along the main street, smoking and talking amongst themselves. They paused at the butcher's shop to comment on the carcass hanging on a gallows out the back, and exchange hellos with the man in a bloodied white apron weighing beef on a scale, surrounded by a cloud of flies that settled on everything, including the meat.

By a round-about way they reached Cashman's store. Tom took in every detail: the solid slab construction of the door, the barred grills on the window spaces. Inside they walked between the rows of shelves, enjoying the sight of a variety of goods they had not seen in a long while. Everything from Lea and

Perrins sauce, patent medicines, flour in drums, soap, horse-shoes, tinned goods to hardware like axe heads and knives. In a cabinet behind the counter sat a selection of Winchester and Martini-Henry rifles, a couple of shotguns and Colt revolvers in wooden cases.

Tom purchased some pipe tobacco and a packet of .577 cartridges so as not to seem suspicious, then led the other two back out onto the roadway. 'I think I've got a plan,' he said.

'Ha' aboot another plan, eh?' said Bob Anderson. 'We could just buy what we need, wi'out havin' to pan in windaes and doors, then be on our way tomorra without any bastard chasing us.'

'Where's the fun in that?' countered Tom. 'Besides, we're going to need every cent we can lay our hands on when we get to Hall's Creek. What now, you blokes, how about a quick peg or two at the pub?'

Without any further urging they crossed the road to the pub, a slab hut with drinkers spilling out on to the street. Tom led the way inside, and as soon as his eyes adjusted he stopped dead. For there, right in front of him, sitting at a table with a glass of rum, was Maori Reid. Beside the half-drunk spirit sat a pile of coins and a grimy old pack of playing cards.

Also at the table was an Aboriginal youth. He looked to Tom like a Jangman from the Roper. There was also something very familiar about him.

Tom would have turned and left, but other eyes had already been raised. Thinking furiously, he walked on past Maori without a word and fronted the bar, where he bought three rums. He led Larrikin and Bob, armed with a glass each, back to the table where Maori Reid sat.

'Hello there, sir,' he said. 'Are these seats taken.'

'Not at all,' said Maori Reid smoothly. He extended a hand, 'Nice to meet you Mr ...'

'Holmes, Tom Holmes.'

'I'm John Smith,' replied Maori, just as smoothly.

The attention of the rest of the bar had moved on, and Maori Reid smiled and lowered his voice. 'I've just been gettin' the good oil from Billy here. Your friends Searcy and O'Donohue are on their way. They might get here at any minute.' Then, in a whisper, 'I'm thinkin' that you and your "gang" won't have the ticker to knock over Cashman's store with a couple of pinks around?'

Tom ignored the veiled insult, 'What about the Katherine traps, are they in town?'

'No, there's only one, and he's out on patrol. Not expected back for a week or two.'

Tom turned his attention to the black youth Maori had identified as Billy. 'Do I know you from somewhere?'

Billy shrugged and looked scared.

Maori sucked in his lip. 'Billy's the one who rode off on George Bowen's horse out at Abraham's Billabong, when youse were knocking off that beef. That means he's on the cross – one of us now.'

Tom snapped his finger. 'I knew I'd seen him before.' He turned to the boy. 'So that's where you met "Mr Smith" here.'

'Yes *Mulaka*. Last time I seen this feller he was hangin' up wrong way.'

Tom laughed, then threw down his rum in one draught. Larrikin and Bob followed suit. There was no question of staying for another with the brooding presence of Maori Reid in the pub.

'We're off,' Tom said. He extended a hand. 'Nice to meet you, Mr Smith.'

'Likewise, Mr Holmes.'

They walked outside, and when they reached the horses, the three men knocked out their pipes and stood taking a last look at Cashman's store.

'Are we still going to rob the place?' Larrikin asked. 'It might not be so easy if those two traps get here in time. I don't like Maori Jack being around, either.'

'Of course we're still going to do it. I don't mind old Searcy and O'Donohue arriving either. It'll add to the fun.'

Tom turned to the stockboy who had been waiting with the horses. 'You orright Blind Joe?'

'Yeah I'm orright, boss.'

'When we get back to camp I want you and the rest of your mob to clear out straightaway.'

'What for boss?'

'We got things to do and don't want you mob mixed up in it. You take the others west, you know the junction, where the Flora River runs into the Katherine?'

'I know that place boss. Plenty sand, and fish n' turtle.'

'You get cracking, walk all night and camp there. We'll follow tomorra, with full packs of tucker and supplies.'

'Orright boss.'

The four men mounted up and maintained a lively trot back towards the camp. Each was silent, filled with thoughts of how the events of the coming night might affect his own future.

# Chapter 13: Billy and the Traps

Up from the Gulf on a mission of revenge, Troopers Searcy and O'Donohue rode side by side, reaching the Elsey in record time, and veering north towards the Katherine.

'You don't think Inspector Foelsche will be angry that we've ridden back all this way when we're supposed to be on duty in Borroloola by now?' Alfred asked.

O'Donohue shook his head. 'Paul is a man o' the world. He'd expect us to punish the ruffians who stole our horses and made us look like dashed fools.' He held one fist up to his face. 'I'll see Tom Nugent and his cronies in chains if it's the last t'ing I ever do.'

'It's a shame,' said Alfred, 'that the very rawness of the Territory attracts undesirable characters. I'm not talking about hard-working farmers and labourers, storekeepers and clerks. We need people such as those. It's these dashed parasites like the Ragged Thirteen that I'm talking about. They care for nothing but themselves, and not for one minute the glory of the British Empire.'

'I agree with ye, Alfie. If only we could close the borders to 'em. The Territory needs to be settled with intelligence and foresight. That's not to say I don't enjoy an adventure as much as the next man, but we don't need robbers and vagabonds.'

The conversation kept them engrossed through the day. Then, just before Abraham's Billabong they saw a rider coming towards them. A string of packhorses followed, attended by a couple of stock boys.

'Hey, isn't that Matt Kirwan?' Alfred said.

'I think so. Yes, it's him, by God.'

They both liked Kirwan. He was a rogue, but a well-bred one, for he was from a good Melbourne family, yet too wild to be contained in that city. His left arm was in a sling, so he rode one-handed. As he neared it became obvious that his face was swollen, and marked with old bruises.

The riders reined in, and the horses nosed around each other, snorted and stamped.

'Hail there,' said Alfred, 'it's nice to meet a good man on the track. Got time for a cuppa?'

'I've always time for a brew with some mates.'

They stopped and lit a fast-burning fire of dry twigs, the hot flames quickly boiling the billy before dying again. It was only once they had mugs of sweet tea in hand that O'Donohue asked the question.

'We heard about your arm, Matt, and I see a bruise or two on your face. The damned Ragged T'irteen had no right to do that.'

Matt's face darkened. 'The devil take them. Can't you put the mongrels behind bars? I heard that you'd captured them and had them down in Roper Bar a few weeks ago.'

Alfred preened, 'We did too. Just the pair of us. And that damned Trooper Donegan convinced us to let them go … but tell us about the fight. How did your arm get broken?'

'I fought the Scotsman, Hughie Campbell, fair and square, and would have ground him down and won, but that fat-arsed Sandy Myrtle sat on me and broke my arm. Now, you tell me, why are you riding back this way? I thought you two were the new coppers at Borroloola?'

There was a long silence then, O'Donohue cleared his throat. 'The Ragged T'irteen stole our bloody horses, which is why we're riding these second-rate neddies. We're on our way to find the bastards and arrest 'em. How about you?'

'I'm heading back to the Roper Landing. Young Bowen will have to fend for himself from now on, God help him.' They'd finished their tea by then, and Matt smoothed out the fire with his foot, grinding a few still-burning embers into the dust. 'Do me a favour though. Keep an eye out for a grey horse that belongs to George Bowen. Young black called Billy rode off with him the same night the Ragged Thirteen raided me for beef. He's a good horse and George wants him back. The brand is a crossed diamond.'

'We'll keep an eye out, for sure,' promised Alfred, and in no time at all they were back in the saddle and riding north towards the Katherine.

Increasingly aware that they were absent without leave from their new post in Borroloola, Searcy and O'Donohue wasted no time covering the sixty remaining miles. The heat intensified as they headed north, the sun burning like a branding iron. By mid-afternoon on the second day they were only an hour away from the town, and had already passed the camps of some lonely travellers, most of them bound for Hall's Creek.

Up ahead through the trees there was a flash of grey, and the thunder of hooves as a horseman spurred his mount off the back legs, springing into a full gallop.

'Whoa,' shouted Alfred, 'That might be the horse Matt Kirwan was talking about. Let's ride him down.'

Leaving their tracker with the packs, the two policemen set off at speed, the tired horses responding well. It was a wild ride through spear and hummock grass, spurs biting deep and the policemen leaning low like jockeys, eyes almost closed to exclude flying bugs and sharp speargrass heads.

This was bad ground for fast riding, however – gilgai country – pitted with hidden clay holes. The horse in front took a stumble, grunting with alarm and almost throwing the rider. The horseman got his mount under control, but by then Searcy had reached him, shouldering the horse with his own and grabbing the reins. A final dart on foot was foiled by O'Donohue who dismounted and ran the horse-thief down, pushing between his shoulder blades so he collapsed in an untidy pile.

With the horses tied securely, Alfred helped pin the fugitive. 'Doan hurt me,' he cried.

'By colour and brand that horse belongs to Matt Kirwan. It was stolen from Abraham's Billabong. Consider yourself under arrest. What's your name?'

'Billy.'

'Have you seen those thirteen ruffians from the Roper? Did you ride with them? Are you assisting the gang?'

'Nah *Mulaka*. Saw nobody. Only Maori Reid.'

Searcy and O'Donohue exchanged glances. 'Maori Reid is in Katherine?'

'An' Tom Holmes. The one I seen down Abraham's Billabong.'

'Holmes?' said O'Donohue.

'Nugent,' smiled Searcy. 'That man wears pseudonyms like normal men wear jackets. He's here, right within our reach. Hey boy, now that we've got the stolen horse we might go easy on you: if you tell us all about this Tom Holmes we might even let you go.'

'They gonna rob the store in Kath-ryne town.'

'When?'

'Dunno. Mebbe tonight.'

'They're staying in town?'

'Nar, out on the river somewhere.'

'You've done well, Billy. But if we do let you go, do you promise to walk back to the Roper and keep out of trouble?'

'Yes *Mulaka*.'

Alfred let go of his shoulder. 'Well go on. Clear out of it then.'

O'Donohue also released his pinioning hands and let Billy up, who loped away without a backwards glance.

Alfred grinned at his mate. 'Tonight's the night ... you and me are going to have those bastards cold.'

# Chapter 14: Before the Raid

With the supply of rifle cartridges replenished, Tom turned his thoughts to the revolvers, or 'squirts' they all carried. These were, in the main, cap and ball weapons such as Tom's own Colt Navy.

Aware that they had just a handful of .36 calibre balls left, Tom set about casting new ones. He rummaged through the packsaddles for some folded lead sheet he had borrowed from a church roof in Toowoomba. He added this to a saucepan, setting it on the coals of a fire made from black wattle sticks – the hottest burning timber around – most often used for heating branding irons. He worked his hat mechanically, like a bellows, and slowly the lead began to melt into a sluggish grey pool.

At this stage he stirred in a spoonful of flux from a tin, and scooped off the dross from the surface. The moulds had handles like pliers, with a spherical cavity at the business end. Working over a flat rock with a steel funnel, he poured the first one full, leaving it to cool while he made a second. The first ball was then ready to drop into a quart pot of water, tinkling against metal as it reached the bottom.

Each ball then needed to have any protrusions filed off, and Tom liked to finish with a glasspaper rub, until they were perfectly round and shiny, satisfactorily heavy. He had more than twenty new balls done when Blind Joe came over, holding the hand of the boy Tom had brought up from Borroloola.

'What's up?' Tom asked. 'I told you to clear out and meet us up the Flora Junction.'

'I'm gonna boss, but this young feller says he don't want to leave you.'

Tom left the business of casting and got down on one knee, so his eyes were level with those of the boy. 'You get going with Blind Joe, for your own good. Things are going to get lively around Katherine town tonight, and I want you safe. Orright?'

The boy nodded slowly, eyes like waterholes.

'Blind Joe's takin' you to a fine camping place. I'll be there before you know it, and we'll tarry a few days there – have a grand old time.'

Another nod, this time fully accepting.

Tom watched Blind Joe lead the boy away, then let out a long sigh, relieved that he seemed to be preparing to join the crew heading west.

Meanwhile, Searcy and O'Donohue were riding hell-for-leather towards the town. They passed a drovers' camp on the southern bank, with half a dozen stockmen keeping a big mob of bullocks boxed in, but Alfred just waved his hat in greeting and rode on. There was something about their arrival in relative civilisation that made him worry that maybe Inspector Foelsche might not be happy with them retracing their steps. It made him conscious that he was on borrowed time.

Crossing the river at Knott's Crossing, the sun was an orange fireball that played on the river surface with reflections of the green flushed banks, while the horses churned through. Both men let their mounts pause to drink in the shallows on the other side before reefing their heads up and moving on, climbing the far bank, passing a noisy group of travellers bathing, skylarking and drinking rum. A little further downstream was a bucket chain of Chinese, no doubt carrying water for a vegetable patch on the high bank.

'This place is going to the dogs,' said Alfred as they entered the township. Most of the population appeared to be on the pub verandah, and there were catcalls from lower types as they recognised the uniform. Dusty urchins glared avariciously as they passed.

'Pity t'ere are so many low-lifes here,' mused O'Donohue. 'A glass of ale'd sit well on my palate this evening.'

'I agree wholeheartedly,' said Alfred. 'But I fancy we have more important things on our plate.'

They found the police station deserted, with a note on the door. This was the only part of the structure made of sawn timber. The rest was of split slabs of ironwood, and the roof of casuarina shingles.

The note was rendered in quill and ink, already a little faded; *Gorn west on patrol. Any disterbance should be reported to Barney Murphy who will telegraf Parmerston.*

'We'd better report in to headquarters directly, then,' said Alfred. And at the telegraph office, he penned a short communication, with O'Donohue looking over his shoulder all the while. In the end, after numerous crossings-out they came up with.

AT KATHERINE IN PURSUIT OF NOTORIOUS GANG
THE RAGGED THIRTEEN STOP WILL RETURN TO
BORROLOOLA IN HASTE ONCE ACCOMPLISHED
STOP SEARCY AND ODONOHUE ENDS

Pushing his way to the front of the line, citing 'official business.' Alfred watched the telegraph operator tap out the message. Then, they had scarcely mounted up again, when the operator hurried out with a reply.

'Constable Searcy, this just come back for you.'

Alfred took the note and read it, frowning.

EXTREMELY DISAPPOINTED YOU HAVE IGNORED
ORDERS AND NOT YET ARRIVED BORROLOOLA,
REPORTS OF MAJOR UNREST IN TOWNSHIP STOP
ORDER YOU RIDE IMMEDIATELY REPEAT IMME-
DIATELY FOR THE MACARTHUR STOP INSPECTOR
FOELSCHE ENDS

Searcy looked at O'Donohue. 'Even he wouldn't expect us
to ride tonight, would he?'

'He sounds shirty, but I wouldn't reckon on it.'

'We've got one night to nail the Ragged Thirteen. We have
to take it.'

'I was counting on the local police officer being here. Can
we take them with just two of us?' O'Donohue asked.

'Well, we bested them on the Roper.'

'Not quite the entire gang, and they weren't in the process
of a robbery. They will have firearms.'

Alfred drew himself up to his full height. 'I did not come all
this way to ride away again with my tail between my legs. We will
wait for those rascals and apprehend them in the act of robbing
Cashman's store.'

O'Donohue patted his belly as if stoking a fire there, 'Of
course we will.'


Back at camp, Jimmy Woodford and New England Jack had
just returned from a trip into town, riding with the reins in one
hand, and a demijohn of rum in the other. They were not the
only ones keen to warm up with the fiery liquid.

'I'll be damned if I rob a store sober,' said Jimmy, his hair
and eyes wild. 'It'll be twice as much of a lark fully charged.'

Sandy Myrtle wasn't so sure. 'Maybe you should ask Tom.
We voted him as leader, remember?'

Jimmy paused with his mug in one hand, and jug in the other, then called across to Tom, who was rubbing his new lead
balls, one by one, with glasspaper. 'You don't mind if we down

a few belts of the good stuff, do you Tom?'

Tom shook his head sagely. 'So long as you can sit on a horse and don't do anything stupid, go for your life. I might even enjoy a nip or two myself before we ride out.'

Jimmy let rip a whoop and touched mugs with New England Jack. Upending these vessels they drained them fast, with a few drops dripping down off their moustaches.

'Here's to tonight,' cried Jimmy. 'And the most daring gang in the land since Ned Kelly and his mates fell at Glenrowan.'

# Chapter 15: The Katherine Robbery

Scattered over a mile of river bank, the settlement of Katherine was deep in midnight slumber. There was no wind, the air warm and smoky from hearth fires that burned beside bark and iron humpies.

Thirteen mounted men rode out from their camp downstream, skilled horsemen all, keeping to the scrub where they could, moving like shadows. Tom Nugent, at the lead, kept every sense on high alert. Somewhere, far out in the night, a pair of hunting dingoes howled. The river was a faint whisper as it ran over the stones around Knotts Crossing.

Up ahead Tom could make out the dark shape of a man on horseback. 'Hold it there, lads,' he said softly. 'There's someone riding towards us.'

'It's a friend,' came a voice. 'I'm riding in.'

Tom did not reply, but the horseman rode out of the darkness of the trees, into the open, where the moonlight illuminated the face of Maori Reid.

'You're not part of this,' growled Tom. 'I've told you to piss off before, so why the hell do you keep turning up?'

'It's a free country. Besides, I came to report that Searcy and O'Donohue are in town and waiting for you bastards. I can sort them out for youse, even now. Just give me the word.'

It was Hugh Campbell who spoke up. 'Nae listen, you dog, Tom's told you to ride on, an' I suggest ye do it.'

Maori Reid turned his face so his eyes were blazing white. 'Shut your gob you daft Scot. Go back to your fucking bagpipes and leave the man's work to real men.'

Scotty started forward, but he was not about to initiate a fight on horseback, and there were more important things at hand than dismounting and scrapping with Maori Reid.

Besides, taking advantage of the confrontation, Jimmy Woodford moved up behind Maori Reid with his Snider rifle reversed. He swung the butt with a vicious, short stroke. Maori sensed the attack and tried to turn, too late. The hardwood struck the back of the New Zealander's head like a pole-axe, felling him so he slid over the side of his horse. His right foot caught in the stirrup until Jimmy kicked it free, allowing his victim to thump to the ground, out like a snuffed candle.

'That felt good,' said Jimmy. 'The horse-murdering bastard.'

'Good work, Jimmy,' said Tom, looking down at the inert form of the man. 'Maori had that coming. Now let's ride in fast from here in case anyone heard us talking. You got that axe ready Sandy?'

'Sure have.'

'Good. Now gee-up.' Tom let his mount have his head in the dark, trusting him to avoid obstacles, controlling only the speed of the canter and a general direction. They were into the town before they knew it, for there were no gas lights here, just the odd glowing fire around the township.

Coming to a halt beside the store, Tom slipped three fingers under the lever of his Martini-Henry carbine, standing guard while Sandy Myrtle dismounted with his axe. Sandy's huge shoulders swelled like tree trunks as he took his stance and swung. The door was a stout construction, Tom had studied it earlier that day – made of slabs of deep red local ironwood

– and it stood up to a pounding. After four hefty blows from Sandy, however, the screws broke through the hinges and the way was open.

'Alright boys,' Tom hissed. 'Everything we can carry, we take.'

As they filed in, Tom remained on guard, watching for any sign of trouble. The dust was rising from their hurried arrival, for the surface of the track had been pounded by hooves and wheels into a deep, fine powder, light as air.

The men were inside now, and Tom heard the clink of cans hitting sacks as they went to work. Horseshoes, flour, tea, sugar. He smiled to himself. He had long ago decided that the system was biased against men like him, and that taking back his share was not just a right, but a duty.

A town-dweller in a night shirt with a jacket thrown over the top approached from one of the nearest bough shelters. He carried a shotgun, broken, over his forearm, and his nose was red with grog.

'What in the name of the Almighty is going on here?' he shouted.

'Go back to bed, this is no concern of yours,' Tom shouted. The man hesitated at first, and Tom raised the rifle to his shoulder and trained it on the man's chest. The nightshirt flapped around his legs as he ran off into the darkness, shouting as he went.

'Hurry now you lot,' Tom shouted into the doorway. 'They'll all be waking now.'

The twelve started to file back out from the store, one after the other, throwing sacks over saddles, booty from the raid. Nervous horses nickered and stamped.

Last came Tommy the Rag.

'Hurry up, fuck it Tommy.' Tom whispered under his breath, but he couldn't stay angry. Tommy wore a grin so wide, enjoying the game more than the rest of them put together, giggling as he mounted up. But that frontier town was waking, lanterns blinking on and shouts ringing out from neighbouring shanties.

Tom Nugent ran his eyes over her ragged band. 'Now mount up,' he called.

But as they did so, two men stepped out onto the road just ahead. Both had rifles ready at the shoulder.

'Surrender, in the Queen's name,' called a voice, loud and commanding.

# Chapter 16: A Company of Thieves

lfred Searcy's legs were steady and his hands did not shake as he peered through the iron sights of one of the most feared weapons in those parts, a Winchester repeating rifle. Beside him stood O'Donohue, with his Martini-Henry locked and loaded. Together they were representatives of the law; a force to reckoned with.

Alfred had always seen himself as a hero-in-waiting. He had recently started writing the story of his life. Now, in this remote outback town, his first real moment of fame might have arrived. He and O'Donohue were the sole manifestations of good in this moment of evil. It was time to act. Still with the rifle to his shoulder he sighted over the heads of the Thirteen and fired into the air.

'Stand to, you ruffians,' he shouted. 'Lay down your weapons and you might yet save your skins.'

For a moment there was dead silence, surprise perhaps. Then, the raiders ran for their horses, leaping onto saddles, giggling and laughing as they went. One even dropped his trousers and showed his buttocks. Searcy felt the muscles of his neck tighten with anger.

As the Thirteen rode away. Alfred was fully prepared to

shoot to kill. He focussed on the bulky shape in the rear of the galloping thieves, surely the infamous Sandy Myrtle, a man so huge that men took pity on the poor creature, reputedly called Jonathan James, that carried him. Yet, these were not good conditions for shooting, darkness exacerbated by dust. Iron sights, moreover, were never much good in the dark.

Alfred fired, swung the lever, fired again. Three times the butt thumped into his shoulder before he realised that his target was nowhere in view. He knew with a trained rifleman's gut instinct that his efforts had flown wide. The first shot had been close, but the others might as well have stayed in the tube.

He lowered the rifle, holding it at the balance point in one hand as he and his mate loped after the horsemen, hoping for one more shot where the track curved. Unfortunately, the Thirteen were already too far away, and besides, men woken by the gunshots were appearing from their camps. The chances of hitting one by accident were high.

'T'ose damn mongrels,' O'Donohue muttered. 'They reckon t'ey are above the law. P'raps we should raise a party to chase an' give battle.'

Alfred said nothing, but as they walked back to the store, he looked dismissively at the half-drunk blowhards who staggered out of their bough sheds and wurlies to see what the commotion was. There wasn't a man among them he would have trusted to ride out with him against thirteen well-mounted rascals.

At the store Jim Cashman himself had arrived, ranting at the damage and depleted shelves. Alfred could not meet his eye, and simply turned to O'Donohue.

'Let's get our gear, we're going after them.'

'Now? In t'e dark?'

'You bet your pension we are.'

Alfred led the way back to where their tracker waited with the horses. The first thing he did was to reload his rifle with heavy cartridges from a box of ammunition he took from his saddlebags. Then, with O'Donohue beside him, he mounted the nervous horse and left town at a walk, before digging in his heels and cantering through some initial side creeps and even a light buck or two.

On the outskirts of town Alfred stopped and addressed the tracker. 'Now Jimmy, there's a good bit o' moon and lots of men in that company of thieves. You reckon you can track 'em?'

Jimmy leaned down from the saddle, examining the trail. Then, without a word he urged his horse on. The track headed southwest along the river, and the camps they came upon were awake and riled, offering shouted reports of the Thirteen riding through.

Downriver ten miles they found a furious gang of ringers, a cattle camp from Elsey Station. They'd shot a 'killer' the day before, and hung the carcass overnight to set, a strong branch serving as gallows. The Thirteen had seen it, and stopped for long enough to strip the carcass to the bone before riding on.

'Those thieving dogs,' the lead man ranted. 'If you catch them I want my meat back, and I'll testify in court against them meself.'

'They can't be far ahead,' muttered Searcy. 'Burdened down by meat, and all those stores, we must be getting close.'

But the Thirteen were not ignorant of the chance of pursuit. Not long after capping the night off by stealing the meat, they had headed down to the river, riding in through a dry side gully, under a canopy of paperbarks, then up along a shallow stretch of running water.

Searcy and O'Donohue had no choice but to follow, urging their horses into the river, pushing through the pandanus. In places the water was deep enough to reach the horses' bellies. Both men were afflicted by itchy grubs from the riverside trees, and were scratching the blotched red skin on their arms and neck that resulted.

'T'is a risk, Alfie,' commented O'Donohue. 'I've heard of

big 'gators around here.'

'Damn the 'gators,' came the reply, but the horses were wary, picking their way around hazardous snags and deeper holes.

The going was slow, with Jimmy forced to examine the banks as they went, looking for exit points. Before long the stream veered left into a channel cut in a veritable lake of sand covering dozens of acres, soon separating into five or six separate deep ruts, any of which the Thirteen might have followed.

Jimmy finally stopped, waiting for the two policemen to catch up. 'We sitdown along sunup, boss. They coulda gone this way, or maybe that way. If we go on we maybe lose them. Too many ways now.'

'Damn,' shouted Searcy. 'But I see that we have no choice. We'll make a light camp and get a few hours' sleep. At dawn we get after them again.'

O'Donohue shook his head sadly. 'Inspector Foelsche is going to kill us when he finds out. We're absent without leave, and I don't like it.'

'He'll be pleased if we catch the Thirteen,' muttered Alfred, but later, lying awake in his swag, he wondered if that was true.

# Chapter 17: Fugitives from Justice

'E veryone alright?' Tom Nugent had called, when they pulled up ten miles south west of the Katherine township.

Sandy Myrtle took off his cabbage-tree hat and thrust his hand inside, extending a finger through a bullet hole in the weave. 'Well damn me for being a lucky bastard,' he said. 'I thought I felt something.'

The gang fell into helpless laughter, full of nerves at the burglary and their rapid exit, remembering the sound the police bullets had made as they parted the air around them.

'Damn near took the top of yer scone right off,' said Tommy the Rag.

'Fancy missing a target as juicy as Sandy Myrtle,' laughed Fitz.

'Beats me why you have to wear that darned hat in the night time anyhow,' breathed Wonoka Jack. 'I thought only ladies wore hats after sundown.'

Sandy replaced the hat on his head. 'Shut yer mouths, you lot, or I'll close 'em for you.'

Tom Nugent grinned to himself. The banter was one of the things he loved about this crew of misfits. They rode on, and when they came upon a hanging bullock carcass next to a glowing campfire and some abandoned swags, it seemed wasteful to hurry past it. Within an hour, with Jack Woods in charge of proceedings, they'd hacked off most of the meat and stuffed it in tucker bags. Even more heavily laden, they headed off downstream along the Katherine River itself, riding through the stream, splitting up when it diverged into a maze of channels, making pursuit all but impossible.

By dawn, however, they were back up on the high banks. It was scrubby country: sandy soil with crackling dry speargrass. Even the woollybutt, shitwood and black wattle trees grew stunted and mean. Every now and then, to cope with the heat, they would head down to the river bed, finding pools of sweet green water interspersed with rapids, and banks of green couch grass that the horses loved.

They lunched on the riverbank, in just such a spot, amongst the writhing trunks of paperbark trees, and a breeze off the water. After some swimming and skylarking, Bob Anderson gathered sticks for a campfire. A bottle of rum, looted from Cashman's store, was opened and passed around, while fresh beef steaks and Scotty's best Johnny-cakes filled bellies.

Tom raised his mug to his mates and grinned. 'Here's to mischief, fast horses and adventure.'

They all drank down their drams, and Larrikin hurried around with the bottle to refill them all, before lifting his mug also. 'And' … he added. 'Here's to a fortune in gold waiting for us at the Hall's Creek fields.'

Laughing and drinking, they talked of nuggets like bantam eggs lying just under the ground ready for them to pick up. Then, while Jack Woods cut beef into strips and hung them on sticks over the fire to cure, Larrikin led his mare into the river shallows.

Cupping water with his hands he wet her all over, brushing her coat down with his fingers. When he was done she trotted out, rolled in the hot gravel and shook herself off.

'Looks like you got your wish, Larrikin,' said Sandy Myrtle. 'I reckon that mare's in foal.'

'Why's that?'

'A pregnant mare shakes only her head and neck, not her body, like she just done.'

This precipitated a long discussion as to whether she was or she wasn't. They had all been involved in the breeding, and thus had a strong interest.

Jimmy Woodford was all set to get out a nail and string, 'to prove the fact for good and all,' but Tom Nugent laughed. 'I haven't seen that barrel of hers start swelling yet. That's when we'll know for sure.'

They were having fun, in no hurry to ride on when there was a loud whistle from downstream.

Tom stood up. 'Cripes, that's Blind Joe. What the hell is he doing back here?' He thrust two fingers in his mouth and whistled back.

Blind Joe rode into the camp, his dark skin shiny with sweat and his horse's side flecked with foam.

Tom walked to meet him, alert and wary. 'What's up, Joe? You haven't seen them policemen, have you?'

'No *Mulaka*. Much worse'n that.'

'Who?'

'That Maori Reid, he follered us mob all the way down along the junction where you tell us to go.'

Jimmy Woodford's face turned deep red. 'I wish I'd kilt the bastard when I had the chance.'

'You might as well have,' growled Tom, 'for you can bet you made him angry.' Then, to Joe. 'What's Maori Reid done? Tell us, quick.'

The black man said nothing, but tears glistened in the corner of his eye.

'Mount up, you lot,' cried Tom. 'I've been soft and I apologise for it. Now we're going to deal with that bastard once and for all.'

Jim Carmody was the first to tack up and hit the saddle. 'Maori Reid might be my brother-in-law, but I'll gladly put a bullet in him myself.'

# Chapter 18: Searcy Turns Back

In the middle of the afternoon, Alfred Searcy and his mate O'Donohue followed their tracker up to the remnants of the Ragged Thirteen's dinner camp on the river. They walked the horses in, carbines in their laps as they rode, inhaling the smell of food scraps and cold campfire.

Some hasty drying racks over the fireplace had been abandoned. Dollops of grass had been turned, thrown by horses spurred from a standing start.

'They left in a hurry,' said Alfred, eyes following a scavenging goanna as it sprinted away and up into a tree. 'Not sure why. We're still a long way behind, and it looks like a lazy camp.' He dismounted and held his hand flat over the hearth to judge the heat. 'Barely any warmth there. I'm guessing they'll be three or four hours ahead.'

'T'e bastards are well mounted,' said O'Donohue. 'It might take another day or two to catch up now. We'll have to let t'em go and ride for the Macarthur. If we hurry we can be t'ere in t'ree or four days, before t'e Superintendent sacks us.'

Alfred thought about it. The Thirteen were long gone, miles ahead, and to follow would mean days on the hunt, most likely losing their jobs in the process. Foeleche was of German descent, and strict on discipline. Besides, Searcy also had the feeling that now a serious crime had been committed, the Thirteen might not be taken easily. Two policemen wasn't enough for a serious pursuit.

'Damn those bastards,' he said, but he called for Jimmy, who was still casting around the spoor, expecting to follow. 'You better lead us back Borroloola way, orright?'

'Orright boss.' If Jimmy thought it strange that he be asked to turn around so suddenly, he gave no sign.

Those two mates rode like the wind. They never came off the trot, galloping when the mood took them and the horses seemed willing. By evening, storms were out roaming the grasslands, with raking winds and the first real rains of the coming wet. Black clouds rose in columns, and lightning flickered like gunfire.

Feeling heavy raindrops, and the moisture-laden air in their nostrils, Alfred and his mate whipped off their hats and whooped and hollered with excitement.

They were half way to the telegraph line, twenty good miles down, when they headed in to a small waterhole called Clem's Pond. Now, for the first time they became cautious, slowing the horses so they could see if any men, white or black, were there before them. There was indeed a man camped at the water's edge, shirtless and still wet from the rain. His right leg was stuck out straight from his body and the other tucked underneath. His face was pained with fever.

'Hey that's the horse thief, Billy,' cried O'Donohue.

'In a bad way by the look of it.' Alfred rode closer, looking down at the leg. There was a bloody wound in the man's thigh, striped red with infection. A hobbled horse had been grazing in the scrub just back from the waterhole, but lifted its head to look at them.

'I hope that's not another stolen horse, is it Billy?'

'No *Mulaka*. This one was gibben to myself. Cranky bastard threw me good back there, an' got a stick through this-feller leg.'

'You're in luck,' said O'Donohue. 'Mr Searcy here is darn near as good as a doctor.'

'I'll do my best, anyhow,' said Alfred. 'We'll see to the horses and get the billy on. Then we'll clean that leg up and have a look.' Jimmy had reached the waterhole with the rest of the plant and was already hobbling them out.

The leg, it turned out, had been pierced by a shaft of green timber, made up of multiple splinters, each as thick as a finger. Billy had managed to remove only a fraction of the total, and Alfred had to use forceps. Each extraction was followed by a seep of blood. The patient grew increasingly distressed, and O'Donohue had to hold him down by the shoulders, while tendons stood out in the dark skin of his neck. The muscles of his leg clenched so tight that they were like boards.

When it was done, with the wound bathed with iodine and bandaged neatly, they ate johnny cakes with treacle together and talked.

'So where are you headed to, Billy?'

'Nowhere *Mulaka*. Just wanderin' about.'

'What do you plan to do when your leg heals up?'

'Dunno, *Mulaka*.'

'Do you feel like doing a job for us?' Alfred asked.

'Where 'bouts boss?'

''Round Victoria River Depot way. That Ragged Thirteen have to turn up there on their way west to Hall's Creek. You could wait 'til they arrive, then get a message to us in Borroloola.'

'Perfect,' cried O'Donohue, applauding. 'Oh you are a clever man, Alfie.'

'Orright, yeah,' said Billy. 'I'll do it. When my leg all fixed.'

'If you help us catch the mongrels, we'll give you so much tobacco you won't be able to carry it all.'

O'Donohue fixed his eyes on his mate. 'I like the way your mind works, Alfie. No wonder every vagabond in the north is afraid of you.'

Alfred nodded, as if accepting only what was his due. 'Yes, once we're established in Borroloola, and we get the word from Billy, we can slip out west and capture the damned Ragged Thirteen. This time we won't let them go.'

# Chapter 19: The Stone Knife

The boy loved being there on the Flora River, where calcium-rich water flowed from distant underground springs, forming a green channel that never stopped flowing. Upstream from the junction the waters cascaded over raft-walls of skeletonised logs, boiling into pools and churning through rapids.

A family group from the local wild mob were settled upstream. Blind Joe went to warn them that some horsemen were coming. These white men, he said, were not interested in staying, but were heading west to hunt for precious rocks, and should not pose a threat.

After this initial contact, the bush people kept clear. After all, these newcomers were different, with white-men's clothing, horses and gear. They were from all over the north. Some of the women had ridden with their men from the Queensland coast. Some wore crosses on chains around their necks and kneeled to a white man's god.

On the second day, the young men killed five ducks. Un-plucked and bloody, the birds were roasted on the coals. Still-kicking cherapin, with their long, pincered claws, along with mussels and water lily tubers, rounded out the feast. The boy ate every scrap he was given, picking clean bone and shell alike.

When the food was all gone, most of the party settled down to sleep, soon woken by the sound of a horseman coming in fast. The Thirteen were expected that day, so at first no one was alarmed. Then Blind Joe grew wary. He ran for the horses.

'Hide,' he shouted. But it was too late.

Maori Reid, mounted on his horse, charged into the camp, carrying a carbine one-handed. The boy remembered and feared the dark-bearded rider. One of the women realised the danger and tried to grab the youngster.

The carbine barked, belching black smoke and fire. The woman's chest tore open and she fell to the ground.

The boy tried to run, but Reid scooped him up, near-wrenching his arm from his shoulder, then dragged him into the saddle. The boy screamed, but the sound of gunfire had scattered the others. Those who managed to fetch spears and stand could not throw for fear of hitting the boy.

Reid smelled of tobacco, sweat and rum. His arms held the boy like iron straps as he doubled back to where the Ragged Thirteen's treasured plant had been left to graze and rest.

Blind Joe was by then saddled and mounted, galloping off as Maori Reid opened the action of his rifle and inserted a fresh cartridge. Blind Joe reached the trees, whipping the horse with the flat of his hand. The heavy bullet took down branches and leaves not far from his head.

Maori did not bother to chase, instead removing a coil of rope that had been lashed to his saddle dees. This proved to be made up of half a dozen individual lengths, each about four-teen feet long.

The first length he used to bind the boy: his hands, then his neck, the loose end tied to the saddle. This done, he hunted up four of the Ragged Thirteen's finest horses, and haltered each, ponying them together in a string. It was neatly done, without fuss, at least as fast, the boy reckoned, as Tom Nugent might have managed.

'You're mine now,' growled Maori Reid. 'An' we're gunna ride like mad bastards. If you try to escape, I'll cut your throat.'

The boy had lately been allowed to ride a spare horse bareback, but now he sat uncomfortably, ahead of his captor, on the pommel of the saddle. They swam the Flora at a gravelled crossing, then followed the western bank of the Daly River, often riding in the shallows, or in the leaf litter and detritus-strewn layers of an old flood level.

It was a difficult path, but Maori Reid did not slow the pace. Branches whipped past at face level in the riverine scrub. It was obvious to the boy that Maori was doing his best to confuse the spoor. He never rode past a shelf of bare rock, taking the horses out where the marks of their hooves would be hard to see, and where the exit points would have to be painstakingly discovered. Yet Blind Joe, the boy knew, would follow. Joe was not blind at all, but had the keenest eyesight of any living man. The name was some kind of joke that the men of the Ragged Thirteen found amusing.

The boy remembered the stone knife, wrapped in rags in his pocket. It comforted him, though with his hands tied, it was impossible to retrieve it. Later, perhaps, he would have his chance.

Maori Reid rode fast, just as he had promised, stopping only to sweep their tracks or change horses. They rode through rain squalls twice, and afterwards the humidity increased so that their clothes and skins were wet from sweat and rain combined. For the boy, that afternoon was a torment. The rain, he knew, would make the work of following them much more difficult.

Just before dark they crossed the Daly, then made camp on a beach of white sand and red pebbles. A fire of driftwood was soon burning, with the river streaming past in a narrow channel.

'We'll get some tucker together and curl up for an hour or two,' Maori Reid growled. 'I won't take no chances with you running off.' He transferred the loose end of the boy's rope from the saddle to a paperbark branch, then cooked johnny-cakes on the coals. He threw a hunk to the boy, who held out his hands to indicate that he could not eat with them tied.

Maori released the knots that bound the boy's wrists. 'You used to be Tom Nugent's but now you're mine. I'll train you up to work, and work you will. The sooner you look me in the eye and call me boss the sooner I'll cut you loose and let you ride your own horse.'

After they had eaten, Maori tied the boy's wrists again, tighter than before. 'Now sleep,' he said.

After a while, when Maori's chest was rising and falling evenly, the boy started working at the ropes on his wrists. The knots held fast. It was impossible to move them. But when Maori woke and went out to catch the horses, he again loosened the bonds.

'You'll ride easier with the use of your hands. See? I ain't as bad a bastard as everyone thinks.'

Back on horseback under a glowing moon, the boy saw a dark bank of cloud, blowing out from the horizon, blotting out stars as it came. They were in thick scrub. The moon disappeared behind the cloud. Then came the darkness.

The boy dug in his rags for the stone knife, and with every ounce of strength he possessed, he drove it deep into Maori's thigh, plucking it out for another blow. Reid cried out like a bird. Pain-strengthened hands clutched and fumbled for the boy and his knife.

As slippery as a catfish, the boy used the weight of his body, falling purposely from the saddle, over the near-side of the horse. He slipped free from Maori Reid's grasp. He hit the ground, rose to a crouch, then used the stone knife to hack at the rope that still bound him by the neck to the saddle. Free at last, he started to run.

# Chapter 20: A Strange Kind of Justice

Tom Nugent was riding beside Blind Joe, when a high-pitched, unearthly wail carried on the air, rising above the sounds of the breeze and the river, the clink of spurs and the creak of leather. He spurred his horse, heedless of the river scrub, reaching the riverside camp at a furious gallop.

There, on a sweep of white river sand, the body of a woman had been placed on a platform of sticks, a fire smoking away underneath. Most of the stockboys were gathered around, some of them naked, having stripped off their Western gear. Others had blood on their faces and arms where they had cut themselves with sharp stones and sticks.

As the pair dismounted, Blind Joe broke into sobs. Tom knew that grief with Aboriginal people was loud and raw, and there was no getting in the way of it.

Closer now, Tom recognised the dead woman's face. He turned back to see Sandy Myrtle and the others arriving, tethering horses and walking in with shocked faces. Most carried weapons, still unsure of what had happened and how to react.

'It's Wonoka Jack's woman,' Tom said, then addressed the mourners. 'Was it Maori Reid that done this?'

One of the women hissed sharply. 'That bad-wan Maori come here alright. He shoot her inna heart, an' take the boy belonga you.'

Tom said nothing, but his lips whitened. He liked the boy, and felt responsible for him. His big hands closed into fists at his side.

A shout came from behind. It was Wonoka Jack, brushing aside restraining hands and coming up to see the dead woman. 'Oh the bloody rat. The cruel swine. He'll pay for this, I swear he will.'

Finally Tom found words. 'I should'a hung the bastard properly when I had the chance. I won't make that mistake again.'

Carmody had ridden off to see to the plant, and came back with more bad news. 'Four good horses missing.' He turned to Tom. 'If you're follerin' Maori I'm goin' with you. If anyone should put a stake through the heart of that monster it's me.'

'You ready to track him for me, Joe?' Tom asked.

Blind Joe nodded very slowly. 'A life for a life,' he said.

Tom studied the assembled men. Apart from being consumed by grief, Wonoka Jack was showing signs that a bout of malarial fever was on its way. New England Jack had the same trouble. Sandy could ride no other horse than Jonathan James, and was thus not able to join a fast chase. The Scotsmen – Bob Anderson and Scotty – had not yet reached the same class of bushmanship as the others.

'I'll take Carmody then,' Tom said at last. 'And Larrikin too, if you'll come?'

'Too right I bloody will,' cried Larrikin.

'An' me as well,' shouted Jimmy Woodford. 'I want to be in at the death o' that horse murdering cur.'

'Righto,' said Tom. 'You too. We'll pick fresh mounts then take up the trail.'

Blind Joe began the hunt with restrained eagerness. One of the younger stock boys showed the party where Maori Reid had crossed the Flora, then headed northwards along the main channel of the Daly.

After that, Blind Joe tracked from the saddle, scarcely saying a word, only pointing or signalling occasionally. There were times when his brow furrowed, and he walked his horse slow, leaning over so his head hung down, scarcely above the earth. At times like this Tom had the sense to rein in, light a pipe and wait while the tracker rode in seemingly nonsensical lines.

At other times they reached a near gallop, and speargrass heads flicked the horses' flanks and stung through the riders' dungarees. Rain squalls came and went, but for now, Blind Joe's keen eyes kept them firmly on the trail.

After dark there was no choice but to wait for the moon, and Tom begrudged every wasted minute. When it finally rose, luminous white over the Daly River valley, Blind Joe went back to work, leading them slowly downstream.

Around dawn, after scarcely any sleep, they were lolling in the saddles, but there was no question at stopping. Cattlemen learn the trick of sleeping in snatches that might last only seconds.

The heat and humidity were insidious. Blind Joe's eyes were bloodshot and his hands shook, but he solved each riddle as it came and kept them moving until mid-morning. Now they reached a chain of muddy ponds back from the main river channel. Horse tracks mingled with those of animals; great three-toed prints of jabirus beside the distinctive mark of kangaroos.

Blind Joe examined the area slowly then spat. 'This tucker taste different than before,' he said.

'What do you mean?'

'Plenty track, different track. More-feller horse. Dunno now *Mulaka*.'

'Follow the freshest ones,' said Tom.

They rode for another hour, away from the river and into a long stretch of woodland. Then, just shy of a creek gully, Blind Joe signalled for them to dismount, then came back and pushed his face up close to Tom's.

'Someone aroun' here. Look out.'

Tom drew his revolver and thumbed back the hammer, then watched as the others did the same. They moved at a crouch. There was a taint of campfire smoke in the breeze that swished and whistled in the casuarinas. One step at a time now, easing forward and swivelling his head, Blind Joe led them into deeper scrub near the creek banks.

March flies landed on the backs of necks and hands, needling deep into the skin, impossible to ignore. Tom gritted his teeth and did not let his concentration waver. He had just rounded a thick paperbark trunk when a Colt .45 appeared, aimed with dead-steady hands at his temple.

'Holster your weapon,' came a voice. 'Real slow and careful.'

Tom was surprised to see that the owner of the Colt was not Maori Reid at all, but a woman with flaming red hair.

He holstered his weapon and stepped back. 'Red Jack,' he said, touching his hat. 'What are you doing here?'

'I had to go up to Pine Creek to look at a horse. Now I'm on the same journey as you. Heading for the Kimberley.'

'Have you seen Maori Reid?'

Red Jack inclined her head. 'That I have.'

'What about the boy?'

'I've seen him too.' Without lowering the handgun, the woman thrust the tips of the first two fingers of her left hand into her lips and whistled.

The boy appeared, responding to the sound. He smiled when he saw Tom and ran to him.

'At least he seems to like you. What's the little bloke's name by the way?' Red Jack asked. 'He won't tell me.'

'He hasn't got a Christian name yet, and he can't remember the one from his own people.'

'Where are they?'

'Dust and ash by now. Wiped out in a "dispersal" on the Macarthur.'

'Enough talk,' said Jim Woodford, walking slowly out of the scrub. 'Now where's Maori Jack? We've got business with that bastard.'

Red Jack lowered her Colt. 'You gentlemen strung Maori Reid up by his ankles and made him a laughing stock. Then, from what I hear, one of you clobbered him on the back of the head in Katherine. You're lucky he didn't put a bullet in your spine one night as you lay in your swag. He's a snake, everyone knows it, and you poked him with a stick.'

Tom looked at her seriously. 'He killed a woman, and took four horses. Just because the boy's back doesn't get the bastard off the hook.'

'You want to see Maori Reid?' she asked. 'Come with me.'

Red Jack led the way through the trees to a camp, with horses hobbled all around, and a campfire burning low. Maori Reid was there, lying on the ground with his head on a saddle. His lower body was a mess of bloody bandages. His eyes were glassed over and the smell of infection hung over him like a toxic cloud.

'This young bloke carries a sharp little knife,' Red Jack said. 'It must have been made by his people before you picked him up. He managed to prick this bastard right through the femoral artery. Maori had just about bled dry when I found him, and now the wound has turned septic. He's as good as dead.' She shrugged. 'But if you really want to shoot a gravely ill man where he lies, don't let me stop you.'

Tom fingered the butt of his revolver, staring at the once piercing eyes of Maori Jack Reid. He turned to Blind Joe, who nodded once. The black man wanted Reid dead, and so did Jimmy Woodford. Carmody showed a trace of relief that he might not be forced to shoot his own kin, and Larrikin shook his head. It just didn't seem right to kill a man who was already fighting for his life.

After a moment of reflection Tom tipped his hat to Red Jack. 'Thank you, ma'am. There's a strange kind of justice at work here. It's not pretty, but I believe that it's fair. I'll leave this bastard in your hands, and to the fate that God decides for him.'

With the boy trailing him like a shadow, Tom walked back towards the horses.

# Chapter 21: Alligator Jim

Tom Nugent and his hunting party reached the main Flora River camp in the late afternoon. Storm clouds glowed yellow, reflecting like gold on the surface of that special waterway as it snaked out of the limestone plains, twining with the Katherine to create the mighty Daly River.

The plant was soon hobbled and grazing on green pick, brought on by the storms. A good fire burned in the hearth, with a pile of firewood stacked ready for the evening.

In the process of collecting wood, however, George Brown was stung by an inch-thick centipede that had been domiciled under a lump of driftwood. Not to be outdone, Carmody stubbed a bare toe on an old log submerged in the sand, and howled for ten minutes solid, at which point Sandy Myrtle grew tired of the noise and promised him something that would really make him yell.

To keep up the entertainment Jimmy Woodford spied the shape of a big barramundi cruising in the deep-water channel below a sand bar. He stood watching for a minute or two, shirt off, muscles relaxed so that his hairy belly pointed to the river.

'Anyone fancy fish for supper?' he asked thoughtfully.

Tom laughed. 'I've got a good length of cat-gut in the packs and a hook or two if you want to give it a try. Or one of the boys will lend you a fish-spear.'

'Bugger that,' cried Jimmy. 'I'll show you bastards how to catch fish.'

Tom watched with interest as Woodford fetched his rifle and walked back to the bank. Working a cartridge in to the breech he raised the weapon to his shoulder and fired.

The surface of the water was disrupted into concentric waves, and the air filled with falling droplets. Birds took flight from trees along the riverbank. The big silver fish floated to the top of the water, kicking feebly.

Woodford turned and smiled. 'How easy was that? You don't even have to hit them, the explosion of the bullet on the water busts their brains.'

Making his way to the water's edge, he stripped off his dungarees, then walked across the sand bar to where the barramundi lay near the surface. The others watched idly, honing knives, mending clothes or oiling leather. One or two were reading.

Woodford had almost reached his fish when it managed to flick its tail, taking it into deeper water, out of reach of the sand bar. 'Hey you blokes,' he called. 'Someone chuck me a stick, will you?'

Tom hunted around for a good green stick, which he threw underhanded, spear-like, out across the water. Woodford collected it, and started using it to prod, poke and drag the fish closer.

The process took a while. It seemed to Tom that Jimmy Woodford was winning. He was almost waist deep now, half off the sandbar and into the swirling current.

'Jesus Christ, a 'gator,' someone shouted.

Tom looked up and saw it coming. A giant of a thing, swinging its tail lazily upstream with the scent of fish blood in its nostrils. The thick snout was partially submerged, ahead of deeply-slitted, armoured eyes.

'He's right,' cried Tom. 'Get out of there.'

Woodford turned, his face showing hope that someone was playing a joke on him. Torn between self-preservation and not wanting to be the butt of a joke, he played it safe with a couple of mighty strides onto the sand bar.

Before anyone had the presence of mind to train a rifle on it, the 'gator burst from the deep water, jaws open, the back of its head slick with water. It scooped up the fish, so big it hung out the length of a forearm on either side. Then, lifting the prize high, it opened its jaws wider several times to force the fish down, before turning and disappearing below the surface.

'Fucking hell,' Woodford spat. 'That was close.' He walked back up through the shallows to dry land, shivering visibly from the closeness of this encounter.

'You're a fool, Woodford,' said Sandy. 'You let that blessed 'gator eat my supper. I was looking forward to it, too.'

That night, when the meal was done, and fresh sticks were added to the fire; flames leaping, lighting up the old paperbarks that grew so gnarled and huge on those banks, the gang passed around a bottle of grog. Only Wonoka Jack was absent, at a smaller fire, with the stockboys, still grieving for his dead lover.

While the others talked and laughed Tom scribbled madly with pencil and notepaper. At some length, he stood up. 'Alright you blokes, I have a little verse to share, if you wouldn't mind shutting yer gobs for a bit. This one's called, Alligator Jim.'

There were a few sniggers at the title, but they waited in silence, as Tom Nugent started to recite his poem, using voice and hands and eyes to command their attention.

> Jim Woodford was a brave man,
> A marksman tried and true,
> Yet the day he tried to shoot a fish,
> Forever he would rue.'

The camp broke up into laughter, and Tom waited with the timing of a showman.

'He held the rifle to his eye,
And took his deadly aim,
The bullet flew in earnest pace,
That fish would never be the same.'

More laughter. Woodford was blushing like a cherry. Bob Anderson punched him playfully on the shoulder.

'But as he reached to claim the prize,
Poor Jim was in for fun,
A 'gator rose to get the fish,
And Jim turned tail and run.'

Sandy Myrtle was shaking so hard, laughter exploding through his lips, that the ground itself seemed to move along with him. Tom finished the verse with a flourish, shouting the last line at the top of his voice.

'And here we've heard tell of a man,
Of vigor and of vim,
Who henceforth will be known as,
Alligator Jim.'

'Haha, Alligator Jim, that's bloody perfect,' someone howled, and more laughter rang through the camp.

The men were now in the mood for poetry. Tom Nugent was not the only lover of verse, though he would often kick things off with one of his own, as he had tonight.

Larrikin Jim produced a battered book from his saddle-bags. Holding it open he paced around and through the firelight under the teeming stars. 'I'm gonna read one from old Adam Lindsay Gordon …'

There was clapping all round and a series of 'Hear, hears,' and 'Aye,' from the Scotsmen.

Jim waited for silence, then, started to read. He was an expressive reader, and by the second verse there was no sound but for his voice, the river waters pushing at the old snags that held against the current.

> 'Lightly the breath of the spring wind blows,
> Though laden with faint perfume,
> 'Tis the fragrance rare that the bushman knows,
> The scent of the wattle bloom.
> Two-thirds of our journey at least are done,
> Old horse! let us take a spell
> In the shade from the glare of the noon-day sun ...'

When it was finished, Sandy Myrtle cleared his throat and said, 'Beautifully read, Jim. It might interest you bastards to know that Gordon was a ne'er do well back in England, and was sent out here by his old man so he might make something of himself. Poor bastard fell off the perch at the age of thirty-seven.'

'May he rest in peace,' Tom said. 'He was one of the best. Now, I say it's time to unroll our swags and get some sleep. To-morrow we ride for the Victoria River!'

They cheered and bickered and carried on as they threw out their swags and settled down to sleep. In addition to the night noises, Carmody was singing a sad old tune, just something he liked to do after a few drinks. No one minded, he had a rich and soothing voice.

The newly christened 'Alligator Jim' took no chances, carefully keeping Sandy Myrtle between him and the river.

'It'd take that 'gator a long time to chew through Sandy an' get to me,' he said. 'So this is where I sleep tonight.'

# Chapter 22: A Town called Borroloola

After a break-neck ride, Alfred Searcy and O'Donohue pulled up at Abraham's Billabong for supplies and a breather. Young Bowen, a little tougher looking than last time they had seen him, fronted the counter of the store, and was happy to see that the policemen had his grey with their plant.

'It's a relief to see some troopers in the area,' he said, once his horse was safety in the paddock. 'You're on your way to Borroloola?'

'That's right.'

'Well you'd better hurry. There's an article in the Times and Gazette about that town.' He picked up a copy from the counter and started leafing through it. 'Listen, I'll read it to you.'

> Drunkenness is epidemic, and drunken men practise rifle and revolver shooting in the open road ways of the township at all hours of the day, whenever their sweet wills direct, to the constant danger of the rest of the inhabitants.
>
> A perfect reign of terror exists; lawlessness and crime prevail to an extent that is quite indescribable, and the

*peacefully disposed people are obliged to submit for fear of incurring the displeasure and vengeance of the roughs and perhaps having their property destroyed, or even endangering their lives.*

*A race meeting had been held, and was largely attended by people from far and near, and of course, such an opportunity could not be let slip without a celebration which, as might have been expected, degenerated into a saturnalia of drunkenness and excesses. Amongst other acts of violence reported was the sticking up of the stores of W. Macleod, and Cameron; Cameron resisted with firearms, whereupon the rowdies retreated out of pistol range and fired rifle balls into the store, but fortunately without wounding anyone. Some of the less patient of the residents are seriously talking of lynch law, and the establishment of a vigilance committee for the punishment of offenders. The following is an extract from a letter from a resident in the district: This town and the district are in a state of terror for want of police protection, all the outlaws from Queensland flock here. Horse stealing, forgery, robbery, violence, and repudiation of debts are included in the catalogue of crimes—one case of sodomy, committed by three brutes in the form of men on a drunken man.*

'That's enough,' said Alfred. 'I care to hear no more.' He turned to his mate. 'We leave now, and must ride all night. No wonder the Commissioner was keen for us to get down there.'

Forty-eight hours later, they rode into Borroloola, seeing first the river on the left side of the track, with the Government wharf jutting into the water. Small boats and a ketch sat at their moorings or alongside the wharf itself.

This was not Alfred's first visit to the town. He had, twelve months earlier, arrived on the steamer Palmerston, in the capacity of Customs Officer for the colony of South Australia. On that occasion he had managed to catch Maori Reid and his wife Henrietta in the act of bringing goods over the border from Queensland, and failing to pay import duties for doing so.

Now, entering the township, they saw camps and bark shelters in plenty, but few houses. White survey pegs were visible in grids out into the distance. A sign identified the main street as Riddoch Terrace.

'A grand name for a strip o' dirt,' commented O'Donohue.

It was so hot, on that December afternoon, that nothing stirred as they rode in, a few bony horses behind bough fences scarcely looking up. It was only once they came upon a building site, where a handful of Chinese carpenters were hammering away at the frame, that they saw any sign of life.

From a white canvas tent in the shade alongside this new structure, a gentleman emerged. Alfred recognised him as a travelling magistrate from Palmerston, a man by the name of McMinn.

'At last,' said McMinn. 'We've been waiting for weeks.'

'I'm sorry,' said Alfred. 'There was a loathsome gang of ruffians on the loose up north that required our attention.'

'I hope you nailed them good.'

'Unfortunately not. But that story is not yet finished. We heard that there have been troubles down here.'

'You could say that. Whatever kind of mayhem you can imagine, you'll find it here.'

'Whose house are t'ose men building?' O'Donohue asked.

'The new Police Station. With quarters for you two gentlemen, and myself when I'm in town. Now come to the tent for a dram, and wash the dust from your throats.'

'That sounds like a capital idea,' said Alfred.

Later, as dusk approached, the little township came alive. Residents left the shade of their bark shelters and slab huts, talking and laughing on the roadways in groups. Shouting and singing was soon heard, carrying from the two shanties that paraded themselves as pubs. Two men galloped past at a ferocious rate.

'I say,' said Alfred. 'They should slow down. Riding like that in a built-up area is dangerous.' He looked at O'Donohue. 'I think it's time we made our presence felt in this place. People need to know that law and order has arrived.' He had drunk just enough whisky to feel infallible.

The magistrate begged off, preferring to sit with his glass and watch, as the two troopers dressed in their full uniforms, mounted up and walked their horses slowly down Riddoch Terrace towards the cluster of pubs and stores. With a view to how the townspeople might see them, they turned their heads from left to right, patently studying every human being they saw.

Though the sun was now hidden behind the scrub, the air was still baking hot. Yet the land was becoming fragrant with it, earthy with dusk, but also some less pleasant smells that come with humans living in close contact.

The Macarthur River was almost always in view down below the bank. More people, black and white, were camped alongside the water. The greatest numbers, however, were clustered under deep verandahs clad with bark, for the pubs were separated by only a couple of small stores.

As Searcy and O'Donohue neared the area, two dozen or so drinkers stopped to stare. The singing and laughter ceased.

Alfred saw this as a sign of the regard these lawless types must hold for the law. 'Yes. You are right to be wary,' he called loudly. 'British justice is here. Prepare for many changes.'

The laughter started with a skinny ringer-type, wearing a cabbage-tree hat that was so old patches of his ginger hair showed through. Others followed suit, until the whole crowd were roaring, slapping each other's hands and proposing loud toasts.

'Did yer hear the stinkin' trap? British justice is here?'

The first man threw whatever missile happened to be handy. A leather boot sailed through the air and landed on the rump of Alfred's horse. If it wasn't so flat it would have skittered. Alfred saw red, and was turning to identify the culprit when a bottle, a stone, then a large fish head were propelled towards him. He was forced to take evasive action.

O'Donohue copped a stick on the shoulder, and within a few moments they were both in full retreat. Reining in, just out of range of the missiles, Alfred turned his horse and tugged his carbine from its scabbard. It was half way to his shoulder when O'Donohue stopped him, with a hand on his arm.

'No Alfie, don't shoot at them. They're all armed, and do we really want to start a gun fight?'

Alfred took a deep breath, and even the drinkers seemed to quiet down while they saw him sheathe the weapon once more. After a long, searching stare he turned his horse back towards McMinn's tent.

'They will live to regret this day,' said Alfred as they idled home. O'Donohue didn't answer.

'Those boys do like throwing things,' said the magistrate when they reached the tent. 'Have another drink and don't fret too much about it.'

After one more rum Alfred said. 'I swear to God that I will clean up this town so that when we hear that the Ragged Thirteen are ripe for the taking, we can leave it in clear conscience.'

# Chapter 23: Beef for Christmas

Riding in a south westerly direction, upstream on the Flora River, the Ragged Thirteen ran headlong into solid Wet Season rain. Some nights the only fire they could maintain was deep between the raised roots of a thick old paperbark, or far back in a rocky cleft with the flames brushing soot onto lichen and limestone.

When the rain eased, mosquitoes attacked every unprotected square of skin and whined around the ears. Nights were a torment – too hot for blankets – but it was impossible to sleep without the protection they provided from the insects.

'I've had enough of this stinking weather,' said Sandy Myrtle. No one disagreed.

Days of sweat, forced rides, wrong turns and detours around flooded creeks followed. Leaving the Flora headwaters to punch south for the Victoria River was a relief, though the rain hardly faltered, and nothing ever dried out anyway.

There were wild blacks in the area, and once or twice a spear or two flew out of cover or the horses were spooked at night.

'They're just warning us to keep moving,' said Tom. 'There'll be no shooting. I won't have it. We're not squatters or traps who seem to think they have the God-given authority to kill-on-sight. We leave them alone.'

Finally, running low on provisions, Fitz shot a 'dropped' bullock through sheer luck, and they camped on the line of cliffs that overlooked the Victoria River Valley. Tom declared that it was the deep, wide gorge was most beautiful sight in the natural world, with the churning brown river in its midst.

New England Jack Woods packed his pipe with Barrett's Twist, and passed the pouch around. 'How the blazes will we get across that?'

Tom had been wondering the same thing. 'The rain seems to have eased off. Give it a day or two, mate. It should drop enough.'

Over breakfast Larrikin announced that his mare was, beyond doubt, pregnant, her belly now rounded in all the right places. The rest of the gang clapped and laughed, for the joining of the mare to Wonoka Jack's stallion had been a group entertainment.

'I feel almost as proud as if I were the father meself,' said Wonoka Jack. A round of cheering and catcalls followed.

'By the way, you lot,' Tom called. 'Did you know it's Christmas Day, and here we are running out of flour. Thank God for that beef! It won't be quite proper without taters, pumpkin and pudding, but I vote we do our best to honour the day.'

A full rump of beef was diced and stewed up by Bob Anderson and Scotty in some old Caledonian recipe that involved copious amounts of pepper and Lea and Perrins Sauce.

Supplies of rum were low by then, but with the Victoria River Depot just a few days away they did not hold back. There was even some gift giving, all second-hand of course. George Brown gave Sandy Myrtle a copy of a Ryder Haggard novel, and Carmody wrapped a sharp little pocket knife in cheesecloth and passed it over to Tom.

'You blokes have been darned good to me, considering my bein' related by marriage with Maori Reid. So that's just a little thing that's been sittin' in the bottom of my saddlebags for a while.'

Fitz made New England Jack a stock whip, which the recipient cracked a few times and declared to be the best he'd ever seen. Some of the others set out to honour Larrikin's forthcoming foal with greenhide tack.

No one had any musical instruments, but later on Larrikin put on his dancing shoes, and to the accompaniment of clapping hands, he put on a jig that would have made a dance hall crowd shout for more.

Carmody leaned against a tree, watching, thumbs hooked in the waist band of his dungarees. 'Where the hell did you learn to dance like that, Larrikin?' he asked.

'Learn?' grinned Larrikin. 'I never learned a thing in me life. I just put on me dancing shoes and move me feet. That's how I do it.'

On dusk they sat on the edge of the cliffs and stared down at the deep valley of stone and its wide river. The rain had settled the dust and smoke, leaving the air as clear as glass and every surface washed clean.

'Tomorrow,' said Tom, 'we go down and cross that bloody big river. Then at last we'll know we're getting close.'

# Chapter 24: Crossing the Victoria

The Victoria River, when they reached it, riding down a spur of one of those jagged hills, was a turbid, flowing lake, rimmed with mud and thick undergrowth. The sun was out, but it cheered nobody, for the heat was almost unbearable.

Horse and man alike saw no pleasure in that day, and tempers flared, insults thrown like hammers and occasionally punctuated with a swinging stirrup iron.

They pulled up on the high bank and Fitz whistled. 'She's running a banker, there's no doubt about that.'

They rode upstream, horses slick with black mud to their chests, looking for a place to cross, but it was hard going. Swearing and cursing, they pushed their way through heavy foliage until finally there was nothing for it but to force a crossing, or embark on a wide detour on land.

Tom lost the usual twinkle of fun in his eyes, showing the wear and tear of leadership. He tried to figure how the river worked; how the current sped on the near bank or when the bed narrowed, or shelved on the broad pebbled bars. With this in mind he led them to wide sweep where stones below the surface could be seen in the rush of water.

A Wardaman family had been on the fringes, one man working a fish spear in the shallows, while women and children grubbed for mussels on the banks. At the approach of the horsemen they grabbed a dead barramundi as long as man's arm from the ground and ran for the scrub.

'I swear it looks shallower here,' Tom said. 'We should try it now before we get more rain.'

'No bloody way,' Tommy the Rag spat, 'I don't swim, you bastards. I'll camp here and you can pick me up when yez all come back with the arses out of yer pants from Hall's Creek.'

Tom Nugent studied the river again. It seemed to him that a good horse should keep its footing most of the way. The best horsemen amongst them could swim their horses across, with only Tommy and Scotty Campbell best off swimming separately from their mounts.

'I'm not riding across that fucking river,' Tommy ranted. 'Go across and to hell with ya.'

Tom Nugent took his last bottle of rum from one of the packs, twisted off the lid and sniffed it. He took a swig before handing it to Tommy.

'Dutch courage, old mate. Have as much as you want.'

Half way through the bottle Tommy had a change of heart. 'I dunno what was in that bottle besides rum,' he slurred. 'But I'd charge hell with a bucket of water right now. Now where's me bloody horse?'

The crossing was longer than it looked, and by the time they were half way across the heads of two or three 'gators were visible, surfacing downstream and making bow waves in the water, before disappearing to God knew where. Even Tom felt the awful fear of those submerged monsters.

One of the spare horses screamed in unearthly pain, and tried to rear, the jaws of a huge 'gator wrapped around its hindquarters, tearing bloody streaks through hide and flesh as those bony, toothed jaws came together.

A death-roll by the 'gator brought the poor horse down, while Tom tried vainly to churn through water to help. He was forced to abandon the chase in deeper water, current tugging at his horse and legs.

No man could stand the sound of a horse in pain, and this one wailed in a human-like shriek that shook them all. Tommy the Rag lost all composure, panicking his horse so it bucked, slowed by the water, showing its teeth and panicking the rest of the plant. It was a rout, a desperate crossing that saw two men thrown and washed downstream with horses and gear floating everywhere so it was a miracle no others were taken by those dark beasts.

Sandy Myrtle, one of the first across, took position, solid as a sandstone pillar, with his rifle. His first shot killed the mare that was still being mauled, silencing her pain at last, then he aimed at the heads of the 'gators, firing until none were in sight.

Tommy the Rag took off his sodden shirt and sat on a rock way up from the edge, shaking like an insect.

'Are you alright?' Tom asked.

'I knew I shouldn't have tried to cross. I hate those damn 'gators, I really do, they make my fucking skin crawl.'

'This is the most dangerous river in the north,' said Tom. 'We were lucky to lose just one horse. Now mount up. We want a dry camp tonight, and a cheerful fire away from the river.'

# Chapter 25: Whisky and Water

The Victoria River Depot, when they reached it, wasn't much of a place, a couple of jetties half-afloat in tidal mud, the usual collection of bush dwellings, tents and rough camps. There was noise enough at first, even some music, but everything went silent as the Thirteen left the women and stock boys with the plant and packs on the fringes and walked in to the little settlement on foot.

Tom Nugent nodded at an Aboriginal man standing beside the track, staring as they sauntered past. There was something familiar about him. Nothing certain, but enough to cause a prickle of worry in the base of Tom's neck.

From the bank above the river, Tom watched a crew of boys unloading goods from an oil-burner launch some thirty-feet long. A gang of miscreants and unemployed watermen hung around in the shade watching the work progress, their women cooking listlessly on open fires or half asleep in blanket-wrapped bundles.

A little further along the foreshore they found a man in the shade of a bough shelter. On the table in front of him sat two or three open bottles of grog. Behind was a stack of wooden crates, a Snider carbine leaning against them.

At another table three men were playing draw poker for money. Judging from the red eyes, sorrowful faces, and a blackened slush lantern on the table beside them, Tom guessed that they had been playing for some time, perhaps all the previous night.

A group of half a dozen men, and one rare, haggard white woman had set themselves up between the bough shed and a broad, grey boab tree. One man had a concertina and another a fiddle, while a third thumped a drum of rawhide stretched over a hoop of iron. The music started again. The woman danced.

Tom noticed that the barman moved his carbine closer as the Thirteen walked up.

'I'm a little thirsty,' said Tom. 'Wouldn't mind a peg or two. Anyone else?'

Sandy Myrtle grinned. 'I think the good Lord would look kindly upon us imbibing of a small quantity of spirits after a sojourn in the wilderness.'

'I don't give too much of a toss what the Good Lord thinks, right now,' said Tom. Leaning on the bar table he barked out. 'Rum, please sir.'

'I've only got whisky,' said the proprietor.

'That'll do then. Line up thirteen glasses and be quick about it. Then you can start pouring the next.'

The shanty-keeper narrowed his eyes, 'You're the Ragged Thirteen, I'm guessing?'

'That's us.'

'Well I hope you've got cash to pay. I hear that cheques from you lot aren't worth the paper they're written on.'

The shanty-keeper's tone was never going to wash with the Thirteen. And it was George Brown who took exception for them all. His face reddened, 'We've got South Australian coinage if that's acceptable in this shit-hole,' he snarled. 'Now get the fucking drinks like the man asked.'

The shanty-keeper scowled but pulled the cork from the

bottle and started filling glasses. A minute or two later, with his second drink in hand, Tom took a seat at the table with the card players, watching the action.

'We've heard of you,' said one, in an Irish brogue.

'Heard of you alright,' said the second. 'Saddle-strap bush-rangers, they call you.'

The third said nothing. He was a dark-skinned European, Spanish perhaps.

'Some people who don't know us well might say such things.' Tom's voice hardened. 'But they don't say it within earshot. What's your business here?'

The Irishman replied, 'Crew of the launch yonder, brought supplies around from Palmerston for Victoria River Downs and Wave Hill. I heard you mob are headed for Hall's Creek. Best you hurry or the gold will all be worked out.'

Tom looked past the card-players and saw that the young Aboriginal man who had watched the Thirteen arrive had walked a little closer to them, staring across a hundred yards of speargrass.

'Who's that?'

'Dunno his name. Been hanging around here for a few days. One of the ringers from the Downs almost put a bullet in him yesterday, trying to get his business out of him.'

The conversation fell away, and Tom sat with his third drink in silence, watching as the Aboriginal youth walked back to his camp, sat with a mug of tea and stared back across the intervening space at Tom and the Ragged Thirteen.

Tom had that niggling feeling that he was a little too interested in them.

Larrikin was known for his fun-loving ways; a swagger, and willingness to try anything. He was not of attractive appearance. His hair was a cap of little woolly curls and his eyes were like slits. But he never had trouble attracting members of the opposite sex when there was a dance floor around.

Sipping his whisky, Larrikin couldn't take his eyes off the dancers under the trees. Occasionally he clapped a hand in time with the drum and concertina.

He had grown up an orphan, on the Norman River, Queensland, he'd once told Tom, raised by a man called Major Colles. 'Singin' and dancin' was all we had. God knows there was never enough food to eat.'

After the fourth or fifth tot he walked all the way back to the pack horses and came back with his dancing shoes. He took off his boots, his feet stark white under the woollen socks, and laced on those hard leather hornpipes.

'You going to have a turn or two, old mate?' Tom said, indicating the dance 'floor.'

'Yep, I can't resist. Whether dust or fancy planks makes little difference to me.' With those words he sprang to his feet, and by way of announcing his arrival, capered his way across to the space before the musicians. Some of the men gathered around, cheering as he started an Irish jig with every nearby hand clapping. The circle widened with some of the layabouts sensing entertainment.

The virtuosic display lasted for a song, at which point some of the others joined in. New England Jack Woods and Bob Anderson dropped their gun belts and took to the floor, grinning like children.

A gunshot broke that scene. Echoes sounded across the river and off those massive cliffs that lined both banks. It was a shock of noise, carving its way through the river air and ringing in the skull.

The music stopped.

The dancers paused mid step.

George Brown stood with the smoking gun, facing the owner of the grog shanty who stood transfixed, a pillow of dust drifting from where the bullet had struck the earth just near to his feet. The silence that followed as the echoes died was absolute.

'You have five seconds to explain why a man who serves watered-down whisky deserves to live,' George snarled at the shanty owner.

Tom, still seated at the poker table, lifted his glass to his nose. He sniffed the liquid inside, then eyed it deeply. 'Why so it is, the mongrel cur.'

Sandy Myrtle nodded grimly. 'It's an old trick – serve the good stuff straight up when a man is on the alert and his senses keen.' He pointed to the bar table. 'That's the bottle on the right. But when a man has had a few it comes from the next bottle, which I'm betting is one quarter clean rainwater. I dare say there's another bottle after that, which has half water.'

George's revolver barked again, and a bottle exploded into a thousand shards. 'Now admit it, you thieving dog.'

The shanty owner scowled. 'It's an honour to be called a thief by a thief of such renown, but you are mistaken. If there's any water in those bottles I didn't put it there.'

It must have been a flash of the eyes that warned George, for the shanty-keeper was in the process of lifting the Snider carbine when the elder Brown brother crossed the dusty earth and pressed the barrel of his revolver to the other man's temple.

'Good work George,' said Tom, now on his feet and making for the bar table. 'First thing I'm going to do is tip that goat's piss out on the ground.' He upended the first bottle and poured it on the ground, then the second and third. 'And now we want our money back.' He opened the cash box and looked inside. A small wad went into his pocket. 'Some of this can be for punitive damages,' he said. 'And now boys, let's see if this dog can swim.'

Strong arms pinioned the shanty-keeper, lifting him out of his chair, supporting him by feet, shoulders, head, back, thighs and legs. He was trying to fight, but they gripped him hard, and while Tom walked alongside, they carried him down to the jetty.

'The deepest end boys,' cried Tom.

'Don't do it, you mongrels,' cried the shanty-keeper. 'There're 'gators out there. Big bastards too.'

At the extremity of the longest jetty they swung the man once, twice, three times, then chucked him far out into the river. There was a splash of water and foam, then his head surfaced, arms floundering at the surface.

Tom found himself a boat hook, and every time it seemed that the shanty-keeper would grab hold of the jetty timbers and pull himself to safety, Tom prodded him off with sharp jabs.

This went on for ten minutes or more, the shanty keeper exhausting himself with his efforts to stay afloat. The rest of the Thirteen went back and plundered the crates of good whisky and swigged as they watched, laughing at the entertainment.

Finally, when the local crowd bored of the game, and wandered off to their work or leisure, Tom allowed the blubbering man to climb ashore. Fitz and Larrikin carried him up the bank and rolled him in dust so that even his face was caked with it.

They left him there, an exhausted mess in the dust. 'That'll teach you to fool good men with your tricks,' Tom said. Then, 'Come on you lot. Time to move on.'

Back at the horses they distributed the looted whisky bottles among the packs. Larrikin was the only man among them who was sorry to leave.

As they rode out of the little settlement Tom looked back one last time to see the Aboriginal youth staring back at him. Something told him that he should have dealt with him right there right then, but he had seen enough violence for one day.

# Chapter 26: Red Jack's Camp

While the Ragged Thirteen rode south from the Victoria River Depot, Red Jack met the river at Gregory Creek and resolved to follow the eastern bank as it dog-legged south to Victoria River Downs and beyond.

As a fiery sunset filled the horizon, Red Jack crossed the creek on a gravel bar, reined in her stallion and swung to the ground. In a short time she had the packs unloaded, and a fire leaping high.

Even as she brushed down the satin black coat of her stallion, Mephistopheles, she never smiled, wearing only a frown of concentration. She gave her packhorses and spares the same treatment, checked for galls where the pack had rubbed and applied ointment where necessary. Finally, she hobbled all the plant, and hung the night-bell only on Mephistopheles, for the others would not stray far from him.

Even then her work was not done. She checked all the tack and hung it ready on handy tree branches. Her last act was to remove the Martini-Henry carbine she carried from its scabbard, and lean it against a tree close to hand. Finally she started on an evening meal.

A couple of days earlier she had spent some time with three

women of the Wardaman tribe, learning many of the natural fruits and delicacies that most stockmen never bothered with. That day, on her travels, she had stopped to pick billy goat plum, and wild grape. She'd also made a citrus-tasting drink from a nest of green ants.

Cooking was not a chore to Red Jack, and she gently sautéed the fruits in a pan. Unwrapping a square of linen she revealed a lump of salted beef she had purchased back on the Katherine. With her folding knife she sliced the meat into squares and stirred them in.

When she had finished she cleaned the pan and plate in the creek, and unrolled her swag. She crawled under the blanket, as always, fully clothed, her rifle beside her under a fold of canvas.

This was the danger period, she knew, in those moments before she fell asleep. When her mind always tried to delve back into the past.

Childhood. Growing up hard on the Darling Downs. Bonded to horses as soon as she could walk, at fifteen she'd become a buckjumping champion. Her reputation spread from Roma to Thargomindah. Riding astride like a man she earned more than a few curses from the flash lads who fancied they could ride and couldn't stand being bested by a girl, and a skinny young one at that.

But that was before the fire. Long before the tragedy that made her a wanderer. Long before the lonely years on the track.

For some weeks now, there had been a new thought that entered her head in these minutes before she slept. For the first time in many years, it was a man. He was tall and well made, big in the arms and chest.

Tom Nugent had called him Scotty. There was something very special about him. A shy smile, that deep Scottish brogue …

She did not think for a moment that she was ready to fall for another man, but the memory of Scotty, leaning on the rails watching her work a horse gave her pleasure, banished the memories that slithered from the dark shadows in her mind.

With these thoughts, Red Jack fell into an exhausted slumber. Under the myriad stars, with a faint breath of welcome cool air moving over the landscape, her dreams were filled with that tall and gentle Scotsman.

# Chapter 27: Billy Reports Back

Every day Alfred Searcy wrote a new entry in his journal. He saw himself as a sea-captain, with the vessel being his own body. Just like James Cook or Matthew Flinders, on land and on water, he set down in detail the events of the day; ground covered, and places visited.

Borroloola had proved to be a difficult posting, and already Alfred's journal was filled with accounts of wild adventures. On just the second day of he and O'Donohue's arrival they had been forced into forming a patrol, following up rumours of a gang of Chinese extortionists who had set up a faux customs post on the border with Queensland. These charlatans were, apparently, charging travellers a fee to enter the Territory.

It was only through the skilful use of their rifles that the two policemen had managed to subdue an angry mob and arrest the perpetrators. Then, just days after dealing with this outrage, a ketch sailed into the Borroloola landing. The crew reported that their captain had been clubbed to death when attempting to 'hire' a young Yanyuwa woman as a house maid.

It seemed prudent to send only O'Donohue to deal with this, but the local men who volunteered as deputies made themselves so drunk on the voyage downstream that they started an all-out war on a bushfire, convinced that the burning trees were black warriors holding burning torches. O'Donohue finally managed to restore sanity, but not until the party's ammunition was near exhausted.

Meanwhile Alfred attempted to maintain the rule of law in the town, a near impossible task. Internal order was hard enough, but raids for women on already persecuted groups of Yanyuwa and Binbinga, reprisals by the same, and regular cattle-spearings saw black-white relations reach boiling point, and the threat of violent confrontation was always present.

One day, a wild local youth, with a bush of black curly hair and a sliver of bone through the septum of his nose, hurried into the newly-completed police station and reported that a big mob of his people had yarded some cattle out at a lagoon and were slaughtering them at will.

'Them bad blackfellas,' he warned. 'Kill plenty cow.'

Alfred formed a party made up of himself, Cameron the publican, old Billy McLeod the storekeeper and a couple of trackers. Guided by the 'informer', wearing chains as a 'precaution', the posse rode off to investigate.

Reaching the lagoon in question, there were no cattle in sight, least of all a large party of Yanyuwa. The informer tried to slip his chains and creep away but his horse bolted, dragging him bodily alongside the lagoon until the chain came adrift from the horse and he escaped into the water. The white men supposed that he had likely become lunch for a 'gator.

'Does this look like a set-up to you?' Alfred asked his companions. 'Did that rascal lure us out here on purpose?'

Old Billy McLeod, who had been around the traps for a while, had no doubt. 'Well I guess we were probably the only sober white men with weapons in Borroloola, and now we're in the middle of bloody nowhere. Yeah, for my money it's a trick.'

'You think the Yanyuwa would dare to take on Borroloola?'

The consensus was that they would.

Riding as fast as possible back to town they found a party of three hundred armed black men advancing on the cluster of shanties and shelters that made up the town. The party of whites charged, firing into the air (according to Searcy's journal, but the truth may well have been more lethal) as they went, forcing the hostile party towards the river, where they swam across to the other side, but remained a threat for some days.

Soon after, with O'Donohue back from his excursion down-river, they were faced with arresting a notorious local ruffian called 'The Orphan' who had set up a butcher's shop, helping himself to Macarthur River Station cattle to provide the beef.

Next came a local race meeting. This 'entertainment' provided many pages of fodder for Alfred's journal. The township had, by then, its own racecourse. O'Donohue loved to ride, mounted on a horse that he had changed the name of three times.

When he first purchased the gelding, he had been named 'Coronation', but after a disastrous race at the Adelaide River, he'd renamed it 'Ruination.' Now, however, when the horse delivered him more wins than losses at Borroloola he rewarded the animal by renaming him 'Reformation.'

The race-going crowd consisted not just of the Borroloola locals, but all the ringers, prospectors, brumby-runners and n'er-do-wells for two hundred miles around. They coped with the heat by drinking the town absolutely dry of alcohol in a three-day binge that left many suffering delirium tremens. Some wandered off, initiated gunfights or fell into the river. Some of the survivors robbed the store, carrying away and drinking every item that resembled alcohol, including Lea and Perrins sauce and cough remedies.

Alfred was recording this latest round of adventures, sitting on the verandah of the police station, when he heard the sound of a horse, driven hard. He turned to look just as it came to a stop outside.

It was their old friend Billy, lean from hard riding and sweating visibly. Alfred directed him to the stables around the back, then, at the verandah table, he poured a pintpot full of tea, and gave the rider a couple of plugs of tobacco.

'So Billy, have you seen the Ragged Thirteen?'

'I think I mighta done, *Mulaka*.'

O'Donohue came through the door in time to hear. 'What d'ye mean you think you mighta done? Those rascals stand out like balls on a bulldog.'

'Yes boss, but I been gone a long time. Maybe I can't remember what I seen.'

'You cheeky beggar,' O'Donohue spat.

Alfred pulled his purse from his pocket, removed a shilling coin and flipped it to Billy. 'Oh I don't mind a bit of pluck, and he has come a long way. Now where did you see the Ragged Thirteen, and did they break the law?'

'I seen 'em at Vic River Depot. They bash 'an half-drown this one *bala*, then steal all his money and grog.'

'Where are they heading now?'

'Victoria River Downs, then longa Halls Creek.'

Searcy smiled and turned O'Donohue. 'We've got those Ragged Thirteen bastards cold. Better pack for two weeks.'

'Do you think it's a good idea to leave Borroloola?'

'It's been pretty darn quiet after the races,' Alfred said. 'We must go where duty dictates, and besides, we'll be back in a week or two. Not only that, those vagabonds made fools of you and I. We can't let that rest.'

O'Donohue grinned. 'To be sure, you're right, Alfie. Let's go get them.'

# Chapter 28: Tom's Trick

'I can't see a bloody thing,' called Tom Nugent.

Sandy Myrtle cupped his hands and shouted up towards the crown of the tree. 'Well climb up higher then, and stop yer blessed complaining. I'd have shimmied up the blasted tree myself if I was as skinny as you.'

After a week or two heading south along the Victoria River, the Ragged Thirteen were half-starved and desperate, gathered under a spreading gum tree, looking expectantly upwards to where Tom Nugent continued to climb, trying not to look down as he moved into the high branches.

A limb made a cracking sound as he moved higher. He gave a start, bringing on a chorus of laughs from the men below.

'Well, you bastards try climbing the fucking tree. I'm not a possum, you know.'

Finally, Tom settled into a fork off the main trunk. Pushing aside a leaf-laden twig, he was able to see all the way to the station homestead of the pastoral holding called Victoria River Downs. One of the world's biggest stations, it had been taken up by Fisher and Lyons, two of the richest of the Territory's land barons. The property sprawled over some of the world's best grasslands, broken up with scrub, stony hills and gullies –

an overall area not much smaller than England.

'What can you see?' Sandy Myrtle shouted.

'Homestead. Yards. Outbuildings. Not much yet. Give a bloke a chance, will you?'

There were dozens of men in the yards, working horses, Tom saw. Others wandered in and out of various sheds. He saw a killer being hoisted on a gallows, and men stropping knives, ready to swarm in. There were wagons, and serving women getting about their duties. Tom took his time, noting every detail, even the trail of smoke from a Bilingara camp on the river.

Tom's eyes focussed on a stout-looking building next to the homestead. The store. Even as he watched, one of the hands walked up, went inside, then returned a minute later with a tin of tobacco in his hand.

Having seen all he needed to see, Tom shimmied back down the tree, then dropped to the ground, examining his ankles and inner forearms where the bark had scraped his skin.

'By God that's a big affair and no mistake,' he said. 'Haven't seen anything like it west of Longreach, except maybe the Macarthur River show.'

'The store's open?' asked Fitz.

'Yes, and it'll be fully stocked for the Wet, I'll warrant.'

Larrikin struck a pose, thumbs in the pockets of his dungarees. 'I think it's our duty to relieve this cattle station of some of their excess goods. It's not fair for them to be greedy.'

'I agree,' Tom said. 'But if the thirteen of us ride in there they'll know exactly who we are, and they could raise an army as soon as click their fingers. Every one of those men has a rifle or a pistol not far away.'

'So what's the plan?' growled Sandy Myrtle. 'I haven't tasted tobacco smoke for a week. I'll kill for it …'

'I'll ride in myself,' Tom Nugent said thoughtfully. 'They don't know me, so I'll pretend to be some rich swell riding around looking for land. These squatters all love a toff, and I'll surely get a chance to chew a bone with them. Someone keep a lookout from this tree here. When I walk out on the verandah and scratch my ear it means there's no one around and you blokes can come in and do your thing.'

'That's a grand jest,' cried Larrikin, 'but they won't fall for your act dressed like you are now.'

'No,' agreed Tom thoughtfully. 'I need to bung it on somehow.'

Each of the Thirteen, it seemed, had a prized item of clothing at the bottom of a kitbag that they figured would be perfect for the occasion.

Sandy Myrtle delved in his packs like a wombat digging a hole, broad arse high in the air, showing a deep and wide crack, so tempting that many a stick or rock had been lodged in there over the weeks the Thirteen had been together. So often, in fact, that Sandy never displayed his rear end without wary glances behind him.

'Here,' he said. 'Tweed trousers. Perfect for the job.'

'Yeah,' drawled Tom. 'And five sizes too big for me.'

Fitz supplied an English riding saddle, stolen off a new chum's horse outside the Burketown Hotel. 'The blasted thing's almost brand new,' he said. 'I stole it only five months back. The owner was just off the boat from Brisbane. I would have taken the horse too – nice looking chestnut he was – but the blessed thing bit me on the shoulder.' His voice took on a haughty tone. 'I won't steal a horse that bites.'

Larrikin sat Tom on a fallen log and used a sharp pair of scissors to trim his hair, then produced a cut-throat razor so rusty and chipped that Tom paled at the thought of it scraping his neck and cheeks.

'No bloody fear, yer not touching my face with that thing.'

'Listen Tom, you're either going to look the part or not. I'll be careful mate, promise.'

When the time came to go, Tom mounted his own horse. He was a fine animal, a gelding with more than a few bad habits, but a dark bay in colour, with clean legs and straight back. Tom's tanned face and wrists were set off nicely by a piratical white shirt. A silk cravat owned by Bob Anderson was the final, distinctive touch.

'I don't mind what you do,' warned Larrikin, 'but don't get blood on that shirt. It's dashed hard to wash out.'

Tom mounted up and looked down at the others. 'I say old chaps,' he said, 'my name is Thomas Holmes, formerly of London town. I'm looking to speculate in this new country. My business partners are keen to invest in land, so I'm here to see what's about.'

The company clapped until the bush rang with it. Sandy Myrtle summed up the general feeling. 'You're perfect. Keep 'em busy and we'll come in and do our thing.'

Tom rode off, and as the sun dropped towards the horizon, Fitz clambered up into one of the tree's top-most branches, making easier work of it than Tom had.

'The plan's off to a good start, boys. I can see Tom and another couple of blokes on the verandah.'

'What're they doing, mate?' Wonoka Jack asked the question for them all.

'Well there's a table and chairs there. Oh Lord, Tom looks every inch the gentleman. Haha, they're sitting down and a girl is bringing them supper.'

'Jesus, real food. What are they eating, Sandy?'

'It's hard to tell at this distance, but I swear it looks like taters, and roast beef, and peas, and gravy ...'

'Oh Gawd, peas and gravy,' someone said.

Collective hunger brought on a long silence, and Sandy sighed wistfully.

After a few minutes of watching the men eat Fitz announced. 'They've got tinned fruit coming, for dessert. Lucky old Tom.'

'Well it's going to be lucky us in an hour or two,' said Sandy, 'because as soon as the signal comes we're going to raid that store. We'll be feasting like pigs before you know it.'

'How are we going to raid the fucking thing?' asked Larrikin from below. 'As Tom said before, there're a lot of armed ringers around.'

'We'll sneak in, lever a couple of slabs off the walls and take what we want.'

George Brown scoffed. 'If we were real bushrangers we'd ride in, guns drawn, take what we want and shoot anyone who stands in our way. All this sneaking around gives me the shits.'

'If we were real bushrangers,' Sandy said wisely, 'we would have been hung by now. A man can get away with a lot in this world, so long as he doesn't cross a certain line. So anyway, shut your trap and let's do this the smart way.'

As darkness fell it became harder for Fitz to see, and he was getting uncomfortable up in the tree. The plates were cleared, however, and a bottle of port wine appeared on the table. Glasses filled. A moment later Tom scratched his ear, slow and deliberate.

'Alright boys,' Fitz called. 'That's the signal.'

They left their horses saddled there under the trees, bridled up with only the bits out of their mouths for a fast getaway. Tommy the Rag was deputised to watch the plant while the raid took place. On hearing this, he screwed his face up like a child.

'Why do I have to wait here, you miserable bastards?'

Sandy Myrtle hardly looked at him. 'Because you walk like you got a shovel strapped to your leg and you've got a big mouth. And if you get caught we're all fucked. If anyone finds you here, just fire off a few shots with your squirt and we'll double-time it back here.' He looked at the others. 'Alright boys, let's go relieve Misters Fisher and Lyons of their surplus goods and provisions.'

# Chapter 29: The VRD Raid

Setting off towards the Victoria River Downs station outbuildings, ducking under ironwood rails into the station horse paddock, Sandy Myrtle attempted to move with stealth, but his bulk made it difficult. Every time he bent over he felt a twinge of pain that shot up his spine and down through his thighs. Moving ahead of him was Larrikin, perfectly balanced, carrying a steel jemmy bar.

The station horses were alarmed by the eleven men moving amongst them at night. Some walked up curiously, nickered and sprang away. The men made soft sounds of comfort as they hurried on, finally reaching the far end of the paddock and crossing the fence.

They paused behind the far wall of a stable to catch their breath. 'Inside will be the best horses on the run,' whispered Fitz. 'We'd better take a look.'

How could they resist? Every one of them loved horses, and particularly good horses, with a passion.

They let themselves in through a side door, and walked along the stalls. It was dark inside, but it was easy to see that these were the cream of the station plant. The best of all was an attractive grey, with clean legs, long neck and high withers –

surely the station manager's or even an owner's thoroughbred.

Jimmy Woodford couldn't stop staring at the animal, even as they moved on towards the open front entrance.

'C'mon you,' hissed Sandy.

'He's a marvel that horse. Have you ever seen the like of him?'

'Alright mate, but we've got work to do. I'm starving hungry, and starin' at horses won't fix that.'

In twos and threes they crossed the dark station track, bent over and moving slowly, thereby reaching the store itself. The raiders circled their way around to the back, which was sandwiched between outbuildings so that they were finally out of sight.

Larrikin knelt with his bar and started to attack the slab wall. The nails were long and stubborn, and he was forced to move along the studs underneath, levering and prying. One of the nails screeched as it came.

'Shut that noise,' hissed Sandy.

Luckily there were some distant sounds, men laughing around some fire somewhere, others talking. A voice broke into song, yodelling out a few lines popular around the stock camps back then.

> She rode into town on a chestnut mare,
> Wearing just her golden hair,
> I asked her please to marry me,
> And took her horse and virgin-i-ty,

The singing was well timed, for it allowed Larrikin to work faster at the slabs, finally opening a man-sized hole in the side of the wall, though Sandy opted to draw his revolver and act as guard while the others went inside.

'I'm not too good on my hands and knees,' he said.

Larrikin went in first with a candle stub and vestas to provide some light. The others followed, one at a time, and after a minute or two they started to reappear, pushing goods ahead of them.

The Ragged Thirteen 'requisitioned' everything away that could be carried – horseshoes, flour, treacle, salt, rum, tinned goods and more. When they were fully laden, Larrikin replaced the slabs as tightly as possible, then joined the others in hurrying off.

Jimmy Woodford took a detour to the stables and returned leading the three finest horses, including the grey, opening the slip rails to get them into the horse paddock.

'Are you mad?' Sandy hissed. 'They'll never pin us for a few horseshoes and the stores, but they'll get us for these nags straight. Especially the grey, anyone with eyes in their head can see he's a stand-out horse. At least leave that one.'

'Alright, I'll leave the grey,' Jimmy said. 'But I'm taking the others. That mongrel Maori Reid shot my horse, and I'm sick of riding old rubbish.'

Sandy held the two horses while the younger man led the grey back, and secured it in its stall.

'C'mon,' he said, when Jimmy came back. 'Let's get moving.'

Back at the camp under the tree, there was a hurried bout of shoving food into mouths, filling packs and preparing for a night run to the Western Australian border, some one hundred miles distant.

They had scarcely half an hour until moonrise. They set off then, heading straight west and travelling fast to put some distance between them and any pursuit.

'I hope Tom's alright back there,' drawled Larrikin.

'He'll be fine,' commented Sandy, 'I'd back that bastard against a pit full of brown snakes.'

At first they followed the Wickham River, then, in the interests of speed, struck out across the plains. It was good country to ride with a moon shining white on the grasslands, and hills capped with pillars of stone on the horizon.

Carmody's navigation skills, honed on the quarterdeck of a ship but equally applicable here on the savannah, proved invaluable that night in choosing the straightest route to the border. The point at which a line through the Southern Cross intersected with another perpendicular line from the pointers showed due south, they all knew that, but Carmody, knowing the relative positions of the stars for this time of year, used two or three other constellations as well.

'It's like a bloody road map,' he said.

Most of the time, however, there was no time to talk. They kept the horses at a jog trot, and for even the best of them it was an exhausting pace, but they ate up the miles.

There was a thrill in watching the coming dawn, then the glory of the sun, lifting spirits of man and horse alike. Poor Jonathan James for all his strength, carrying Sandy Myrtle's great bulk, had slowed to a walk during the night, and the others loitered to let him catch them.

'For pity's sake let's stop for breakfast,' moaned Sandy.

'Not yet,' said Fitz. 'Not until we cross the Negri River, then you can eat all you bloody want.'

# Chapter 30: Across the Murranji

'There's only one way to save time,' said Alfred. 'We'll have to take the Murranji Track.'

After a frantic ride from Borroloola, up through Anthony's Lagoon and Brunette, they had reached Newcastle Waters in four days. Arriving at the homestead, they'd enjoyed the hospitality of the manager, a friendly man by the name of Giles, with comfortable cots in the ringers' quarters, half empty because of the Wet. They had just finished a hearty meal of beef and fresh garden produce.

From here they had two choices. North to the Elsey then across the Dry River country, or west from here on the dreaded Murranji stock route, pioneered by Nat Buchanan a handful of years earlier. Over a hundred miles of narrow track through limestone country, with hollow ground that spooked cattle and made stockmen's lives a misery. It was a last resort.

O'Donohue paled. 'Good Christ, Alfie. T'ey call it the death track. They say t'ere's graves and ghosts at every stop, and from all reports t'ere's only two waterholes of any note – no water otherwise for fifty moiles or more.'

'That's in the Dry,' Searcy argued. 'There's been some rain, Giles said so. Besides, we're not drovers, forced to cover only eight or ten miles a day at best. We can get through as fast as we want.' He paused, then, 'Do you want to catch the Ragged Thirteen or not?'

'Of course I do.'

'Then we can carry water and get through that damned track. Lesser men than us have done it.' Alfred turned the wick down on the lantern until it was barely glowing. 'Let's get a couple of hours sleep then head off in the cool of the morning.'

'If you t'ink we should.'

'I do, my friend. I think we must.'


They were saddled up and ready long before dawn, the two policeman leading, and Jimmy, the tracker, bringing up the spare horses and packs in the rear. At first the going was easy, a formed station road, and wide grasslands. By sunrise, the scrub had started to close in, and the trail narrowed. The January sun gathered heat like a storm gathers cloud. By noon it was a fireball, and both men pulled their hats down low.

When they stopped for the midday meal the track was a mean and insidious scar, through scrub so thick on either side that Alfred jokingly suggested that not even a snake could penetrate. Lancewood they were used to, but the bullwaddy was a brutal plant, thick and strong as a pole, but equipped with thorns like daggers.

They did indeed pass graves, one at a shallow little waterhole. O'Donohue crossed himself and hurried on, and even Al-fred said a prayer.

The horses did not like this place, not one little bit. And neither did their owners. The superstitious O'Donohue kept himself together until near dark, when swarms of mosquitoes came from nowhere, descending in relays of a hundred or more at a time.

'We'll ride all night,' said Alfred, 'but let's stop and eat now while we wait for the moon to rise'

They had already dismounted and had a camp fire burning before either of them noticed a nearby rough cross of split timber and the raised mound of a grave nearby.

'Jaysus,' said O'Donohue. 'Did we haf't stop right on the resting place of another poor sod?'

Alfred leaned close with a lighted brand and read the words that had been scratched in to the cross. Here lies Jack Hall. Dyed of fever, July 23 1883.

'See!' he said. 'He's been dead for a couple of years.'

'Yeah,' agreed the Irishman. 'Just long enough for his shade to get stirred up and look for mischief.'

They ate corned beef and fresh bread from Newcastle Waters. Instead of cheering them, the meal made O'Donohue look more worried than before. To make matters worse Jimmy was jittery and impatient, throwing down his food as if to hasten their time of departure.

Alfred walked off into the bush for a leak, then as he came back the landscape seemed to have closed in darkly around the fire. Even the silhouettes of their horses in the firefight seemed still and mysterious.

Searcy was not a man to allow such things to get him down, and seeing his mate huddling at the fire, looking this way and that, he decided that it was necessary to lighten the mood.

With this in mind he started creeping around so he was directly behind O'Donohue, but hidden by a bush from view. From this position, Alfred began a low and mournful wailing, slowly increasing the pitch. The effect on O'Donohue was dramatic. He jumped up, drew his pistol and cried. 'Sweet Jaysus, what's t'at noise?'

At this point Alfred strolled into the firefight. 'What noise? I didn't hear a thing?'

'How could you not, Alfie? It was bloody 'orrible.'

'Probably a bird.'

'A bird?' He spat. 'Not even a curlew could make a deathly

sound to touch it.'

'I think you're hearing things,' said Alfred. 'Let's get going.'

O'Donohue seemed much happier back in the saddle, but Alfred could not resist a little more fun.

He dropped back so he was riding alongside his mate. 'It's strange,' he said, 'but I keep thinking I can see someone following us.'

O'Donohue's voice dropped to a whisper. 'Blacks?'

'No, not blacks. A horseman, but a strange one.'

'You're talking shite, Alfie. How can t'ere be a horseman? Jimmy's up ahead of us, out on the flank, I just seen him meself.'

'I don't know. Perhaps it was only a fancy. A trick of the night.'

'What did this horse look like?'

'The horse was kind of silvery. Strange. The rider's hat looked like that same colour too.'

They rode on for a little further, with Alfred constantly looking searchingly behind him. After a few minutes of this he stopped his horse, turned one hundred and eighty degrees in the saddle, then shouted at the top of his voice. 'Gawd help us. It's coming for us.'

Alfred Searcy later boasted that he and his mate had set a new record crossing the Murranji Track: just three days after leaving Newcastle Waters they arrived at Victoria River Downs.

The policemen and their tracker were lean from the saddle, eyes in dark pits from lack of sleep. O'Donohue had recovered his composure, but no one mentioned the terror of that night.

The manager walked out from the homestead. 'Good to see men in uniform here, we've been done over and no mistake.' He extended a huge and work-hardened hand. 'My name's Lindsay Crawford. Get your boy to run the horses into the yard there and I'll tell someone to bring them some feed. They look near perished.'

'Nice to meet you,' Searcy said. The manager was tall and rangy, with a bunch of black curls escaping from his hat. 'Done over? Have the Ragged Thirteen have been here?'

'Been here is a damned understatement,' said the manager.

The two lawmen watched as Jimmy led their horses into the house yard, removing the saddles and hanging them on the rail. A stock boy brought in a bale of hay and spread it around. Crawford watched with a critical eye. 'Now you blokes come and get a bite or two into you, and we'll talk about the thieving mongrels who paid us a visit.'

They sat on the verandah while a young black woman brought tea on fine crockery and fresh baked scones. Searcy, ever polite, ate delicately, but O'Donohue couldn't resist stuffing the warm food into his mouth so fast he could scarcely talk.

Crawford, observing this, said, 'A hard trail then, fellas?'

'Yes, soon as we heard that the Thirteen had assaulted a shanty keeper at the Victoria River Depot we saddled up and hit the road.'

They ate and drank for a bit, accepted a second cup of tea, and O'Donohue's eyes turned to the young black woman as she came to clear the cups and plates. As she was about to walk away the policeman cleared his throat.

'Don't go just yet, lass, stop here for a moment.'

She stopped, and there was a tremble in her, for one of the cups rattled on the saucer.

'Nice features on t'is one,' O'Donohue said to Crawford. 'Is she local stock?'

'I think she's a Walbiri from down Wave Hill way. One of the men found her and her ma wanderin' after a shootin' party had been through. Her ma died years ago but this one's been brought up by my missus.'

'What's yer name, girl?' O'Donohue asked.

'Judith, Mister.'

O'Donohue leaned forward on his chair and placed the flat

of his hand on her belly. 'You gettin' plenny good tucker or you growin' 'im picaninny in t'ere?'

The three men laughed, but Crawford stopped and grew serious. 'Let her go now, she's got work to do.' He stood. 'Now come and have a look at the mischief the Ragged Thirteen have managed to wreak.'

The two lawmen followed the manager down to the store. It was a standard place of white-washed split slab walls, with top-hinged windows propped open with sticks, and a bark roof. A couple of station blacks were sitting in the shade outside, looking quizzically at the newcomers as they wandered up.

Searcy walked through the ransacked store, noting the slabs that had been removed to gain entry. 'Typical of the Ragged Thirteen, they display a low animal cunning,' he said.

'Cunning, alright, one of them presented at the station and pretended to be a land speculator. I weren't here, being out on the run at the time, but Lockhart the book-keeper was in charge. The fool gave the king of thieves a top-notch feed and every possible entertainment.'

'That would have been Tom Nugent. He's the only one with the smarts to carry that kind of thing off. They've got a good start towards the border, but you never know with these riff-raff – they might have stopped to get drunk just twenty or thirty miles away.' Searcy thought for a moment, they really needed more firepower to take on the Thirteen. 'If you would lend us a couple of ringers who are handy with their rifles, and another tracker, we'll get after them.'

Crawford shrugged, 'I should think that volunteers won't be hard to come by. Would you plan on leaving at first light?'

'We won't wait that long. It'll be dark soon, but the moon rises before midnight. I'll send our tracker out now to get a fix on their route, while we try for a couple of hours of sleep. Then we'll assemble at the yards and move off as soon as there's light to see.'

# Chapter 31: On the Border

R eaching the Negri River was like a homecoming for the gang. There, camped on the opposite bank, were the stock boys and women they had sent ahead. Blind Joe stood watching the Thirteen ride in, one hand on the shoulder of Tom Nugent's orphan from Borroloola, who looked disappointed when the leader did not appear.

'Don't worry lad,' called Larrikin, still wet to the leggings from crossing the river. 'Old Tom Nugent will be along shortly.' He looked at the camp, then back across the brown, swollen waterway. 'This here river is the border, but I think we need to ride another ten or twelve miles to be safe from the traps.'

'No bloody way,' snapped Sandy Myrtle, swinging out of his stirrups and hitting the ground with a lurch. 'I'm stopping here for a feast, and ain't moving again 'til tomorrow, and even then only when Tom Nugent rides up.'

'The wallopers might still follow us, don't you reckon?' asked George Brown.

Sandy Myrtle shook his head, 'Not much chance of that. They're hundreds of miles away. Besides, the bastards aren't supposed to follow us over the border. Now, enough talk. It's time to cook up a feed and enjoy the fruits of all that hard work.'

Scotty, as usual, took up the job of chief cook, and before long there were plates of johnny cakes and treacle, tinned peaches, hot tea and tinned beans. They ate until they were full, and restlessness soon took over. Jim Carmody got up a game of mumble the peg, the stock-camp favourite involving pen knives being flicked from various positions into the ground.

Later in the afternoon, Tom Nugent arrived on a grey stallion, leading his own horse. Sandy Myrtle watched him cross the river, unsure at first, but as he neared the quality of that stallion became apparent. 'The bloody idiot,' he turned and shouted to the others. 'Tom stole the fucking grey.'

Jimmy Woodford crossed his arms over his chest, annoyed. 'That's because he didn't have a fat old woman there telling him not to.'

Normally Sandy would have reacted to this, but now he kept his attention on Tom, waiting until he rode up and dismounted. 'Are you mad?'

'What do you mean?' Tom said. 'I hope you left some tucker for me, I'm famished.'

'You took the grey.'

'You lot nicked a couple for yourselves from what I can see, and besides, we're safe over the border.'

'Safe are we? Your new friend at the Downs won't let that horse slide, and Searcy hates our guts. Best to turn him loose now.'

Nugent dismounted. 'Not a chance, Sandy. Now shut your mouth, there's a good bloke. He rubbed his hands together. 'Now for some tucker.'

'Well don't listen to me then,' said Sandy, 'but mark my words. Duffing that horse was a mistake. A man can get away with a lot in this life as long as he don't …'

'Cross a certain line,' Tom finished for him. 'I've heard you say it before. Now lead me to dinner, before I pass out.'

Late in the afternoon, at Tom's suggestion, Scotty Campbell and Larrikin forded the Negri again and climbed a nearby slope to watch for anyone who might be in pursuit.

They settled themselves down about half way up the hill, sitting on a natural contour, surrounded by turkey bush and tussocks. Seeing nothing at first, but spying a bull ant nest ten paces down the slope, Larrikin collected small stones and threw them at the insects. The first missile landed just shy of the entrance, and the ants went mad, climbing all over the stone.

Scotty joined in the fun, sending first one stone then another.

'I reckon you hit one,' said Larrikin. 'I seen it jump in the air and fall down.'

'One tae meself then,' Scotty said.

They were so busy raining missiles down on the ants that they didn't, at first, notice a lone rider in the distance. It was only that Scotty, tired of the game, finally flicked his eyes up and saw the raised dust in the scrub to the east.

'Och, Larrikin, belay that for a taim. We 'av company.'

'Looks like you're right,' drawled Larrikin, and they watched in silence as the form of a lone rider, with two spares and three packs strung out behind, became clear.

'Shid we be calling the others?'

'Nah, one walloper wouldn't come after us alone. It's just a traveller. But we'll watch just in case.'

The rider was not hurrying, but came closer slowly. Finally, when they came abreast of the hill Scotty saw red plaits hanging down from the broad cattleman's hat. 'That's Red Jack,' he blurted.

Larrikin whistled, 'By all that's holy I think you're right.'

As they watched she crossed their sign, and reined in. Scotty could almost see her eyes following their trail heading up the slope, scanning the hillside until, at the distance of half a mile she had picked them out.

'She's spied us,' cried Scotty.

'Well she's not exactly dangerous, who cares?'

'Hell an' all, she's comin' this wae.'

Larrikin seemed to forget his bravado, and together they wriggled into the thicket of turkey bush, raising their heads just far enough that they could see her canter up the slope, directly towards them.

'That lass can ride,' breathed Scotty. There was something about her, he thought to himself. Something like the faeries in the illustrated Scots books that his mother had read to him. This woman had that glow. Not just beauty, but inner goodness. Hugh Campbell wanted her in a way that wasn't only physical. He wanted to make a sacrifice for her. Prove himself.

'Christ, what's she doing?' Larrikin muttered. 'Is she working for the traps?'

'Nah,' Scotty said, 'she's only curious.'

At that point Larrikin jumped sharply. 'Fuck,' he hissed.

'What is it?' Scotty asked. But just then something sharp pierced the soft skin behind his knee. Hugh looked down to find that their hiding place was only a short distance from the ants they had been stirring up. Now those ants were swarming over them, crawling up their dungarees and biting bare flesh, finding the gap between trousers and shirt.

The red-haired woman momentarily forgotten, they both jumped up, swatting at their legs like madmen.

Finally, when Scotty raised his head it was to look straight into the eyes of Red Jack as she stopped, just a few paces away from them.

After a long silence she said, 'Well damn me. I don't think I've ever seen two jackasses so overgrown before.'

Then she wheeled her horse and trotted away, her packs and spares following obediently behind.

Scotty slowly picked himself up, and stared after her. 'Ach she's bonnie. Ah only jes' seen her and already me pair heart is achin' for the lack.'

Larrikin shook his head sadly. 'That's only because you're young and stupid. Red Jack leaves broken hearts behind her wherever she goes, and she doesn't give a fuck who they belong to.'

# Chapter 32: Changing the Brand

'Listen to me Tom, and listen good,' Sandy Myrtle said after breakfast, still licking crumbs from his beard. 'You have to do something about that horse.'

'What can he do, apart from turnin' it loose?' asked Fitz

'I'm not letting the horse go,' Tom said, 'and that's flat.'

'You know,' said Larrikin, relighting his pipe and taking a deep puff, 'last year I was working at Alexandria Station over on the Barkly. Their brand is a capital A in a box, this one has a B in a circle. When I left I bought three horses, one of them was a grey stallion. He was a poor old bugger that I used as a packhorse until he died. It seems to me that with a hot knife and a steady hand the brand could be changed. It might be enough of a story to keep a man out of gaol.'

Tom shook Larrikin's hand. 'You, my friend, are a genius.'

They heated a knife in the fire until it glowed red, and the handle had to be wrapped in a rag to be held. Since altering the brand was Larrikin's idea he was deputised to do the work, and he oversaw the project, demonstrating with a stick in the dust just how he might make the change most efficiently.

The stallion, meanwhile, was no idiot, and he watched the

proceedings with a wary eye. When Larrikin took the knife from the fire and walked towards him, the stallion reared. He was a big strong horse, and was not going to be held while the hot knife was in proximity.

'There, there mate,' Larrikin cooed. 'It'll all be over in an instant.' The high-spirited beast responded with a kick that would have taken Larrikin's head off if he hadn't moved.

They tried everything, but the horse would not let the knife get close to him.

'We'll have to throw the bastard,' said Larrikin. 'It's the only way.'

The Thirteen gathered around while Larrikin made a loop in a rope and firmed it up around the stallion's neck. The ends went down through the forelegs, in a complicated arrangement around the rear fetlocks. Then, while the animal fought and kicked every inch of the way, Larrikin had Tom pull from the front rope-end and he on the side. The stallion's rear legs gathered up, and he went down, held by willing helpers while the knife burned into the hair and skin of his shoulder.

When it was done, the area was thick with dust raised from the activity, and the air smelled of singed horsehair. They all agreed that the brand looked much like Larrikin had promised it would. He'd fined up the top of the B to resemble an A, and rounded the square into a circle. It was messy, sure, but not all brands were applied expertly.

'What was the name of that old nag of yours, Larrikin?' asked Tom. 'The one with this brand.'

'Gumnut.'

Some of the men laughed, but Tom shrugged. 'Well I guess we'd better call this one the same then, though it don't really suit.' He looked at Larrikin. 'We might as well do the other two horses you blokes took from the homestead, while we're on the job.'

The Thirteen were too busy to notice when riders came up on the other side of the river: Searcy, O'Donohue, eight armed ringers from VRD and two trackers. The horses were blown from hard riding, and the men were weary but alert. They were veterans of stock camps and long droves, more at home in the saddle than any feather bed.

Leaving the horses and creeping up to the edge of the scrub, the police party gazed out at the Negri and the slow rise of stale smoke on the other side.

'That's them,' growled O'Donohue. 'But that river's the border, damn it. They're in the sovereign colony of Western Australia and there's nothing we can do about it.'

Searcy grinned. 'That's not the case. All these bushmen think that the Negri River is the actual border. It's not. The real border is the 129th meridian, which the river runs along, here and there. I'm telling you right now that the Ragged Thirteen are still half a mile within the Jurisdiction of the Northern Territory of South Australia. And the best thing is that they don't even know it.'

O'Donnell smiled. 'Alright then. How are we going to take them?'

'I've got a brilliant idea,' said Alfred, 'of how we can have the whole lot of those rascals in chains. But it will only work in the morning. Let's go back a ways and sleep well. There's men's work to be done in the dawn.'

# Chapter 33: The Call of Nature

An hour before dawn Alfred Searcy led a line of horsemen across the Negri, half a mile upstream from the
Ragged Thirteen's camp. Moving carefully in the dark,
armed with coils of rope and loaded carbines, the police party
worked their way back down on foot, taking up their positions
around the camp, spaced at regular intervals just a long stone's
throw from the sleeping men.

Searcy chose a boab tree as thick around as a garden rotunda
as his post, waiting for the Thirteen to stir. The instructions
he had given to the men in his party were simple. The gang of
ruffians had been gorging on stolen food. They would wake
around dawn, and the call of nature would take them, one by
one, out of the camp. When they did so, a quick gag and a few
lashings of rope would allow them to be spirited away, back
here to the boab. Searcy would guard the captives while the rest
of the gang were taken.

'Won't Tom Nugent get suspicious when people keep disap-
pearin'?' O'Donohue asked.

'Eventually, yes,' answered Searcy, 'but by then their numbers will have been whittled down and we can take the rest by
force.'

It had rained during the night, but the sun rose clear and burning yellow, just as two of the Victoria River ringers brought in their first captive. This, Searcy saw, was the lad called Tommy the Rag, wrists secured around his back with his own stockwhip. His eyes were furious, and he attempted to kick at them with his feet until they too were lashed together, and he had no choice but to lay down.

'What's that smell?' Searcy asked suspiciously.

'Well now,' said the ringer. 'You can't expect to apprehend a man er, performing a call of nature without things getting messy.'

'It's a weakness in the plan,' said the other.

Searcy bristled, 'Stop griping and get on with it. Before long we'll have the whole lot of them in custody, and they can wash themselves off in the river.'

For a while nothing happened. Searcy was forced to watch Tommy the Rag trying to chew through his gag for entertainment, but the next two captives came together. George Brown, then 'New England' Jack Woods. Both were strong men, fighting the ropes and those who carried them like 'gators caught in a net.

O'Donohue was just as strong, however, and he brought each of these men in with the help of the trackers and some ringers, throwing them under the trees, binding their feet, then giving Brown a kick in the side for good measure.

'I must admit, Alfie,' the big Irishman said, with his chest heaving. 'I doubted yer plan at first. Yet it seems t' be working.'

Sandy Myrtle had experienced a troubled sleep, and laid abed a tad longer than usual. Finally, however, he lumbered to his feet, found a pannikin of water and a pipe he had packed ready the night before. He swallowed the water thirstily, then walked to the fire, leaning over to light the pipe on a burning stick. Tom, Fitz, Carmody and Larrikin were warming themselves and toasting lumps of damper.

'Where is everyone?' Sandy asked.

'Dunno,' said Fitz. 'Out and about.'

When the pipe was finished Sandy's bowel started making its presence felt. He stood and walked from the camp, into the scrub, scouting around. Being such a big, heavy man, nineteen stone last time he checked, he did not like to squat. His preferred latrine was a fallen trunk that he could sit on. He would often spend some time looking for the right one.

The search was hastened by the growing urgency in his gut, and in the end the best he could do was an old fallen sapling, no thicker than his arm, supported at knee height by its spindly branches. Stripping off his dungarees he perched himself on the trunk, sighing with relief.

He had eaten well the previous day, wolfing down johnny cakes and treacle until he felt sick, along with tinned beans and salted meat. The result was a fully ripe discharge, depositing in a rush below his perch.

A sudden noise from behind had Sandy turning. He saw two men, strangers both, carrying carbines. One also held a length of cloth ripped into a gag. Sandy tried to get up, but at that moment the old trunk he was sitting on broke with a sharp crack, and down he went, plumb into a hot pile of his own effluent.

The men rushed forward with the gag. But not before Sandy managed a loud shout of surprise. He rose like a bear, howling with rage, lashing out with a huge arm, so unbalanced and unsteady that he fell back into the same patch of filth he had just risen from, now mixing with reddish mud from the previous night's rain.

Bellowing and lashing out mindlessly, Sandy got up again and rushed at the two Victoria River ringers, who turned tail and ran, thinking now of nothing but their own safety.

Tom, back at the fire, heard the sound and stood up, holding an enamel mug of tea in his right hand, every sense attuned. 'What was that?'

'Dunno,' replied Fitz, 'sounds like old Sandy Myrtle just lost his temper.'

A moment later the sound of a gunshot echoed through the bush and they were all on their feet, scrabbling for weapons.

'Hey Blind Joe,' called Tom.

'Yes Tom?'

'Get the rest of the stockboys, women and horses together and ride west until noon-time. We'll catch up with you there. We've got trouble.'

Then, to the gang members who were at the camp. 'Mount up, boys, we'll find out what the devil's going on out there.'

Sandy Myrtle charged like a bull through the bush after the two men. He wore no trousers at all, and a singlet that had once been white was stuck to his torso. He was a fast runner, over a short distance, and it wasn't far to where Alfred Searcy waited with his prisoners. Sandy was roaring, face red with anger, his half-naked body covered in foul-smelling brown and reddish slime.

'Good God,' shouted Searcy as the two ringers ran in, with this apparition behind them. He had time to lift his rifle and fire a warning shot over the huge man's head. It had no effect.

'Arrest him,' shouted Searcy to the ringers.

'Arrest that?' one of the ringers shouted back. 'You've got to be bloody joking.'

Searcy was forced to run for his life, Sandy's huge fist swinging wildly and missing his head by a whisker. The smell was intense. Terrible. Almost life changing.

Laughter rang out around the boab tree, as the prisoners in their bonds laughed at the sight. But Sandy was not distracted, his heart set on punishing the men who had interrupted his morning ablutions. He ran with every ounce of strength, fists clenched, eyes narrowed, and droplets of sweat flying from his forehead at every stride.

Alfred Searcy was smart enough to double back, but the two ringers ran on, terrified and disgusted, all the way to the horses, and it was only when Sandy saw them mounted and swimming back across the river that he recovered some of his composure, walking back to where Tom Nugent and the others had just arrived on horseback.

Only Searcy and O'Donohue had rallied, with Jimmy the tracker, their carbines trained on Tommy the Rag, George Brown and 'New England' Jack.

'These men are our prisoners,' shouted Searcy. He was hoping for the rest of the contingent from Victoria River Downs to turn up, but the sound of horses sloshing their way across the river told him that they had already joined their mates in making a retreat.

'The devil they are,' replied Tom, holding his heavy Snider rifle like a toy. 'Turn around and walk away. If you're still on this side of the river at the count of fifty we'll throw you in.'

The tracker, having a sense for which side was on the ascendancy, turned and went after the ringers. Searcy and O'Donohue stared at each other. Then slowly lowered their weapons.

'This won't be t'e end of t'e matter,' warned O'Donohue.

At that moment, however, Sandy Myrtle emerged from the trees, still bare of clothing in the lower half of his body, sheeted with sweat and filth from top to toe.

Seeing Searcy and O'Donohue, he roared with rage, and gave chase. The two policemen had no choice but to run, and while Tom and his mates untied the ropes, the riverbank rang with laughter, and the slowly receding sound of Sandy Myrtle yelling as he chased his prey to their horses and over the river.

'I don't think I've seen old Sandy lose his temper before today,' said Tom.

'It's a sight,' said Wonoka Jack, rubbing his wrists. 'I seen him go berserk once in the town of Stuart. Damn near killed five men, he did.'

Tom smiled, 'Still and all, I think it's best that we all get mounted and ride some distance into Western Australia, away from those damn traps. They're going to be spoiling to get us after this little fracas. Besides, we're so close to that darned gold I can smell it.'

# Chapter 34: Hall's Creek

The Elvire River wound down towards Hall's Creek, with an established trail on the high ground beside it, marked with heavy wagon ruts and bush camps along the way. Graves were common, as were cairns of stones and timber crucifixes.

On a short cut between loops of the river, propped up at the foot of a boab tree, the Thirteen came upon the body of a man. There were no kite-hawks or crows circling in the air above him, for they were busy on the ground, pulling the flesh from his cheeks and the eyes from their sockets. The sharp beaks had also found entry through a hole in his chest. Clouds of flies crawled like a living mass over his body and swarmed in the air.

Tom used his revolver to dissuade the kite-hawks, shooting one dead and scattering the others into slow flight, dragged down by the weight in their bellies. The Ragged Thirteen, either standing or mounted, looked down on the remains of the man.

'Poor bastard,' said Larrikin. 'I wonder what got him.'

'A bullet or a knife, I'd say,' said Fitz. 'Those birds got into his chest easy enough – must've been a wound to start them off.'

'Let's bury him,' said Tom. 'No man deserves to be eaten by

a pack of damned birds.'

The others agreed, and while Larrikin and Scotty started off, Tommy the Rag went through the dead man's pockets and swag. There was a battered old chequebook from the Bank of South Australia, and Tommy examined it briefly and slipped it into his top pocket. He caught Sandy Myrtle's eyes.

'He won't be needing that where he's going.'

The grave was a shallow one, and they compensated by piling rocks on top. No one talked or smiled until they had moved on to the river, where the main track ran, busy with men hurrying to the diggings. Others were leaving, eyes sunken with fatigue and disappointment. Many offered to sell information or the few shovels and pans they still had.

'I've got a hand-drawn map of the diggings,' one of them offered. 'Two and sixpence for hard-won intelligence that'll save you time.'

They crossed a dry tributary, the Black Elvire, and struck the first diggings soon after: hundreds of men hunched over their sluices and shovels. A waterhole on the main junction was clogged with men and horse teams taking water, washing gravel. No one stopped to talk, but hurried like ants in that world of mullock heaps and shafts, pistols at their hips, watching through narrowed eyes as the newcomers rode in.

'Friendly bunch, aren't they?' Wonoka Jack muttered.

'Diggings are all like this,' Tom Nugent said. 'Anyone with a decent patch is dead certain someone's going to jump their claim, or strike it rich next door, or steal their gold. Don't expect the time of day from these people.'

It was another seven or eight miles ride to Hall's Creek itself, and the Elvire River now became a rocky gully, with flat topped red hillocks in a landscape dry as dust. The creek that gave the town its name was no better, apart from a couple of small pools here and there.

'No wet season here, as yet,' commented Tom. He noticed

quite a few abandoned claims, testament to the fickle nature of greed, as he led the Thirteen half a mile north of the township, looking for a campsite. Blind Joe scouted out some poor-quality blue grass, located above a bend in the river bed that held a reasonable puddle. With the exhausted horses hobbled, and unlikely to stray, the men dressed in their best clobber, and strapped revolvers to their waists.

Leaving the stockboys to watch the camp, they walked in a group back towards town. The sun was starting to sink into a dusty horizon when they arrived. It was a village of shanties, lively and noisy with lanterns up on poles and half a dozen grog shops. All the stores were open into the night, even the mud-brick post office and police station.

One man was offering a patch of common on which new arrivals could water and feed their horses, for there was not a blade of grass to be seen. Silage worked out to a shilling a horse per day.

'That's why we left the horses back at camp,' Tom said, and they walked down narrow streets lined with shanties and bough shelters. The original inhabitants of these dry ridges sat in the dust under the few surviving trees, and their children played with cast-off things from the miners.

In one of those alley-like streets they came upon the darkest den in that dark den of Hayes Creek, a twenty-four-hour cesspit of drink and opium. There was a card game going on in one corner. The croupier was a man with one eye, a sawn off double barrel on the green felt table in front of him, and a wall of split logs to protect his back. He dropped cards with monotonous practice, always perfectly in place, talking only when necessary.

The players were diggers. Most played with small nuggets or bags of pure gold. They scarcely glanced up as the Thirteen arrived.

The other drinkers in that dingy bar were more interested in the gang's arrival. One was a whiskered old Irishman, drinking often from a jug of ale, yet with a canny look in his eye. There were two young men at the bar itself, and judging from their clothes, they were fresh on the fields. Another was too well dressed to be a local, with the look of a remittance man about him.

There was a mean-eyed rascal with a huge Colt strapped to his hip, glaring at the newcomers as they walked in. A table of Chinese played mah-jong on ivory tiles, opium pipes lying idle in a tray.

Tom fronted the bar and shouted to the mangy-thin attendant. 'Bring us thirteen bottles of rum and thirteen glasses,' he called. 'And food.'

The Thirteen dragged three tables together and planted their elbows down. When the rum came, Sandy Myrtle poured his glass full and raised it. 'Here's to a long journey's end, and a successful quest for gold.'

The others followed suit, and soon a waitress was bringing plates of beef and real yeasty bread, dripping with butter. Fresh produce too! Tomatoes and cucumbers from the Chinese market gardens. The Thirteen ate hungrily, while, with the coming of night, the shanty started to fill with diggers coming off their claims, thirsty and tired.

One such man had scarcely walked in the door before he spotted Tom, and shouted, 'Well if it isn't old Tom Nugent from the Hunter Valley.'

Armed with a tumbler of rum the new man squeezed in with the Thirteen.

'Hey you blokes,' said Tom, 'this is Luke Frey, I used to work with him in the Gulf.'

There were some handshakes and murmured greetings, but the new arrival didn't divert them much; the food and rum, and yarns between themselves being of more interest.

After a while a prostitute started working the bar, leaning over the men, slapping hands away from her bosom, disappearing now and then with a man for a small nugget of gold or a half crown.

'Are yer tempted?' Tommy the Rag asked Sandy Myrtle.

'Not at all, boy. I'm happy with she who waits for me back at camp. Let these daft yokels waste their nuggets and get a dose of the clap as the price of their pleasure.'

Pleasantly content with the food and rum, Tom Nugent got down to quizzing his mate about how things worked at Hall's Creek.

'The diggings are winding down,' opined Luke Frey. 'You blokes have missed the best of it.'

'That remains to be seen,' said Tom. 'Who's to say there's not a rich reef just yet undiscovered and that this place will end up like Hill End or Ballarat?'

'That's very true,' said his mate, 'but such a reef an't been found yet.'

'So what's the best way to get a claim?' Tom asked. 'Find new ground to peg?'

'Just take yer pick from what's been abandoned. Under the rules here, once the claimants been gone for seven days they're anyone's. You just have to check with the Mine Warden and register it for your own self. You feel like a walk?'

'Why not?' said Tom.

And the Thirteen took their half empty bottles and walked down the narrow lanes that wound between the claims, following gully and dry creek, hill and tailings heap while Luke Frey talked and took swigs of their rum.

'See that place there? Old Roly Phelps from England hung himself from the headgear after working it night and day for months, garnering barely a speck for his trouble. Had no funds even to get home. The claim over there was worked by two Russians, then two Adelaide lads. A few nuggets was all that was took.'

'But there's still gold here?'

'Yes there is, but it's patchy. The blokes who are still here are mostly finding enough to keep afloat … just. Every now and then someone strikes it rich, but it's the exception, not the rule.'

'So where do we start looking for claims?' asked Tom.

'Anyplace, really. Take a ride around tomorrow. Most of the productive diggings are in an area from Holes Creek in the south, to the Black Elvire in the east, and to the China Wall in the north.'

'The China Wall?'

'An exposed quartz reef that runs for a couple of miles, like the backbone of a beast standing proud from the earth. It's rather spectacular; take a look when you get a chance. Anyhow, there's the diggings south of here, along Hall's Creek itself, but the main action is now to the south east – Nuggetty Gully, Rosie's Flat, and the Twelve Mile. Most of these have no water so you'd either have to buy it in or dry blow your ore. I'd be panning some of the gullies 'til you find some encouragement – choose your claim where you find colour.'

They came, finally, to Like Frey's own claim, with a candle light winking from a slab hut and a dark woman's face in the glassless window. The Thirteen took turns to shake his hand and thank him for the information. Then, neither sober nor drunk, they walked back to their camp, full of the scents of rum, dirt, gold, and adventure.

# Chapter 35: Staking a Claim

Just as the sun's first rays touched the gully, a cupped handful of water from the shallow brown waterhole hit Tom Nugent's face. When the ripples had stilled he used his reflection on the surface to comb his hair with his fingers. He had washed his shirt the night before and hung it on a branch. It was almost dry but not quite, raising goosebumps on his skin in the morning cool.

Sandy Myrtle walked across to join him. 'Important day, Tom Nugent.'

'Oh I don't know,' said Tom. 'I like to take days as they come. Yet, we need to find some ground to work, that's true, and the boys are all keen.' He nodded towards Tommy the Rag, who was already dressed, 'bandicooting' for nuggets on the surface. Back up around the camp, most of the others were throwing down a quick breakfast.

When this was done, they gathered around, tacking up the horses and stowing hunks of Johnny cake and corned beef in saddle bags. None of them knew whereabouts on the diggings they'd be at dinner time, and no one wanted to go hungry.

By the time Tom had walked back and mounted his own horse he looked around at the rest of the Thirteen. 'You blokes ready?'

They replied with a series of nods and quiet murmurs of agreement.

'Then let's go find the piece of dirt that's going to make us rich.'

Together in a group, all on fine horses, the Thirteen were a sight as they rode from claim to claim across the diggings, at once both desolate and industrious. Most of the flats had already been excavated to one degree or another, and some had shafts to various depths.

One such mine, sited on a hill of tilted slate, was for sale, and the owner took Tom below ground, where they crawled down narrow tunnels that seemed even hotter than the land above. By torchlight Tom saw the reef for himself, a variable yellow line cased in quartz, and surrounded by layers of soft, red sandstone.

Sandy refused to enter the shaft. 'I'm a man, not a fucking wombat. I'll work as hard as any two normal blokes, make no mistake, but I'll do it on the surface.'

The Thirteen briefly discussed buying the claim, on the basis of proven, payable gold, but it would have taken every cent they could raise between them, and leave nothing for equipment. Besides, with claims free for the taking, apart from a registration fee, no one in the party was keen to part with cash.

'I was born lucky,' said Larrikin. 'We'll find the gold, don't fret about that, and without having to sell every damn horse we own.'

Everywhere they went – Macphee's Camp, Hall's Gully, and all along the Elvire, they found miners busy digging, panning, hauling and dry-blowing. Few were willing to offer the time of day. Those few who talked called them fools and told them to ride back to wherever they had come from.

'Enough gold to buy a loaf of bread a day,' said one. 'This place isn't a rush, it's a damned fraud.'

Dispirited but still determined, in the middle of the after-noon the Thirteen reined in, overlooking a set of claims on the edge of an area called Rosie's Flat.

Tom ran his eyes over the site. There was water in a gully, and even a couple of reasonable shade trees had survived the work. To look at, this spot was a cut above most of what they had seen.

'Let's see if we can turn anything up,' Tom said, dismount-ing and removing the spade and pan strapped to the saddle. It was one of the few claims with enough water to be able to pan, rather than separate the gold dry.

Down in the gully, with Sandy on the shovel, they took a few pounds of gravel from a likely-looking natural trap. With the pan half-filled, Tom moved to the water and started swishing the load, scouring like a wire brush on the hard metal.

Tom was good at panning; fast but careful, and he was not even to the last fines before he caught the glint of yellow in the pan. He turned to Sandy and smiled. When he had finished the pan held a dozen or more specks of gold, but best of all a tiny nugget the size of a match head.

Larrikin bent over to look, then whooped. 'What a thing it is to pull a little nugget out of your first pan-load! I told you I was lucky.'

'It's a good area,' said Fitz. 'Those trees for a start – the horses will be grateful for the shade.'

'They can take turns at it,' smiled Tom. 'But I agree. Gold in the first pan is a good sign.'

The Thirteen walked the area, locating the pegs for eight adjoining claims. Then, while the others reset the boundaries, Tom wrote down the claim numbers and went in with Sandy to the Warden's office to register them.

As they rode back towards town the batteries were stamp-ing, the sound carrying across the landscape. This heavy beat was matched with the swish of gravel being worked through home-made shakers. These were used on claims with no access to water, the resulting fines being winnowed to separate gold from dust.

Down past the mud brick post office, they left the horses at a public hitching post and walked towards the Warden's office. They were passing a shop when Sandy spat on the pavement, at which time the storekeeper appeared at the door.

'Hey you, fatty, spit somewhere else.'

Tom laughed, but Sandy turned and hissed. 'I'll spit where I bloody well like.'

The altercation would have developed further, but Tom Nugent pushed Sandy hard between the shoulder blades, away from the store. 'You want to get us arrested?'

When the big man still wanted to have a go at the shop-keeper Tom dragged him bodily down two doors and into the Warden's office. The interior was well lit, due to windows fronting both the street and a narrow alley on the far side.

A very thin man, decked out in black and whites, with a hanging watch chain, rose from a desk littered with papers, a pot of ink and a good supply of quills.

'Good morning gentlemen. Let me introduce myself, I'm Charlie Price, the Mine Warden.'

'Nice to meet you, Mr Price. I'm Tom, and this is Sandy.'

'You blokes want coffee?'

'Yes, why not.'

A face appeared at the alley window. The urchin's cheeks were as grimy as that of a coal miner's, but tinged with red in line with the local dirt. He wore clothes many times too large for his frame, and the once-white shirt was now grimy with grease and dirt.

'Hey you,' shouted Charlie. 'Got an errand for ye.'

The child scurried around the corner, through the doorway and into the room.

The Warden tossed a shilling in the air, and the urchin caught it with a flick of his right wrist, opening his hand to view the coin. 'So whaddya want with this?'

'Three coffees from Esau the Afghan, an' a coupla them little cakes too.'

'Before ya can blink, Mister,' said the urchin, and tore off through the door.

'Esau the Afghan?' Sandy inquired.

'Yeah. That man makes the best bleeding coffee in the gold-fields, providing you like it strong. Raises a few quid for the hospital with his sales.'

'Strong is good,' Tom agreed. 'Now, tell me, when does the "wet" start around here?'

'We've had a storm or two, but no serious falls just yet.'

They were still discussing the weather when the urchin re-turned with coffee and cakes, as bold as brass with them, 'Here you go gents, coffee fresh-made from Esau's pot.'

Tom took a sip, enjoying the strong flavour with a hint of cardamom. 'Handy lad,' he said, when the child was gone, 'but talk about filthy.'

The broker lowered his voice. 'No lad that one – she's a girl – but the general riff raff around here don't know that.'

'A girl? What's she doing here?'

'There are three kids working a claim, two girls and their older brother Jake. He's about fourteen or so – works like a bloody Trojan. I keep a bit of an eye on the poor buggers, and the girls often pop over and see if I've got any odd jobs to run – honest little imps they are. Between you and me they're not see-ing much sparkle off the claim, and sometimes the only money coming in is a few pennies from errands.'

Now that Tom thought about it he could recognise the more feminine aspects of the child's features. There was a softness to her eyes, and something about her lips. Partly because of his kindness to a struggling little family, Tom felt himself warming to the Warden.

'Now,' the official said finally. 'Now that we have coffee, I wonder if you gentlemen would enlighten me as to how I might be of assistance.'

Tom took out the sheet of paper with the claim numbers on it. 'We'd like to register these abandoned claims.'

The Warden looked up the numbers on a sheet. 'Two of these belonged to a young bloke from Perth, and the others to a syndicate that split up a few weeks ago. Those blokes are gone for good as far as I know, so I have no objections provided you have the ten pounds claim fee per plot.'

Tom fished in his pocket. 'You'll accept a cheque, of course sir?'

'Provided it's a good one.'

'Oh it's a good one, alright,' said Tom.

'Good-o then. What might be the full names of you gentlemen?'

'Thomas Nugent and Alexander McDonald, more commonly known as Sandy Myrtle.'

The mine Warden's face fell. He put down his pen and fell to rummaging through the papers on his desk. He located a paper and started reading it. 'Oh dear,' he began. 'This isn't good.'

'What do you mean?' complained Tom. 'Can we just register the claims and get to work?'

'No, I'm terribly sorry, but we've had a letter from the Northern Territory police stating that you two gentlemen, along with five other named men and six unnamed, are of unsound character, wanted for serious offences in the Territory, and are not to be issued with licences or be allowed to register claims.'

Tom locked eyes with Sandy. 'It's that damn Searcy, who's done this,' he said. Then to the Warden, 'This is bloody unfair. We have committed no crime on Western Australian soil.'

'That's as may be, but under the terms of the Mining Act the Commissioner may refuse to issue permits or claims to persons believed to be of unsound character. That he has done on the basis of the letter. In other words,' he said. 'I can no longer help you … much as I would like to of course.'

Tom saw the rage building in Sandy's eyes, and shot him a harsh glare. Putting this man off side would be a mistake. 'We're disappointed of course,' he said, 'but thank you at least for your consideration. And please do allow me to pay you for the coffee.'

'No, I won't hear of it.'

'Then we'll be heading off.' Tom shook hands with the Warden and managed to get Sandy out the door while the steam was still building.

Out on the street the big man pushed Tom's restraining hand away. 'That snivelling bastard Searcy. I wish I'd killed him. He must have had that letter delivered by hand for it to get here before us.' Seeing that they were passing the shop again, Sandy paused to spit on the front window.

'Wishing won't help us,' said Tom, 'and neither will pissing-off shopkeepers. We have to work out how to get those bloody claims signed up to us somehow.'

# Chapter 36: The Silent Partner

The next afternoon, back at the camp in the gully north of the town, the Thirteen mused over the problem of legally registering the claims. Most had pipes between their lips, while a rum bottle made a slow journey from one hand to the next.

'Why not register the claims in Scotty's name, or me own?' asked Bob Anderson. 'The traps doan 'ave a skiffy who we all are. You sayed so yourself, Tom.'

'The Warden knows that we're together,' replied Tom. 'We're not going to get away with it. If we try to do something like that they can declare the whole transaction null and bloody void. We need someone we can trust, outside the gang, to register the claims for us.'

'What about your mate we ran into at the grog shanty, Luke, wasn't it?' Fitz asked. 'He seemed like a straight-up bloke.'

Tom shook his head sadly. 'I trust Luke so far and no more. If we struck it rich he'd have the deeds in his hands and we'd have no leg to stand on if he tried to take over.'

Carmody, who had been listening with his usual long face, stood. 'Well we need someone who ain't interested in mining on their own account, but is happy to be cut in for a share.'

'A share?' asked Sandy. 'Who said anything about a share?'

'Carmody's right I reckon,' said Tom. 'We need a silent partner, someone who'll be happy to take a share for holding the deeds and shutting their mouth.'

Tommy the Rag had been thinking hard, coiling and uncoiling his stock whip. 'Well I seen that red-headed woman with the big black horse earlier. Maybe she'd do it for us?'

Scotty was the first to reply, head up like a wallaby in the grass. 'You saw Red Jack? Where?'

'She rode past with her plant this morning. I was wanderin' around lookin' for nuggets while you blokes were sittin' by the fire like youse are now. She said she was headin' fer a spot they call Caroline Pool, she's settin' up a horse breaking camp there.'

Just then Larrikin arrived on the scene. He'd been busy brushing his mare down by the waterside, now leading her with a greenhide halter, the muddy water still glossy wet on her swollen belly. 'That sounds like an idea,' he said, having overheard the conversation. 'Red Jack would never rip us off. She don't care about anything 'cept for horses. The only thing would be convincing her to do it.'

'I'll do the blathering, if ye all are agreed,' said Scotty. 'I daena ken if she'll care fer the plan or not. But I'd as like to try.'

'Can't hurt to ask,' said Tom. 'Are we all agreed, that we'll ask Red Jack to register the claims for us, in exchange for a one-fourteenth share of every ounce of gold we win?'

Only Sandy wasn't keen, but he was so fully out-voted that he accepted defeat. 'If you lot are all dead keen on giving away our hard-won gold to a mere lass then don't let me stand in yer way.'

'Without a silent partner,' Tom warned. 'There won't be any bloody gold.'

Scotty rode off with just Blind Joe leading the way, both of them on horseback, enjoying the twists and turns of the Elvire.

A bank of black cloud was building in the north, and the smell of rain was a heady delight for them both.

'Will it be goin' ta rain, Joe?'

'Yeah Scotty, maybe plenty rain dreckly.'

They had no idea exactly how far it was to the Caroline Pools, but before long they saw the glistening surface of a good waterhole, and a number of horses surrounding it.

Red Jack was sitting at the fireside, plaiting greenhide into rope. Scotty rode up close, then reined in and dismounted, while Blind Joe pulled up to wait, holding both the horses.

'Strange,' said Red Jack loudly. 'I don't remember inviting anyone into my camp.'

Scotty stopped dead. God she was bonny, red hair hanging in waves down the side of her face. Eyes like limestone pools. He could hardly get his tongue to work. It was like a dry piece of leather in his mouth. 'I'm 'ere fir tae ask a fa'our.'

'Well alright, spit it out then. Unlike some people I like to concentrate on what the hell I'm doin'.'

'The boys an' I, being on some manner o' police black list, canna register claims in our own names. We need a virtuous soul like yesel' tae sign up for 'em in our place.'

Red Jack stopped what she was doing. 'An' what would I get fer helpin' out a bunch of ruffians who I hardly even know.'

'A one-fourteenth share a' the proceeds of the mine.'

Red Jack threw back her head and laughed. 'One fourteenth share of nothing is nothing. I've got a better idea.'

Scotty stayed for a cuppa, and when he rode back to camp it was almost dark. Blind Joe stopped him once to let a king brown snake slither off the path ahead of them. The Scotsman hardly cared, for his heart was singing with love, drunk on the sound of Red Jack's voice and the texture of her skin.

Finally they reached the camp, enjoying the smell of roasted johnny cakes, firesmoke and rain, for a few heavy drops had started to fall, turning to balls in the dust.

The men gathered around as Scotty rode in, giving him time to get down off his horse, and for Blind Joe to lead it away. They made room at the fire and placed a mug in the Scotsman's hand.

'Well,' said Tom Nugent finally. 'What did she say?'

'Red Jack has agreed tae act as our silent partner,' said Scotty. 'First thing temorra Blind Joe an' Tom's boy will gae'p tae her camp with the claim numbers. They'll mind her plant while she rides intae the Warden's office an' registers for us.'

There was scattered applause and murmurs of approval from the others, but Scotty hadn't finished yet. 'There's one wee problem,' he said. 'Red Jack daena want a fourteenth share a' the mine.'

'Well what on earth does she want?' asked Tom.

Scotty's eyes met Larrikin's. 'Red Jack is wantin' the foal out'a Larrikin's mare, when the taim comes.'

'The hell she does,' spat Larrikin. 'That foal is mine.'

'That's better than giving her a share of our bloody gold,' said Sandy.

'Since when is it better?' demanded Larrikin. 'I've been looking forward to raising that one meself. How does Red Bloody Jack even know about it?'

Tommy the Rag spoke up. 'She saw your mare when she rode through this morning. I remember her saying how she likes the look of her.'

'Well of course she would,' grunted Larrikin. 'Anyone would. But that doesn't mean I'm giving her foal away. You blokes wouldn't expect me to, would you?' No one answered, and he picked up a small stick and chucked it into the fire so hard a shower of sparks went up. 'Bastards,' he muttered under his breath.

Tom winked at Scotty, as if to say. 'Leave Larrikin to me.' And as the rain started to fall in earnest it was as if the camp breathed a communal sigh of relief. They were not just a bunch of deadbeats sitting in a gully. They were about to become the owners of a real gold mine.

# Chapter 37: Missus Dead Finish

When the Ragged Thirteen took possession of those eight adjoining claims, they had minimal experience with mining. One or two had swirled their pans around Hahndorf in the Adelaide Hills, or rocked a cradle on the Palmer, but none of them had any idea about chasing reef gold; sinking shafts. Their mindset was on adventure, not gold mining as a business, and Tom soon realised that the success of their venture depended on the latter strategy.

Thinking things through, he let them have their initial frenzy of panning the gully and specking for nuggets, then soothed them through their grumbles when these efforts bore little fruit. It was Bob Anderson who grasped the need for a concerted, professional effort, and possessed the mind of an engineer, to boot. He and Tom spent those first days snooping around other mines, studying operations at two shafts owned by one of the big companies.

'The reef they call the Heartbreaker,' Tom told the others around the fire, 'runs around this area, but it peters out, breaks into smaller veins here and there. If we sink a shaft and hit a thick streak of it we'll make real money, otherwise we're stuffed. We have to work together from here on, and any man who isn't prepared to spit on his hands and work like a dog might as well speak up now and ride off.'

Tom waited and watched, but apart from some shuffling of feet no one moved.

Bob Anderson produced his plans and they were passed from hand to hand gravely. Questions were asked and answered. Finally Sandy said, 'I have to say, young Bob, that you've a flair with the drawing pen.'

Bob's grin was as wide as the mine shaft in the drawings. 'It looks right easy on paper, but will nae when we're shovellin' rock. Tha gold is down there, it must be, yet it cannae always be easily won.'

The first need was timber for the poppet head and shoring. They swarmed out into the scrub on horseback, looking for cypress trees. These termite-resistant trees had been cut out for miles around but they found a stand on the Elvire.

'This one,' Tom shouted. 'Nice and straight. And Fitz, there's two or three towards that ridge that look the goods from here.'

After marking the trunks, Tom took up the axe, swivelled it through his hands once, then swung with a practiced long stroke that buried the broad head deep into the sapwood, sending chips flying.

Before long the men had pulled off their shirts, and glossy with sweat they competed to bring down trees with the fewest number of strokes. To reduce haulage weight, they stripped and roughly squared the timbers with broad axes, and to bring in the logs Missus Dead Finish rolled up with her wagon in a cloud of dust and curses.

Missus Dead Finish was a woman in her fifties, hunch-shouldered with skin tanned by the suns of wild plains and valleys. She drove a four-in-hand team, carrying freight and the odd passenger from Wyndham to Hall's Creek and back single-handed, twice a week. The price was fifty pounds a ton, landed at the fields. If that was too high, 'You can damn well find some

186

other fool to haul yer shit.'

Rumour had it that she had bashed her husband 'down south' to death with a candlestick holder, but got off with manslaughter because he was a drunk who kicked her 'round the kitchen every evening. Other gossips had it that he was teamster, who'd died on the road over from Queensland. Sitting up on the box seat, with a shortened double barrel in the tray directly behind, if she was waylaid by armed robbers her method was to empty both barrels then whip the horses into a frenzy, leaving the scene at a rate too fast for whatever was left of her would-be attackers.

Instead of using the regulation lead shot in the cartridges, she packed them herself with less expensive missiles, including fine but hard Kimberley gravel, small nails, and scrap sheet steel cut into fragments with tin snips.

Missus Dead Finish took no humbug from anyone, man or woman.

She hauled the Ragged Thirteen's logs and helped unload them back at the claims, unharnessing the horses with a firm hand and sharp tongue. 'Lo, back up there, Roly. Behave yourself.' Her voice snarled and crashed around the horse team like a lightning storm. Then came the sound of a slap as her open hand landed hard on a horse's rump.

Before long the Thirteen and their visitor had settled around the fire. Missus Dead Finish drank rum with the best of them, and told yarns of successes and failures on the fields. The men were themselves flushed with the good feeling of a hard, productive day.

When they had drunk and yarned for a bit, exhaustion took over and they wandered away to their swags.

Missus Dead Finish chucked hers out atop the wagon, then snored like a whip-saw until dawn. The sound was strangely amplified and deepened by the body of the wagon like the bowl of a guitar.

For the Thirteen who were wakened by the noise there was plenty to think about. Tom, with the help of Bob Anderson, had given them a vision, and they wanted it badly.

Sandy Myrtle wished for a fine home in Kensington, Adelaide, with a drawing room and library. He pictured a garden for him to walk in, attended by an army of men in grey overalls.

Carmody wanted a tall ship, sailing with some beautiful woman at his side from one end of the world to the other, gold in his pocket and a diamond earring in each earlobe.

Tommy the Rag wanted a new horse. Jimmy Woodford loved horses so much he'd only be satisfied with a whole stud. Bob Anderson wanted a bit of land to make a start on. Jack Woods made plans to start his own butchering business. Fitz just wanted to make a pile and piss it up against a wall.

Larrikin wanted to own his own public house in Toowoomba or Roma. He pictured himself walking downstairs in his dance shoes to an adoring crowd. Jack Dalley wanted a Colt revolver and new boots. Wonoka Jack imagined how it would feel to travel the world. His brother George just wanted to go home.

Scotty thought only of Red Jack; imagined himself riding beside her on a horse equally as magnificent as Mephistopholes. He imagined sliding a ring onto her finger; being with her all day and night; loving her.

Tom had seen his mate Harry Readford settled on Brunette Downs, and he too wanted a cattle station of his own – not as big as Brunette, mind you – just a few hundred square miles he could call his own. He liked the country around Newcastle Waters, and there was a bush block he knew of, that the cattle kings had passed over.

While Missus Dead Finish snored through the night, the Ragged Thirteen fell back to sleep, dreaming of what life would be like when they struck the reef.

# Chapter 38: Jake and the Girls

H ard work on the claim brought on a fierce hunger. Fitz had seen a mob of station bullocks on their logging forays and rode out with Jack Woods, three pack-horses, and a .577 calibre rifle to investigate.

Twenty-four hours later they were back, loaded down with Durack beef, and Jack soon had tongue, rounds and briskets soaking in his own special corning solution.

'We had to ride a fair old distance,' said Fitz, 'but there's plenty more where this came from.'

Eye fillets went straight into a searing hot pan, and full bellies contributed to a sense of confidence and well-being. 'Best feed since Christmas day,' said Sandy.

'This here is the tenderest beef I've had for many a month,' reckoned Larrikin, talking with difficulty through a mouth chock-full of steak.

The easy availability of beef, there for the taking, gave Tom an idea. He tacked up his gelding in the dawn, filled a water bag and rode out of camp alone, against a sky fringed with black, purple and yellow thunderheads, lying dormant but threatening on the horizon.

It was a while since Tom had been alone in the bush, and

within a mile or two he was enjoying himself a great deal. Recent storms had brought on a goose-picking of new grass, while the dry husks of last year's speargrass crackled under his horse's hooves.

For a time he followed a meandering dry creek bed. It was easy riding, with hardly any vegetation on the floor. Tom liked old creek beds: the layers of clay and quartz in rows, ancient logs embedded in the banks and bones of long-dead marsupials. It was cool, too, shaded by paperbarks, the air somehow older and richer.

He saw wells that had been dug by the local Kija people on a bend, brimming full. He filled his water bag and took the smallest of his gold pans from his saddlebag, washing the gravel from some likely looking spots.

Other prospectors, he was certain, had already swarmed over this area and rejected it, so Tom was not surprised when his efforts were unrewarded. He didn't care – he was enjoying himself. Twice he saw signs of Kija food-gathering along the creek, but they melted away long before his approach, leaving just footprints in the sand, and once, a still-smoking cooking fire.

By smoko time the sun was high and it was time to head home. Reaching the first and only substantial waterhole on that creek, he quickly panned a few more loads of gravel without success, then packed up.

He climbed the grey up the steep right-hand bank, and, consulting the folding compass that he always carried, took a bearing on a distant high pillar of stone that climbed high into the air.

Even at the trot it took a while to reach the landmark, and when he got there, Tom gentled his horse up the slopes to the summit. Once there, he could scarcely believe his eyes, there was not one, but two pillars of stone. Between them was a sunken circle of ground.

Tom knew that this was exactly what he was looking for – a natural holding yard. With steep sides over most of its length he decided that with the addition of some rough fencing it was a perfect place to hold a few head of cattle, maybe twenty or thirty.

No water, of course, but still Tom tucked away the location in his mind and rode on, taking a new bearing to the north east as he again rose to the trot to eat up the miles in a direct path home.

As the Warden had suggested, a nearby claim was worked by a teenager called Jake and his two little sisters. It was a poor claim, elevated and dry, far from water and filled with boulders that had to be shifted with pick and crow bar.

Tom walked over late in the day. The boy stuck his crowbar in the earth and came to meet him. Wearing only a pair of dungarees, and pint-sized to begin with, he was a lean as a whip, with not a skerrick of fat on his frame.

'Hi there young fellow.'

'Hullo Mister.'

'My name's Tom Nugent. Me and my mates have taken up a bunch of claims in the gully yonder.'

'Yeah alright, good to meet ya. Well … I've got a bunch of work to do.'

Tom pointed at one of the two slim figures at work winnowing fines. 'I met one of the young'uns in the Warden's office. I know all about you and … well … I just wanted to say that you've got thirteen new mates now. Ever have any trouble and we'll help out.' Tom hefted a cloth-wrapped parcel in his hands. 'Brought you something too.'

Jake turned, 'Hey Nellie, fetch that billy off the coals and get a cuppa for the visitor.'

They sat on stumps and drank tea from chipped enamel mugs. It was a poor camp, and the sugar jar was empty. One of the girls unwrapped the cloth from Tom's gift. Inside was a big lump of silverside, and she couldn't resist a little cry of excitement. Tom guessed that they'd be eating well for the first time in days.

'So why are you three here all alone?' he asked.

'Mother and Pa brought us up from Perth, all the way to Broome. Mother was going to stay in town while Pa came to the diggings.' The boy's eyes settled on the ground, studying it intently. 'They went out one evening for a sail on Roebuck Bay and never come back. They was both drownded. We had the deed for the claim Pa had bought, sight unseen, and some diggin' equipment, so I brought the little 'uns here. I didn't know Hall's Creek would be like this – it ain't like Pa was describing it.' Jake looked out on the desolation of those fields.

'I'm sorry to hear of your bad fortune, Jake, but I'm guessing,' he looked upwards, 'that they'd be proud of what you're doing here.'

Jake had a tear in his eye. 'Sorry I weren't so welcoming when you first turned up. I admit I was a bit scared when I seen you men arriving. You look pretty rough – all them beards and swearin' and yelling and carryin' on.'

Tom smiled, 'Yeah, we're a bit of a wild bunch, and none of us care much for the so-called laws of the state. But we've got our own laws, and they're iron-hard. We look after each other, and help out people where we can.' He drained his mug. 'Thanks for the cuppa. I'd best get back to shovelling, or the other blokes will think I'm a shirker.'

'I hope you find some gold soon.'

'Well, we've been finding a little, here and there.'

Jake looked at the big lump of beef and seemed to be on the verge of tears. 'Of course you have, but I hope you find a nugget the size of your bloody heart.'

# Chapter 39: The Heartbreaker

The shaft went twenty-five feet straight down before angling back towards Halls Creek. The work was done square and neat; well-shored and precise. Tom had seen how successful miners cut their shafts and he was keen to emulate them.

After weeks of sweat and ten hard-won yards on the flat, speculation mounted that the leader might not be far away, but when they finally found it, there were no shouts or carrying on. The Thirteen knew enough about goldfields to keep good fortune quiet.

Larrikin emerged from the shaft, shiny with sweat, took a long pull from a water bag, then walked over to Tom, who had come off his shift an hour earlier.

'Hi there Tom,' Larrikin said quietly. 'I think you'd better come down and take a gander at something.'

Tom put down his mug and followed, down the shaft-ladder, then walking bent over, near crawling at times until they reached the face.

In the light of a slush lantern Tom saw veins of yellow and red, in thick seams of blue quartz, running in jagged, random lines in the sandstone parent rock.

'The red is hematite,' said Tom, 'and the yellow is gold.' He turned and grinned back at Larrikin. 'Looks like you've just found the Heartbreaker.'

Within an hour the Thirteen made up an anxious group pretending to be nonchalant, hanging around the camp while Tom and Larrikin brought the first bucket-load of ore out. They crushed a few handfuls with a hammer in a pan, then took it down to the water.

Tom used one of the bigger pans to do the work, taking his time, sluicing it back and forth so a little spilled each time. It was a hot, still afternoon anyway, but the heat seemed to go up a notch, and the world stood still.

When it was done they could all see the gold in the pan. Not as much as they might have hoped, but it was real gold, not pyrites or mica. Tom took a pinch of it on the end of his finger and held it up.

'Now at least we've got something worth taking up to the battery,' he said. 'We'll get two or three ounces to the ton, quite likely.'

The others stared back, adding and subtracting figures in their heads. Taking into account crushing fees at the battery, and gold at three and half pounds an ounce, there was profit at the end of the process, but nothing wild unless the leader thickened.

'Maybe the find will get richer as we go along,' said Tom. 'Let's hope so anyway.'

The following afternoon, fresh from a dinner-time argument with Sandy Myrtle over horses, Tommy the Rag swung his pick at a lump of quartz, missed and buried the point in the middle of his foot. The wound spurted blood like a hose, and he sat, gripping the area and cursing Sandy for upsetting him. Bob Anderson wrapped it in a clean rag and helped him up to camp.

Despite the application of 'Moore's Sovereign Remedy', the

only medicine they had to hand, Tommy's lower leg was soon swollen, streaked with red and hot to touch. Within a day or two the wound leaked pus, and the gang started wearing worried frowns.

Missus Dead Finish arrived on her weekly run and was at Tommy's bedside as soon as she heard. With a useful medicine kit to draw from she tut-tutted at the dirty bandages and 'medicine' Tommy's mates had used.

She cradled the sick man's head in one huge elbow. 'You poor little barsted,' she said. 'C'mere and I'll have yer on ya feet in no time.' She set to wiping his brow on her hands and knees, made him soup, delivered spoonful by spoonful, followed by shots of neat rum.

The rest of the gang were touched by the devotion in that night-long vigil. Tom Nugent commented several times that it was like there was a yellow shaft of light shining down from the moon, directly on the pair. 'I never thought the old girl had it in her,' he said.

But even these ministrations failed, and the next morning Missus Dead Finish stalked to the main fire, where the men were lounging around, eating Johnny cakes and smoking pipes.

'Get up, one of yez, and help me carry Tommy to the wagon. I'll be taking the poor barsted to Wyndham. He won't get better without a doctor.'

It had been a while since Missus Dead Finish had lost her husband, and since then she hadn't seen much in the way of attachment. Now, for some reason, the injured Tommy filled her heart. It was a strange feeling but she liked it, and the thought of him dying made her afraid in a way she hadn't felt for while.

The four draught horses, that she normally nursed on the journey, she now drove with single minded determination, talking to them long into the night. They had hearts as big as their bodies, part-Shire, part-Clydesdale and a touch of Irish. They plodded on, while Dead Finish used the big moon as her guide.

'We can't let Tommy die, boys and girls. He's a good one. So pick your pace and hold it, for we won't be resting 'til we hit the Ord.'

It was early in the morning before she saw the river shining like polished steel, and the horses strained against their harness to reach it. There, on the stony banks of that fast-running waterway, Missus Dead Finish found her usual camp. There were other fires there that night, prospectors heading to and from the diggings, but she kept apart from them.

She left her patient in the wagon while she took the horses down for water then hobbled and belled them to graze. Then she lifted Tommy down and propped him by a cheery campfire, fed him with broth she had brought in a cooking pot.

'How you holding up, young feller?' she asked.

Tommy found the strength to nod while his carer piled both their swags on top of one another, to increase his comfort. When the time came for sleep she stretched out beside him on the bare ground, with only her pillow and a spare garment or two for bedding. She slept but lightly, waking to his every noise, dribbling water or rum between his lips.

# Chapter 40: Bow River

Missus Dead Finish and her patient, Tommy the Rag, passed through Baobab Wells at noon and reached Anton's Landing a little after two pm on the third day. A crowd gathered while the big woman carried the once slight, now wasted, young man into the Wyndham hospital – a stone building run with a skeleton crew of nursing sisters and a single doctor.

The doctor examined the patient and turned to Missus Dead Finish. 'Are you his mother?'

'Nah, just a mate,' she said, too worried to be offended.

'You've done well in getting him up here alive, but he's a sick boy. That foot has turned septic and the poison has all but reached his heart.'

Tommy tossed fitfully, burning with fever in his hospital cot, while the freight piled up for Missus Dead Finish, and her customers pleaded with her to hitch up her team and get back to work. This she refused to do, but stayed doggedly, defending Tommy's interests. When the sisters tried to take his stockwhip away from the bedside she shook her head.

'Don't touch that whip. It stays by Tommy's side day and night, sick or well. He'll get better quicker with it than without it.'

After five days, Tommy was sitting up in bed, and finally, back on his feet. Now they loaded up the cart and headed back towards Halls Creek. As they trundled out of town a group of disillusioned diggers lined the track, passing a demijohn of rum from hand to hand and lip to lip, singing a song popular then in the town.

> *Behold in me a digger bold, I've just come down of late,*
> *I spent my time just like the rest, midst spinifex and*
> *slate,*
> *Of tucker it is plentiful, and more than can be sold,*
> *There's lots of pebble and other metal, but the devil's*
> *run away with the Gold.*

> *For the Bow runs into the Ord,*
> *And the Ord runs into the sea,*
> *And we rushed down to Cambridge Gulf,*
> *To clear from Kimberley.*

Missus Dead Finish had always been proud of her speed, but that journey back to Hall's Creek took on a dream-like quality that threw a blanket over any desire to hurry on.

The first day they managed just thirteen lazy miles, to Parry's Lagoon. The second they did better, but lingered on the Denham River crossing 'for the damned horses to get a good feed.' The third they camped on the second branch of the Bow River, where granite boulders made handy camp furniture.

The next day, in the stony hills towards Turkey Creek, Tommy saw a blaze of brown movement just off the track, and through the trees. It was a spot sometimes used as a camp, stony and sparse, but useful because of a number of old wells made in days of yore by the Kija people.

Getting gingerly down from the box, Tommy heard the sound of buzzing flies, a horde of them. The brown shapes he had seen turned into kite-hawks, squabbling over something, with the flies rising and falling in clouds as they moved in or out of the way. A wedge-tailed eagle was also on the scene, and there seemed to be a battle developing between that giant bird and the kites.

The smell hit Tommy at the same time as the kites scampered onto the wing and away.

'What is it, lad?' came from behind him.

Tommy slipped his stockwhip from his belt. 'Don't move, Missus, for Christ's sake. And get yer shotgun handy.' He swallowed down rising nausea, for there on the ground was the body of a man, his body transfixed with a spear through the chest, both hands gripping the shaft as if trying to pull it from his body. The birds had opened the skin and torn strips of flesh from his cheeks, neck and upper chest. One of his ankles above the boots had also provided an entry point. A revolver lay on the ground beside the corpse.

The wedge-tailed eagle was the only one of the birds who had not yet taken flight, staring back at Tommy as if to say. 'This old meat is mine now.'

Missus Dead Finish came up beside Tommy, with the shotgun in her hands. 'The Kija got the poor bastard.'

'Yeah, looks like it.'

'Do yer know him?'

'Nah. What about you?' Tommy uncoiled his stock whip, took aim at the wedge-tailed eagle and let fly, cracking it not a yard from the proud head. The bird admitted defeat, flapping those stately wings and flying off to the nearest branch.

Tommy kneeled beside the body, not daring to breathe through his nose. The spear would not come out, and Tommy used a hatchet to sever it where it left the chest cavity.

'Should we just bury him here?' asked Dead Finish. 'Gawd knows I've done it before.'

'We dunno who he is,' said Tommy. 'Best we get him to

town, someone will know him.'

Wrapping the corpse in a blanket they placed it in the back of the cart. The smell was horrendous.

'How far to town?' Tommy asked.

'Probably eighty mile.'

'Let's not stop again,' said Tommy.

Missus Dead Finish agreed. Neither of them could countenance spending a night with a dead man for company.

A crowd gathered in the street when they stopped the cart opposite the police station. Sergeant James Sherry took charge of the body, but allowed the people of Hall's Creek to view it, in the hope of an identification.

'By God, that's George Barnett,' someone said. 'He's a good man, and I knew his Ma back in Queensland. I know him well enough to dig a hole for the poor bastard.'

'Can we count on you to write a letter back and let his family know?' Sergeant Sherry asked.

'Well I would, but I can't write a word except me own name.'

Charlie Price, the Mine Warden, scratched his beard. 'Come with me, I'll take the words down for you and you can sign it.'

The policeman turned to the crowd and said, 'Go back to your claims, all of you. Be assured that justice will be done. With Big Johnny Durack barely cold in his grave just two months past, this proves that the Kija have not learned. I will track down the killers of this man and bring them to justice.'

Sherry was true to his word. He rode out with two trackers looking for the killers and came back a week later with five black men in chains, walking behind his horse in a line.

'That's not the end of this,' said Tom Nugent to Sandy Myrtle. 'From what I hear Barnett came from a big family and they're yelling for blood.'

# Chapter 41: Desert Rose

The Hall's Creek area, being on the northern fringes of the Great Sandy Desert, was sparsely vegetated except along the river courses. Much of the ground was bare: soils of red, white, grey, or shades in between, relieved by hummocks of grass, curly spinifex and mean acacia shrubs.

After rain, however, green pick came through from the burned or dried stubs of last year's grass, along with some flowers. The most beautiful of these was called the desert rose. It had green leaves, and mauve-coloured blooms, bright red at the centre.

These flowers weren't common either, but after working like a fiend all morning, when the others settled down in the shade to wait out the hours where the heat hammered down in unbearable waves, Scotty saddled up a reluctant horse and set off into the scrub.

'Where ya headed?' Tom Nugent asked.

'Nowt in particular, Tom. Jest a ride.'

Sandy Myrtle shook his head sadly. 'The sun has gotten to your head, lad.'

Scotty didn't care, he just rode away, not minding the sweat that ran down between hat and forehead, down over his neck and even the deep channel of his spine.

Leaving the diggings, he rode the sweeps of ancient sand ridges, eyes scanning for a splash of colour. In an hour of searching he found just two of those wild roses in bloom. He cut the stems carefully with his pocket knife and wrapped them in cloth dampened from his water bottle.

In the evening, when Red Jack came out of the shade to work her horses, Scotty was watching, leaning on the rails. He saw her eyes fall on the flowers sitting on a fencepost. The vase was an old bottle of Lee and Perrins sauce but it worked well enough.

Scotty watched her walk across to the flowers, pick them up, and lift the delicate blooms delicately to her nose. Then she turned and looked at him. There was something in her eyes; wistful and disturbing. He could have sworn that she came alive in that moment. As if her head suddenly filled with possibilities; regrets banished. Then, a curtain closed on her face, and she nodded once. Thanks. Acknowledgement.

Still without speaking she took the flowers into the basic little bough shed she inhabited. A moment later she came out without them, did not look in his direction and started working the horses as if nothing had happened.

One thousand miles away, in the Northern Territory capital of Palmerston, Alfred Searcy nursed his gin and tonic as he looked out across the lawns of Government House, past Fort Hill to the harbour dazzling in the afternoon light. To his left was a long row of trestles covered with spotless white tablecloths. The bar staff, all Larrakeyah youths, shook cocktails and dropped ice in glasses with tongs, scarcely saying a word.

The lawns were trod by leather shoes belonging to the cream of the city of Palmerston. No Lords here, but certainly gentle-men and their ladies, station owners, mine owners, merchants, ships' captains, senior public servants and ranking police officers. For Searcy and O'Donohue attendance at the reception had been well worth the three-day voyage on the steamer from Borroloola.

Standing in the shade beside the gazebo, crowned by a maze of bougainvillea flowers, was the Government Resident, the Honourable John Langdon Parsons and his wife Marianna; Darwin royalty. Like Alfred himself, the Resident and his Lady wore clothes that were inappropriately hot for the afternoon. Everyone tried to pretend that they weren't sweating – much too stoic to take out a kerchief and dab the sweat away.

Food was being carried around the crowd on silver platters by Larrakeyah girls in prim white aprons and matching pinafores. Searcy, as he chose a sausage-meat-filled pastry, couldn't help but admire the serving girl's glossy dark skin and liquid eyes. Out of scientific interest only, of course.

Turning away from the platter Alfred realised that the young architect he had been talking to had drifted away. Scanning the crowd he saw a man in the uniform of the West Australian Police, replete with medals and of military bearing. He had obviously just arrived, received a drink but had not yet attached himself to any of the groups on the lawn.

Alfred walked across and held out his hand. 'Well met good fellow. My name is Alfred Searcy, former customs Inspector and incumbent officer of the law, stationed at Borroloola.'

'Ah, Mr Searcy, why I have heard of you, of course. I'm Sub-Inspector Lawrence. Of Fremantle and more lately, Roebourne. I've spent time in the Kimberley in recent weeks and I've been meeting with Paul Foelsche here in Palmerston about how you fellows do things.'

Alfred could hardly believe his luck. 'The Kimberley, eh? Then I imagine you've had occasion to visit Hall's Creek?'

'Most certainly, why do you ask?'

Alfred narrowed his eyes. 'Have you had anything to do with a gang of vagabonds called the Ragged Thirteen?'

'Ah yes, I remember your letter to the Commissioner about them. Our gold warden did stop them from registering any claims, but unfortunately they found a third-party to do it for them. From all reports they've been fairly quiet … so far.'

Alfred looked around for O'Donohue. To his dismay he saw that his friend was earnestly in conversation with one of the young waitresses. He turned back to Lance. 'Please don't go anywhere, I have a comrade who should join this discussion.'

Striding over, Alfred pinched O'Donohue under the armpit and dragged him away. 'If you are determined to disgrace yourself … then do it, but not in front of the Resident, confound you.'

'I wasn't doing anything. I was only talking …'

'Leave it please. I want you to meet someone. Hurry along.'

After the introductions O'Donohue still, infuriatingly, cast predatory glances back at the girl he had been grooming. Searcy kicked him in the back of the ankle.

'Now,' said Alfred, 'my dear Sub-Inspector Lawrence. As I stated in my letter, on their way west the Ragged Thirteen robbed Victoria River Downs Station. I neglected to mention, that the theft included a valuable grey stallion. I have a warrant for the arrest of Tom Nugent, as the man who stole the horse in question. If I give you the details of the animal will you arrange to have Nugent arrested?'

The WA policeman smiled. 'I'll have Sergeant Sherry down at Hall's Creek and his men bring him in at once. We can try him at Wyndham if you'll have witnesses brought over.'

'Excellent, excellent,' said Alfred, then took a moment to recall how the Ragged Thirteen had humiliated him, and O'Donohue: talked their way out of custody at the Roper Bar, then chased away the police horse plant in the Gulf. Out-foxed and out-paced them at the Katherine, then finally made fools of them at the Negri River. Now at last, Tom Nugent, the ringleader, was in his sights.

'I'm so pleased to have met you,' Alfred said finally. 'Good men are hard to find in this land of ruffians and ne'er-do-wells.' He paused, puffing out his chest. 'And I can't wait to see Nugent in chains; in fact I do believe I'd cross hell barefoot to testify against him myself.'

# Chapter 42: The Vengeance Seekers

The Wet Season arrived for two weeks in February. Less work was done, replaced with horseplay and drinking. Some days the rain was so heavy that the best course of action was to cover the shaft with canvas, find some shelter, and open a bottle.

There was never a dull moment. Jake and his sisters became fixtures around the camp, and the Thirteen lent a hand with a shovel or a gift of beef when it was needed. Missus Dead Finish hung around between carrier jobs, swearing and smoking and drinking rum with the best of them.

Some Irish lads had a claim nearby, always fighting and getting into trouble, and everyone knew Russian Jack, the man who had once carried a mate all the way to Wyndham in a wheelbarrow for medical help. It was a fascinating community to be a part of, and the Thirteen enjoyed the company and laughs while they fought to make a living from stone, gravel, and an erratic gold leader called the Heartbreaker.

The rain lifted as fast as it had arrived, and the land turned dry again, burned mercilessly by a sun that seemed to have rejuvenated from the pause. At least now the gullies and creeks were full of water, and the work of panning and cradling carried on apace.

One afternoon, when Tom came off his shift, he saddled up and rode into Halls Creek for a beer. He was enjoying the cool feel of the glass against his hand when some horsemen came down the road. Six riders in all. Lean horses and hard men, with rifles in leather scabbards, trailing packhorses.

Even the busiest diggers paused to watch them arrive. There was no doubt they'd been on a long road, and had ridden hard. Tom sipped his beer as he watched them dismount outside the shanty. The only one of the six he recognised was a lawman for hire called Lucanus. Tom's sense of unease deepened.

Old Joe Templeton owned the stables across the road and offered a public trough for a penny a time. Tom watched the newcomers take the horses across.

Joe was out in a flash. 'That's my water, gentlemen. You want it, you pay up.'

For a moment Tom thought they would refuse, but after much scowling and angry looks some coins were produced and thrown to the dust at Joe's feet.

'No manners!' cried Joe.

'Shut ya gob you old bastard, or I'll give you more than you bargained for in return for the cursed water.'

Finally, with the horses watered, unsaddled and tied to hitching posts, the six riders headed for the bar. The leading man, older than the others, face twisted into a permanent scowl, nodded his head at Tom, then said, 'Whoever heard of a shithole where a man has to pay to water his horse.'

Tom explained. 'Water's at a premium here – even after rain it has to be carted up from the river in a dray. What's your business? You don't look like diggers.'

'No we ain't. My name's Edward Barnett. It was my brother George who got murdered by the blacks up near Hell's Gate. We've just been fixing up his grave.'

'It oughtn't take six of you to do that,' Tom said. 'And you blokes look girded for war.'

The man grinned wickedly. 'We plan to unleash hell on the Kija for doing what they did. We're just in town to wet our throats, stock up on cartridges, and fill the packs with tucker. Those savages will wish they never messed with my brother.'

'Five of them have already been arrested, by Sergeant Sherry, and sent up to Wyndham in chains.'

'All five were released,' spat Barnett. 'The judge said there weren't enough evidence to convict them.'

'Well how the hell are you s'posed to work out which one's guilty or not?' asked Tom.

'Oh, we'll know.'

'And what's the point, anyway?' Tom put down his glass. 'Revenge isn't going to do anybody any good – just stir things up.'

'I don't know who you are and I don't give a flying fuck. Just get out of my way.'

Within two or three days refugees started to arrive at Brockman, a settlement about seven miles from Halls Creek. Esau the Afghan came from town to assist the midwife Susan O'Neil, who was busy tending the wounded in her shanty there. When Tom heard he rode out to see for himself.

Gunshot wounds were ugly things, Tom decided as he viewed them, the .452 projectile fired by the Martini-Henry rifles opening gaping wounds in belly, thigh or arm. Anyone struck closer to the vitals, Tom guessed, would already be dead.

He asked one of the lesser wounded, who had once worked as a tracker, and thus knew some English, what had happened.

'All-up proper finish. Fambly all g'wei or prop'ly dead.'

'Can you tell me where the white men's camp is?'

The black man nodded grimly. 'Magoombarra Country. Panton River you white mob callim.'

Tom rode back to the claim in a rage. 'Stop work you bastards. We've got a job to do. Mount up, load your weapons, we're going to do what the so-called authorities in this part of the world are too gutless to do.'

It was the first time the Thirteen had ridden together in a while, and Tom wasn't the only one who wondered if it might be the last. Blind Joe rode bareback in the lead, for he'd learned the local country well, and had not lost the keenness of his eye.

On the way north they found a Kija camp, the wurlies torched and the ground disturbed from fresh spade-work. Tom felt a lump of anger in his throat that he just could not swallow down.

They found Edward Barnett's camp less than a mile away, on a good Panton River waterhole. The Thirteen surrounded the Six, who were lounging around the fire drinking rum.

'Go back to where you came from,' Tom said. 'You've had your revenge, and I hope it sickens your heart until the day you die. I'm Tom Nugent by God, and I'm slow to anger, but if you push me I'll bring hell down on you fast enough.'

August Lucanus rose to his feet, hands in the pockets of his dungarees. He looked around at the horsemen and sneered. 'The Ragged Thirteen! I've heard of you – breakers and enterers – horse thieves. Tea and sugar bushrangers. Not the smartest crew in history. If you think you scare me – or any of us – you've got it wrong.'

The Thirteen trained their weapons on Barnett and his men. Sandy Myrtle had a double-barrelled shotgun. He raised it also, tucking the butt under his armpit.

'I haven't shot anyone with an eight-gauge before,' he commented. 'I'll be interested in the results.'

'Get out of here,' whispered Tom. 'Now.'

Sullenly, the Six caught their horses, packed stores into saddlebags and rifles into scabbards. The Ragged Thirteen followed them as far as the Nicholson River, and lined a ridge, watching until they had passed away into the East.

'Good riddance,' said Tom. 'But mark my words. We'll be paying for the actions of murderous bastards like that for a long time to come.'

# Chapter 43: The Ragged Twelve-and-a-Half

No one said a word when Missus Dead Finish started sharing Tommy the Rag's swag, her draught horses hobbled and wandering with nosebags of oats, and some to spare for the rest of the plant, who were rarely well enough fed.

As fond of rum as the rest of the crew, Dead Finish never failed to produce a bottle from under the driver's box. She and Tommy would sit up after the others had wandered off, telling jokes and yarning. The bond between the pair seemed too ludicrous for words – scrawny young Tommy, and a woman at least three decades older than him (no one really knew) – with white bloomers, washed and hanging from a line stretching from wagon to tree. These, Larrikin mused aloud could, with the addition of a pole or two, be used as tents.

In any case, the relationship continued to develop, and Missus Dead Finish's arrival came to be a regular thing. Those who grumbled about a woman in the camp were sweetened by the horse feed, free grog, and the lack of any need to moderate their language or behaviour. This was a woman who could curse like they did.

Tom Nugent said to Tommy one day, 'You and the old girl

seem to get on uncommonly well.'

'Yeah, not too bad.' Tommy looked embarrassed. 'Dunno why. But she aren't like other gals I've known. I feel like she's watching my back. That she'd never give up on me.'

'Cripes Tommy, sounds like you're in love with her.'

'Maybe I am.' There was a long pause, while Tom took a cigar from his pocket, straightened it and bit the end off. 'Do you think the other coves are laughing at me, because she's old, and not real pretty.'

'Maybe a bit, but don't let that bother you, Tommy.'

'Hey Tom?'

'Yeah.'

'You've been around. How does a man know when he's in love?'

Tom smoked his pipe in silence for a few moments, watching the swirling smoke reflectively. 'Love's a bit like wind. Sometimes it blows in hot gusts that last an hour or two, making a lot of dust and noise. Other times it twists and turns all over the place, changin' direction all the time. Real love, now that's another thing. It blows like a trade wind, almost all the time, so steady a man can rely on it.'

Tommy the Rag grinned, and quicker than the eye could see he uncoiled his stock whip and cracked it so hard Tom's ears rang and a pair of foraging pigeons took to the wing and flew off into the sky.

The diggers and townsfolk of Halls Creek could tolerate Sergeant Sherry. Mostly he was content to sit on his verandah, sometimes investigating a serious theft or murder, but he never worried too much about a brawl or even a riot at one of the shanties.

Things changed, however, when a full police patrol came into town. No one liked it. Word spread on the bush telegraph, shouted from claim to claim, or carried by running children.

One afternoon when Tom was down the shaft, working away at the face with a hand pick, he heard the high ringing tone of a length of iron pipe being beaten with a hammer at the entrance. It was the usual recall signal, able to penetrate the depths for some distance.

Crawling in his hands and knees for the first part of the shaft, Tom reached the ladder and started to climb, filthy with rock dust and sweating like crazy. He was half way up when he saw Larrikin leaning over, his head surrounded by the cloudless blue sky.

'What's the problem?'

'You'd best get up here. Word is that there are two out-of-town 'pinks' with some armed boys asking for you, and now they're riding this way.'

Tom thought for a moment. He and the boys had lately been stealing a few Durack cattle and stocking the hidden valley he had found. New England Jack had even butchered one or two and sold the meat. Still, it seemed unlikely that the police would be able to pin that on him.

'What the fuck do they want with me?'

'I dunno. But here they come now.'

As Tom emerged into the sunlight, Larrikin aimed a finger back along the track that weaved its way down the gully between the claim boundaries. Two policemen, still in clean enough clothes to indicate that they hadn't been on patrol for long, were walking their horses towards the Thirteen's claim, and behind them rode a bunch of police boys with rifles.

The police party didn't enter the camp at first, but diverted down towards the base of the gully, where the horse plant were munching on a few scraps of grass. Tom watched, wondering what the hell they were doing. He hoped for a moment that they might keep riding on. Then, he felt a prickle of unease as the trap pointed out the grey Tom had taken from Victoria River Downs. One of the police boys put a halter on him.

Leading the animal, they rode across to the camp. 'Are you Tom Nugent?' the policeman asked Tom.

'Yes, that's me.'

'Is this your horse?'

Tom knew that he had two choices, either take responsibility for the horse or implicate some or all of the others. It was important, he decided, that the others stayed here to work the claim.

'Yes, he's mine. His name's Gumnut, and I bought him from a bloke who said he was branded at Alexandria Station, and that's the brand there.' Tom flashed a glance at Larrikin, who had told the story originally.

'I put it to you that the animal's name is actually Wickfield Chesterton,' said the trap. 'The brand has been cleverly altered, but he is actually the property of Charles Brown Fisher, joint owner of Victoria River Downs station. You, Tom Nugent, have been accused of stealing him.'

Tom's eyes went wide with mock-innocence. 'Why, that's a terrible accusation to make. Here I am, a dedicated miner and member of the Halls Creek Digger's Committee.'

The policeman grinned wickedly. 'Spare us the fine words attestin' to your virtue. A colleague of mine was talking to Alf Searcy of the Northern Territory Customs Service. He told some pretty tales about you and your so-called mates.'

'I beg to differ sir, they are real mates, not so-called mates, but I doubt you'd know about such things. Neither would Searcy, I dare say.'

'Enough talk. The horse is stolen property. You are under arrest for the theft of this horse, worth over four hundred pounds, property of CB Fisher.'

Tom looked across and locked eyes with Sandy, whose eyes had moved to the shotgun propped against a tree nearby. Tom shook his head, telling the big man clearly not to think about it. 'Lads,' he said. 'We all know this is a mistake. I'll go quietly, clear my name, and be back digging gold before you know it.'

The police gave him time to roll his swag and saddle a spare horse, then fixed iron bracelets to his wrists.

Tom, having mounted his horse awkwardly, turned back to the others. 'Isn't it strange how these gentlemen allowed a gang of killers to ride here and commit bloody murder unchecked for a week until we stopped them, but they'll drag a man away in chains over a horse.'

Just as Tom was about to ride off, the boy from Borroloola ran out from the woman holding him. He grabbed on to Tom's leg, tears rolling down his cheeks. Tom leaned down and mussed his curly hair.

'Don't fret, lad. I'll just go along with these men. It's only for a day or two.'

Sandy came forward and unclasped the boy's arms, holding him firmly but gently as the police column moved off in a swarm of dust, on the long road to Wyndham.

When Tom had gone the others gathered around the fire. Sandy said sombrely, 'By God, that wasn't good. I guess we're just the Ragged Twelve now.'

Missus Dead Finish stood up from her place beside Tommy. 'You're wrong there,' she said. 'I'm here too, and I'm as good as any man, even if I'm only half as tall.'

Sandy inclined his great head. 'Right you are Madam, the Ragged Twelve-and-a-Half it is.'

# Chapter 44: Wyndham Prison

Tom Nugent knew a bit about prison cells. He had once been thrown in the Blackall lock-up with his mate Harry Readford, accused of possessing eight stolen horses. It took three days for Harry's bribes to filter out to all the witnesses. The charges were dropped and the pair walked free. Tom had also earned a night or two in police cells from Brisbane to Burketown, usually for being disorderly or fighting.

His Wyndham cell, Tom decided, was not too bad. His first act was to pace it out with long strides from wall to wall. Six paces wide and eight deep, with a sleeping bench along one side, and a drum that served as a latrine. The floor was coated with greasy bones and other scraps from past meals.

Once his investigations were complete, he set about cleaning up, rolling the grimy blanket and using it as a broom, sweeping the scraps under the bars and out of the cell. The gaoler watched incredulously throughout.

'Hey you! Stop making such a Godawful mess for fuck's sake.'

'Ah shut your fat mouth,' said Tom. 'You should be ashamed of putting a gentleman in a filthy shithole like this one.'

'I don't see no gentleman, just a horse-thief.'

'That's yet to be proved.'

'An officer has been sent out to Alexandria Station to check your story about the horse being a gift. Unless it checks out, which I highly doubt, you'll be facing a magistrate soon enough.'

'If they find enough evidence to convict me I'll dance naked on the Anton's Landing jetty at sunset,' Tom said.

'No you won't, because you'll be locked up, right where you bleeding well belong.'

'Just get me a clean blanket,' said Tom, 'and you and me will get along well enough.'

The policeman, disarmed by the overture, dropped the belligerent stare and turned away.

'Make that two blankets, would you mate?' Tom called after him. 'I'm fond of using one as a pillow.'

The best thing about that cell was a large, barred window. It was possible, Tom discovered, to stand on his latrine-drum and look outside over a small grassy park, and a neat white-painted building, all the way to the Cambridge Gulf.

The stone window was a good yard square, and though broken by eight thick, vertical bars, the sea-breeze, once it got up in the late morning, flowed easily through the spaces, and Tom swore he could smell the spice of distant islands. Either way, it sparked his imagination and passed the time.

On the third morning he noticed a bustle of activity in the building in the foreground of his view. Standing on his chair he realised that this must be a school house. Children started arriving at eight-thirty, escorted by parents and siblings, many riding double on horseback or sitting up in carts, most walking up from the close-packed shanties. They were a boisterous lot, boys and girls alike, the children of lugger skippers, store keepers and publicans – many shades of brown and white.

From nine until eleven there was strict silence, and little to see, as the children attended their lessons inside. Yet Tom heard for the first time a species of voice he had not heard for a while.

Cultured, feminine, yet undoubtedly in control. Tom breathed as soft as he could so as to hear all the better. Even when the fat gaoler walked past and attempted to needle him with a comment, Tom ignored him.

At eleven a handbell rang, and the children erupted into the yard. A young woman swept after them, and Tom stopped breathing altogether. She was tall and blonde, bustling around the children. Tom decided that she was the singularly most beautiful human being he had ever seen. And from that moment on, he thought of nothing else.

Back in Halls Creek, the Ragged Twelve-and-a-Half were cleaning their tools and putting them away for the night. Bitterness permeated the camp like a drug. They all still dreamed, but those dreams had gone stale.

Three really big nuggets had come from other claims in the last two weeks. Life-changing nuggets, plucked from the surface, while the gang had sweated their guts out underground for months, for a few ounces of colour. It hurt too much to speak of.

Sandy Myrtle was sipping weak tea when he saw the figure of young Jake sprinting over the mullock heaps and scrub between the claims. Being so thin of frame, he was instantly recognisable.

Knowing something was wrong Sandy sat his mug of tea on a rough lump of sandstone that served as a table and came slowly to his feet.

'You alright?'

Jake shook his head. 'Have you blokes seen young Nellie?'

Sandy felt a chill in his chest. 'No.'

'She was here around noon and I haven't seen her since.'

'Have you ridden in and asked the Warden?'

'Yes, he said he saw her once, around one. She borrowed a map off him, said it was for me, then booked up some flour and matches from the store. One of me waterbags is missing, and a spade and pan. Last night Nellie was bangin' on that we needed to find a new place to dig. She'd heard about those damned nuggets those lucky bastards found.'

'Jesus,' said Sandy, while the others gathered 'round. 'She's gone into the bloody desert? Right you blokes, we split up and look for her. Meet back here in two hours if no one's found her in that time.'

'Me and Bob Anderson will go around the main camps,' said New England Jack. 'If she's there we'll find her.'

'I'll ride north,' said Fitz.

'South,' said Sandy.

Scotty: 'East.'

Larrikin: 'West.'

Sandy called out. 'Hey, Blind Joe. Get up here, we got work to do.'

# Chapter 45: The Second Stone

The dingo pack were starving, with rib bones sharp as knives and shrunken, high bellies. There were five altogether, led by the matriarch, with dugs as black as night, and her teeth worn with age.

The pack had recently taken to shadowing the camps of prospectors, existing on bones or scraps left behind, and even, when desperate, eating shit and sullage. When the old bitch found the scent of blood on the wind she knew it as a human smell. This made her wary, but hunger was a powerful force.

Still unsure, she led her offspring in a winding course, following the tracks that led aimlessly into the arid landscape.

Blind Joe was as keen-eyed a tracker as Sandy Myrtle had ever seen, but he struggled to locate Nellie's trail. They did not know her departure point from Hall's Creek, and it was necessary to cast wide around the diggings.

Sandy, Jake, Tommy the Rag and Larrikin followed Blind Joe in silence, reliant on the senses of this master bushman. By late afternoon they were tense with frustration, and when Blind Joe pointed out a lone man's tracks, Sandy told him to follow it up.

'Let's see who it is, anyway,' he said.

The tracks were like a highway to Blind Joe, and at a jog-trot they soon came to a swagman's camp. He was long-bearded, and lean, busy at the fire, standing when they rode in.

'Welcome, brothers, come and have a cuppa. The billy just biled. Or a tot of rum if youse would prefer.'

The five men stayed in the saddle. Sandy spoke for all of them.

'We're looking for a girl? Have you seen her?'

'What girl? D'ye mean black or white?'

Tommy flicked his right wrist, releasing his stockwhip, but Larrikin's hand struck out like a snake, seizing the whip just above the ironwood shaft, stopping the blow.

'Let's not start taking our frustrations out on the innocent,' said Larrikin.

Sandy cleared his throat, and addressed the prospector again. 'Thanks for the offer, but we've no time for drinking. It's a white girl gone missing from her camp.' He pointed to Jake. 'This feller here's sister. If you see her, kindly take her in to the Mine Warden.'

'I'll do that. What's the lass's name?'

'Ellen, but we mainly call her Nellie,' said Jake.

'Good luck then, to you fellers. This aren't a good country to be lost in.'

The search took on a frantic urgency. They all knew that Blind Joe could follow a track after dark, but only if he was on it in the first place. By sheer good luck, not far from an abandoned claim on two joined hills called the Red Widows, Blind Joe gave a shout.

'Hey Sandy. I seen Miss Nellie been alonga here.'

Jake confirmed it. He knew his sister's print and there it was in the dust, clear as day.

'Good work, Joe,' said Sandy. 'There'll be a pouch full of tobacco for that. If you find her alive it'll be an armload.'

Blind Joe took to the trail with dogged flair, and even in the hours before moonrise he never lost the spoor for long. Around midnight they found much of the equipment the girl had been carrying. A pan, a spade, and much of the food, lying abandoned on the ground.

It had been a while since Sandy had spent so many hours in the saddle, but the old muscles were still there, creaking and groaning. After a few hours the aches and pains had hardened into resolve.

Ah, he thought to himself, it was like a grave yard that night, the moon-silvered plain of termite mounds and small trees, glowing like diamonds, and so silent that it was like some nether world between life and death; past and future. The bush at night held no fears for Sandy, but he had learned to be watchful. He was alert for shapes and shadows that seemed out of place, for movement and sounds. A little ahead and to the right Blind Joe was a constant, sometimes riding, sometimes walking with the reins bunched in his right hand, and occasionally dropping to one knee.

Even more rarely the tracker would toss his reins to one of the men, or secure his mount to a tree, while he cast around the area, muttering to himself before reporting to Tom and pointing. 'Here Miss Nellie run into a branch,' he said once. 'And leave blood on the ground, see?'

'Poor little mite,' said Jake. 'But the blood ain't hardly dried. She can't be far away.'

But another hour passed before the next change in the trail.

'There Miss Nellie make water,' Blind Joe said. 'Just li'l bit water. No more blood.' Then he creased his brow, pointing out an unmistakable dog print in the red dirt.

'Yella dog foller alonga Miss Ellen,' said Blind Joe, then held up five fingers. 'This many.'

Sandy spurred his horse. 'That's it, you fellows. Go! As fast as Blind Joe can lead us.'

Nellie stopped walking and sat on a stone on a rise. First she took a drink from her canvas water bottle and then she allowed herself to cry, partly from fear and loneliness, and partly from the pain of her bruised and bloodied nose.

The sound of howling made her freeze inside. She saw the shapes of five dingoes out in the moonlight, sitting up, and howling with snouts pointing up towards the moon. She was frozen in fear. She had seen them many times before, but not at night and alone like this. The sound of their howling crawled inside her skin.

Finally, the howling stopped, and the dingoes gathered courage. The old bitch slunk forward. The girl picked up a stone and threw it hard. It fell short, and the wary old matriarch scampered back. Not far, however.

Nellie picked up another stone, satisfyingly heavy in her hand.

In the distance Sandy saw something. Was it a splash of white? He wasn't sure. Blind Joe gave a shout too, and the riders put their spurs to their mounts. They all saw the yellow dogs flee into the night, but there was no time or light to shoot at them.

Jake was there first, off his horse and with Nellie in his arms, cooing at her and letting her sob with relief against his neck. 'There, there,' he said. 'Don't ever scare me like that again. Thanks to Blind Joe and these gentlemen here.'

Later, when they took her home, Jake prised the second stone from Nellie's fingers, and found it streaked with rich native gold.

# Chapter 46: The Long Arm of the Law

Billy had been waiting under a lancewood tree, just outside the Newcastle Waters Telegraph Station, since the new moon. Sometimes, at night, he slept. During the day he smoked his clay pipe, or boiled up a billy of tea, but most of the time he just waited, like Mister Searcy had told him to.

Finally, early one morning, the operator wandered outside, holding a sheet of paper in his hand. 'Hey Billy,' he called. 'There's a message here addressed to Mr Searcy. All the way from Wyndham, Western Australia. Is that what you was waiting for?'

Billy took the message, folded it, and buttoned it carefully into his top pocket. This done, he hurried off to catch his horse, an energetic chestnut filly, with a striking, flaxen mane and tail. Billy had stolen her from a brumby-runner's bush yard and broken her himself. She came trotting up to his whistle, and he saddled her up for the ride of her life, wheeling her away towards the Gulf.

In thirty hours of alternating trot, canter and walk, Billy reached the rugged cliffs of the Abner Range, then followed the Kilgour down to the Macarthur, riding into Borroloola at noon on the third day. His filly was spent, but still alert. He loved her more than ever.

Alfred Searcy, spotting Billy from his verandah, walked down to meet him, taking the telegram in hand. 'Good work, Billy. See to your horse, then head out the back, and the cook will make you some tucker.'

Alfred, unable to wait another moment, unfolded the paper out on the street, taking in the words eagerly.

TOM NUGENT ARRESTED AND DETAINED STOP
UNFORTUNATELY PROOF OF CRIME DIFFICULT
DUE TO ALTERED BRAND STOP ADVISE OTHER
AVENUES STOP J LANCE WA POLICE

Alfred frowned and headed back in to his desk to think, calling out for O'Donohue to help him do so, while Billy sat in the lean-to kitchen and ate his own weight in beef and Johnny cakes.

Now that the rat was in the trap, Alfred thought, there had to be a way to keep him there.

Meanwhile, in Wyndham, after a day or two of watching the school mistress in the playground, Tom Nugent borrowed a quill and sheet of writing paper. After thinking through the words he wrote:

> Dear Madam,
>
> I hav ben admiring from a distence the exemplery way in wich you conduct your school, and also the manor in which you comport yourself. If only I was not forced by vile circumstance (no fault of my own) to be constrained by the constabulary (only temporary I assure you) then I would be most pleased to make your aquaintaence.
>
> Yours Truly
> Thomas Nugent

Later that day one of the senior girls, opening the playtime batting, slogged a slow delivery Tom's way. The hard cork cricket ball rolled to the grassy area just below the barred window of his cell. A boy jumped the low police yard fence, long limbed, carefree and unafraid. As he approached Tom called out. 'Hey lad, will you run an errand for me?'

The boy nodded his freckled face. 'I reckon so.'

'Will you take a note to your teacher?'

'I guess I will, if you want me to.'

Tom folded the note tightly and threw it out between the bars, watching it flutter to the ground from where the boy picked it up.

'What's her name?' asked Tom. 'Your teacher, I mean.'

'Miss Byrne it is, mister. I'll give her the note directly.'

Tom settled down to watch while the boy hurried back, chucking the ball to his mates in a long, looping underarm, just as the school teacher appeared on the verandah with a hand bell. The lad walked up and handed her the note, pointing back towards the police lock-up.

The teacher took the note without reading it, pausing only to look Tom's way. As he watched, she folded and tucked the message up her sleeve. This done, she raised the handbell and began to ring it. The children streamed into two lines at the foot of the stairs, then marched inside. Peace settled on the school house, and Tom went over to lie on his bed, staring at the ceiling, a strange little smile fixed on his face.

Later in the day, long after the students had gone home, Tom watched as the school mistress came out from the school house, locking it behind her, staring at the lock-up, narrowing her eyes as if trying to see inside. He wasn't sure if she could see his face in the darkness of the cell behind the bars, but he stared back at her nonetheless.

With Blind Joe, and the boy leading the way, it was a strange procession that readied themselves for a move out to 'Nellie's Reef,' as they were already calling it. Preparations, though, had to be made without attracting too much attention, for the diggers roundabout were always looking for signs of a new strike.

'Why have me and Carmody got to stay behind?' complained Tommy the Rag.

Sandy flared. 'Because if we abandon the claim, the Chinese or some new chum will take it – we've put too much hard work into it for that.' Then, to the others. 'Right you lot, let's move out.'

Sandy took the lead, riding Jonathan James, followed by Jake, Nellie and little Mary. Fitz rode with Bob Anderson, then Larrikin, leading his now heavily pregnant mare. Wonoka Jack and George Brown came next, with New England Jack. The rest of the camp followed – mostly women, some of whom had been with the Thirteen all the way from Queensland or the Centre. Right at the back rode Scotty, looking constantly in the direction of Red Jack's camp.

By noon, they had reached the dry hill where Nellie had fended off the dingoes, and with the gear dumped and the horses grazing, the men were soon out specking. Within an hour, two more gold-bearing fragments had been found.

'There's no damn water so we'll be dry-blowing,' said Fitz, 'but there's gold here, no doubt.'

Sandy agreed. 'Let's peg every square inch for half a damn mile. This one is ours.' He glanced at Jake. 'You happy, partner?'

Jake grinned while little Mary hugged his leg. 'Haven't been happier for a long while.'

That evening, back at the old claim, Tommy the Rag poured two full pannikins of rum for he and Carmody. The fire was a lonely place with just two of them. Missus Dead Finish was out carting from Wyndham, and Carmody had no woman, like most of the others did.

'Those bastards are trying to cut us out of our share of gold at the new claim,' drawled Carmody. 'It just isn't fair.'

'D'you reckon?'

'I do. I've never felt too equal with this gang, no matter how they talk it up. This whole Ragged Thirteen thing, when you get down to it, is all for the benefit of Sandy Myrtle and Tom Nugent.'

'Oh I dunno,' said Tommy. 'They're good men – and Tom's in bloody gaol – took the rap without a word.'

Carmody gulped at his drink, and a drip of rum ran down from each corner of his mouth and into his beard. 'Those horse thievin' charges won't stick – that brand change was as slick a job as I've ever seen. Nugent will be back here to take the lion's share of any gold in no time.'

'I don't reckon you're right there, Carmody.'

'Let's wait and see, eh? They'll never forgive me for Maori Reid bein' my brother in law. They've cut me and you out of this new claim, and left us here on this useless square of ground to scratch our balls. You might be too dumb to see it, but it's clear enough to me.'

'Ah, have another rum, complainin' won't help,' said Tommy. But the thought of the rest of the crew out on a rich new field made him feel sick inside.


Tommy slept badly enough as it was, but the following morning, over a late breakfast of Johnny-cakes and treacle, nursing splitting rum hangovers, the beat of horses' hooves had them on their feet and watchful. A moment later, Bob Anderson and Jake rode in at speed, pack horses trailing.

'Hey,' Tommy cried as they reined in, 'back so soon you two?'

'That's it,' said Jake. 'Don't say a word, of course, but the new claim is alive with gold. We've got eight ounces in my saddlebags to buy supplies, and we're here to register the claims.'

'And whose name will the claims be registered under?' sneered Carmody.

'Jake an' 'is twa lasses,' said Bob. 'Thet belter o' a Warden won't gee'z us our own.'

Carmody stood back, arms crossed over his chest. 'That's what they say. Well don't let us keep you. Tommy and me are riding out to this new claim to make sure we get what's ours.'

Tommy stared at his mate. 'We can't just leave this place, after all those months.'

'Let the damned Celestials have this God-forsaken slice of hell, I say, but listen: it has to lie unworked for seven days before it's classed as abandoned. Someone can ride in once a week and turn a hand for an hour or two – dead easy.'

Bob Anderson shrugged. 'Whit's fur ye'll no go by ye. Jake 'an me hev work to do.'

After they had gone, Carmody tacked up his horse and assembled his gear. He turned to Tommy. 'Are you coming with me, mate?'

'Yeah,' said Tommy at last. 'I'm coming.'

# Chapter 47: Mud crabs and Mullock heaps.

When Tommy the Rag and Carmody rode up, accompanied by a cloud of their own dust, Sandy swore so hard he had to stop and spit. 'You bastards are s'posed to be watching the old claim. What the bloody hell are you doing here?'

Carmody swung off his horse. 'Well that was a fair cow of an idea. If you think we're going to wait on a heartless piece of rock at Rosie's Flat while you mob fill your pockets with gold, you'll have to think again.'

'Everything we find is shared between all of us,' Sandy explained.

'Oh really?' said Carmody. 'I've had a wide experience of sharing, over the years. It usually means that someone else gets everything, an' I get fuck all.'

'You still shouldn't have ridden off,' spluttered Sandy. 'We agreed—'

'No,' said Carmody. 'You agreed, and the rest of us had to go along with it. Anyhow, why can't we just take it in turns to ride in and throw some dirt around for half a day? That'll keep us in proper legal ownership.'

Sandy scratched his beard, 'Well I suppose you've got a

point. We'll have a chat about it later. In the meantime you'd best get yerselves a feed.'

'Bugger food,' said Tommy. He pointed to his eyes. 'I'm gonna speck me up some of that gold before I do anything else.'

The new claim was different to what the gang were used to. Within a few days they had panned or dry-blown alluvial gold in the gullies, and found more gold-streaked stones on the ridge. Nellie's Reef had been exposed, reckoned Bob Anderson, by the parent rock weathering away, leaving the gold there for the taking.

After months of living close together, working as a unit on the same shaft, here the gang all had different theories about how to approach the dig. Without Tom to hold them together, they split off into twos and threes.

Wonoka Jack and his brother George choose a spot half way down the hill and began a deep scrape along the line of the gold they'd found to that point. Bob Anderson camped at the top and tried to enthuse the others about chopping trees for shoring and beginning a deep shaft.

'If t'were one line a'gold here, there cuid be more, 'neath the ground, like.'

'Never again will I squirm like a worm underground,' swore Jack Dalley. 'Not when there's gold to be plucked from near the surface. If there's to be a shaft you can dig the bastard yourself.'

Still, they were all happy enough, and the gold came in, ounce by ounce, first on the surface then scraping the upper layers with picks and shovels. The result did not amount to a fortune, but it was better than the disappointment they had left behind. The gang decided to take it in turns, as Carmody had suggested, to ride in and work the old claim, but after a few days, no one bothered. It was a long ride, just to work in the sun. The chances of finding a big nugget were more promising here, and everyone talked about the prospect.

Word came back to the Wyndham police, from Alexandria Station, that of course there had been the gift of a grey horse, and yes he had impeccable breeding. The manager and head stockman there were old mates of Tom and Larrikin, and owed Tom a good turn or two.

'Tom Nugent. We're releasing you for lack of evidence,' the police constable said, jangling the keys. 'But every man from here to Camooweal, and south to bloody Burra knows that you're a lying dog and you should be in gaol for life if not hanged.'

'Fetch my things for me,' said Tom, ignoring the tirade. 'There's a good chap. I hope you've looked after my horse for me.'

Tom had no intention of riding straight back to Hall's Creek. Instead he rode down to the landing and sold the grey to a new chum for twenty guineas, with a lesser horse thrown in – a bay gelding with clean legs and a deep chest. The grey was worth many times that, of course, but now, with Tom's proof of ownership all over town, was the time to sell.

With money to spend, Tom visited Black Pat Durack's store, where he purchased a new pair of moleskin trousers, heeled riding boots and a couple of striped Crimean shirts. Thus prepared, he booked into the Cable family's pub, paying up front for a hot bath.

Tom spent an hour in the tub, soaking and scrubbing himself. When he was done there was almost as much dark-brown water on the floor as there was in the tub.

He dried himself, shaved, and walked back to his room with the towel wrapped around his middle. He dressed in new clothes and smoked a pipe before walking to the post office, where he asked at the counter for the address of Miss Byrne, the schoolteacher.

'Why she lives in the boarding house over yonder,' said the

postmaster. 'But if you've taken a shine to her, let me just mention that you ain't the first … and no one has succeeded yet.'

When Tom knocked on the boarding house door, it was four in the afternoon according to his pocket watch, the perfect time to catch her, being at the end of the school day. An older woman answered the door, and when Tom asked for Miss Byrne she disappeared without a word. He waited a minute or two before the young schoolteacher appeared in the doorway. She was no longer wearing the bustled gown she wore to work, but a simple dress that had seen better days, and a practical outdoor hat.

She seemed younger than he had imagined, up close. Her skin was lightly freckled, with mocking eyes and happy lips. Her hair was blonde and tied back in a sensible pony-tail.

'Hello Miss,' he said, holding his hat in his hand. 'I'm—'

'I know who you are, well enough,' said Miss Byrne. 'I got your note. Besides, everyone's talking about Tom Nugent, captain of the Ragged Thirteen and famous horse-thief.'

'Are they really?'

'It's all I've heard about. Even the school children know who you are.'

Tom wasn't sure what to say next. She saved him the trouble.

'What are you like with a pair of oars?' she asked.

Tom started with surprise. 'Well, not bad I guess. I've rowed a bit, here and there in me time. Why's that?'

'I'm just heading off to check my pots. You can help.'

'Your what?'

'My crab pots. The tide's just right about now. I can row myself, but crabbing's lighter work with two.'

Tom tipped his hat. 'I'd be honoured to help you out, Miss Byrne.'

'Oh, bugger calling me that all the time. I get it all day and it becomes tiresome. My name's Emily. Just wait a moment, I've got a bucket of bait.' She reappeared a moment later with an

233

evil-smelling pail. 'Here, you can carry it, if you like.'

'Don't mind if I do,' said Tom.

Emily Byrne, it turned out, kept a dinghy down by the landing – a sturdy, clinker-built unit of about ten foot in length, flat-bottomed so she drew 'barely as much water as a duck.'

The tide was in over the flats, and Tom slipped the oars into the rowlocks, watching wide-eyed as Emily lifted her dress to her waist, and tucked it into her bloomers. 'Don't look,' she said, seeing the direction of his eyes. 'They're only legs, and I can't have my dress sitting in bilge water the whole time.'

Emily pointed out the direction of travel, upstream along the mangrove-lined banks. Tom bent to his task, making a show of keeping straight and pulling powerfully into the tide.

'You're a fine rower, Mr Nugent.'

'Thanks, but if I have to call you Emily, you'd better address me as Tom.'

They continued up the channel, and Tom was enjoying the burn of his chest, arm and shoulder muscles. Ahead, around the inlet of a small creek, he could see the first coloured cork float, bobbing on the surface.

'I heard they let you out today,' she said. 'I was glad about that … and hoping maybe you'd come and introduce yourself.'

'I haven't been able to think of nothing else,' said Tom, just as they reached the pot. He used the oars to hold position in the tide, while Miss Byrne bent over, plucked the cork from the surface, and started pulling in the rope. Up came the trap, woven from wicker cane. Trapped inside was a single mud crab as big as a dinner plate – dark brown, almost black, with an armoured carapace and claws that looked like they'd cleave through a man's finger.

'A beauty!' cried Emily, expertly pinning the crab, bringing it out through the trap door, then using twine to bind its claws. Disarmed, the crab was then free to clamber around the floor of the dinghy wherever it liked. Tom regretted having taken off his flash new boots.

He couldn't help thinking what an amazing woman he had chanced upon. Miss Emily Byrne thought nothing of balancing on the gunwale with bare feet and bare legs, hauling in the pots, heedless of the 'gators that slid in off the mud bars and raised their jagged heads nearby.

They got eight more crabs, with Tom rowing all the way up to the mouth of a river Emily called the King. Thankfully, the return journey was assisted by a rollicking tide. The water had dropped a little over the flats, and Tom had to drag the dinghy through shallow mud to the stake that served as a berth.

They boiled the crabs in a copper, on a fire in the backyard of the boarding house – joined by some of the other guests for a feast of sweet crab meat, using hammers and nutcrackers to split claws and legs. They drank bottled beer and laughed over nothing, ignoring the mosquitoes and sand flies, sharing yarns for an hour or two, before Emily announced that it was time to retire for the night.

'School day tomorrow,' she said. 'I'm as shirty as hell when I'm tired so I try to get a good night's sleep for the sake of my pupils, bless them.'

She walked with Tom to the front gate of the boarding house, the air thick with fragrant air moving off the tidal flats. Tom loved rivers. He loved riding with the Ragged Thirteen. He loved the plains of Western Queensland, the Gulf, and the grasslands of the Barkly. He loved being free, but tonight he was feeling something else. Something even stronger.

'Do you reckon I can see you again?' he asked.

'Of course you can,' she smiled. 'You're an artist with those oars.' She reached out with her forefinger and touched him on the tip of his nose. 'See you tomorrow, Tom Nugent, if you're willing.'

'I'm willing,' said Tom, smiling. He watched her walk inside, then turned back down the street towards the pub.

# Chapter 48: Red Jack and the Mare

When a Cantonese syndicate moved in on the old claim at Rosie's Flat, most of the gang pretended not to care. But it was generally agreed that such an act wasn't 'right.'

'It's not that I bloody liked the place,' spat Sandy Myrtle, 'but I don't like the idea of them just walking in and taking that mine we worked so hard to build.' He glared at Carmody and Tommy the Rag. 'This would never have happened if you two had just done what you was asked to and stayed put.'

'Why didn't you stay, if you liked the damn place so much?' glowered Carmody.

This ill-feeling was compounded by the slow but steady drying up of gold in the new claims. By the second month they were scarcely winning five ounces a week. Just enough for tucker and tools.

Larrikin and Jack Woods were soon riding out in the late evenings, dodging Durack cattle, holding them in that secret niche that Tom had found, and butchering them in a bough-shed slaughterhouse. The sly meat business not only fed the gang, as well as Jake and the girls, but brought in some much-needed coin at the same time.

Larrikin's mare, now some eight months pregnant, was one thing that the gang was still excited about, but there was concern in this direction also. Fitz was the first to notice that she seemed to have bagged up way too early, and then, a week or two later, started discharging. Not much, but enough to spark some worry.

'Maybe it's just the poor grass here,' said Tommy the Rag. The dry season was underway, the rains now just a memory.

'Feed isn't the problem,' said Larrikin. 'Someone should go fetch Red Jack. It'll be her foal after all, and they say that what she doesn't know about horses isn't worth knowing.'

'I'll ride fer Red Jack,' said Scotty, beaming at the chance. He had a horse saddled in record time, and was back not long after nightfall, with Red Jack beside him on her black stallion.

Red Jack started by running her hand slowly along the mare's flanks, then stopped and turned to the bystanders. 'I can't do this with you bastards ogling me.' Then, at Larrikin. 'She's yours isn't she? Just hold her head and keep her calm.'

The examination took around thirty minutes, after which time Red Jack washed her hands from a steel bucket, then joined the gang around the camp fire.

'Bad news,' she said. 'The poor old girl's carrying twins. Most times a mare will absorb the extra foetus. This one hain't done that.'

The more experienced horsemen shook their heads sadly at the news. They knew what this meant. Sandy had even suggested twins as a possibility. But they all wanted to hear the verdict from Red Jack's lips.

'Two things will happen from here,' she said. 'Either she'll miscarry both foals, or they'll go full term and be born weak and sickly. Both will probably die.'

'Jesus, that's rough,' said Tommy the Rag, and none of them looked at Larrikin's face.

A couple of hundred miles to the north, Northern Territory trooper Alfred Searcy stood at the rail of the schooner *Levuka*. He was full of nervous excitement as they rounded Adolphus Island, took the Western Channel, tacked carefully around a series of shallow sandbars, then finally anchored in seven fathoms off the bustling township of Wyndham.

The landing here was of tidal mud, planked all the way to deeper water, several teams on hand for the unloading. Another two-masted schooner, the *Simla*, had just finished discharging horses, and they were being yarded up from the landing, many of them caked to the flanks in mud.

Searcy did not look for a porter, but carried his own swag and portmanteau. He was impressed by the activity all around – carpenters building shops or houses and travellers hammering in tent pegs. There were at least three stores, and some jerry-built grog shops along with the impressive Wyndham Hotel.

Despite a hefty thirst, inspired by a fast steamer trip to Darwin, then a berth on the first available ship heading for Wyndham, Searcy ignored the hotel, walking straight to the police station. The place seemed deserted, but a solid rap on the door brought a tired looking sergeant to the door, seeming somewhat surprised at Alfred's uniform.

'We weren't expecting a visit from the Territory police?' he said, stifling a yawn. 'To what do we owe the honour?'

'My name is Alf Searcy. I'm here on a mission of some urgency ...'

'Alfred?' came a booming voice from inside. 'Is that you?'

A ramrod straight figure appeared in the passage. Alfred recognised Sub-Inspector Lawrence, who he had met on the Resident's lawns in Palmerston.

'Why hello, it's good to see you here!'

Five minutes later Alfred was sipping tea in a cool stone room, exchanging pleasantries about his journey and the situation in the Kimberley. Finally, on the second cup, he cut to the chase.

'Now I know you'll be wondering about the purpose of my visit. I'm here with fresh new charges against Tom Nugent. I take it that he's still in custody?'

The two WA cops looked at each other, then Lawrence answered. 'We had to release the man, unfortunately. The manager and head stockman of Alexandria Station backed him up on the horse story. And since the grey's real owner, Fisher, is currently in London, the prosecution case couldn't proceed. We know Nugent changed the brand but just can't prove it.'

Alfred shook his head as if in silent condemnation of their inability to do their job. 'Well, please oblige me by arresting him again. I have evidence, and witnesses.' He unbuttoned a document from his top pocket. 'This here is an extradition order for Thomas Nugent to be returned to the Northern Territory in chains, there to face charges of robbery, assault, and malicious damage at Abraham's Billabong, the Katherine River and the Victoria.

'You have eyewitnesses?' Lawrence inquired.

'Yes,' said Alfred. 'The case is watertight, I can assure you.' He frowned, 'You haven't allowed this criminal to leave Wyndham, I hope?'

Lawrence shook his head quickly. 'No, not yet. He's still here, chasing after the young school teacher from what I understand.'

'Then let us strike now,' said Alfred, 'before he hears that I'm in town.' He puffed out his chest. 'Every criminal has his nemesis, and I am Tom Nugent's.'

# Chapter 49: Too Close for Bloody Comfort

Almost every afternoon, Tom rowed Miss Emily Byrne up the channel: crabbing and sometimes fishing. By the third week he was permitted to kiss her on the cheek. By the fifth they were holding hands when he walked her home after dinner at the pub.

While Emily was teaching, Tom worked shifts down at Anton's Landing, unloading steamers and sail craft as they discharged stores, cattle or horses. He'd also broke-in a couple of nags for Mr Katiford, the Government Surveyor. All in all, things were looking up, though he missed life on the track, and the constant fun of riding with the Ragged Thirteen.

Late one morning, Tom was in the bar of the Wyndham Hotel, with a glass of beer in hand and a pipe drawing nicely, when one of the stevedores from the port hurried in, leaned close to Tom and lowered his voice. 'I was just talking to the skipper of the *Levuka*. A Territory "pink" just arrived in town – name of Searcy. It sounds like he's got it in for you.'

Tom's beer turned sour in his throat. 'That jumped up, arrogant dog! Why did he have to land here, of all places? Just when things were going right for a change.'

'Searcy told the *Levuka*'s skipper that he's ah, assembled …

fresh evidence against you. Something about robberies over in the Territory, and an assault at the Vic River Depot.'

'What?' spluttered Tom. 'All we done there was throw a thieving sly grog seller in the river. How can that be called an assault?'

'Well I dunno, but this Searcy was boasting that he's got an extradition order to take you away in chains. They're havin' a cuppa in the police station, then they're comin' for you.'

'On the level?'

'Yeah, worse luck.'

Tom drained his beer and slammed down the glass. 'Thanks mate. Life was just gettin' too bloody good.'

Leaving the bar, he hurried down to his hotel, using the side entrance to avoid the desk. He couldn't see any point settling his bill, if the police were going to chase him anyway. Besides, he'd need every penny he could get his hands on for life on the run.

Back in his room, Tom rolled everything he owned up into a swag, then opened the window. Throwing his gear out ahead, he jumped to the ground, then hurried out back, catching his gelding from the horse yard. Before riding out he checked that he had, in his pockets or saddle bags, all the things he valued most – pocket book, folding knife, and two small volumes of poetry – Adam Lindsay Gordon and Henry Kendall. Most precious of all was a ferrotype image of his mother in a tiny bronze and glass frame, wrapped in waxed paper.

Leading his horse down dusty back streets, he visited the Adcock brothers' store, where he provisioned himself for a couple of days. With one more stop in mind, he walked another half block, then tied his horse's reins to the schoolhouse gate. He adjusted his collar and walked to the open door.

The school students turned as one to see Tom Nugent standing in the door frame. Silence descended. Miss Byrne herself was frozen, chalk in hand. To Tom she had never looked so beautiful, her hair tied back, but with some lighter strands remaining free, falling around her neck. She wore a cream-coloured dress with silk sleeves and a modest bustle.

Tom cleared his throat. 'Excuse me for interrupting, Miss Byrne. But I must see you on a matter of importance.'

Some of the children now whispered and giggled, until Miss Byrne shut them up with an icy stare. Finally, when silence reigned again, she passed her chalk to a nearby older girl and turned to the children. 'Seniors, please complete the third and fourth exercises on your slate, juniors carry on with your letters. Mary, you will stand and record the name of any pupil who talks, or otherwise takes advantage of my absence.'

Every young eye was on Miss Byrne as she walked to the schoolhouse entrance, passed through, and closed the door behind her.

Tom led her by both hands further away, out of earshot. 'Bad news,' he said. 'I have to run, the Territory police have lobbed in, with more charges against me.'

'Oh … Tom. That is bad news.'

'I'm thinking that I'll find a place for us. Somewhere safe where life will be grand. Will you come, if I send for you?'

'That depends,' she said, lifting her hand and laying her palm along his cheek. 'I won't live with you in a gaol cell.' She was smiling now, but he could see that she was trying not to cry.

On impulse, Tom kissed her on the lips. A long and deep kiss. Their first real kiss.

There was a shout of delight from a boy with his head glued to the schoolhouse window. Then uproar from inside.

'Oh God,' she said, breaking off but still holding his hand. 'The cheeky little devils. I have to go.'

'Goodbye, Miss Emily Byrne.'

'Goodbye, Tom Nugent, Captain of the Ragged Thirteen.'

'I'll send for you, when I'm fixed.'

'Make it soon,' she cried, then hurried back through the door and inside.

Tom was about to mount his horse when he heard activity from the police station just down the block. He ducked deeper into the shade and crept forward to watch two Wyndham 'traps', along with a narrower figure that could only be Searcy, and a couple of armed trackers, march off towards the hotel.

Tom waited until they were well down the street before he mounted up and rode away. He was full of mixed feelings: anger, a touch of panic but most of all, surprise and excitement at the love that had just burst into full flower outside that school house.

Tom knew better than to try and leave town by the back roads. The safest way to get distance under his belt, and to fool the trackers, was to head down the main road. Of course, as he rode, he kept well away from the Landing or groups of people, keeping his hat low.

The new gelding started out with a will, but after an hour he had slowed appreciably. Tom cursed the man who'd offered him as part-exchange for the exceptional grey. He was a nice enough animal, but without the wind needed for a fast escape. Tom cursed the gelding, cursed Alfred Searcy, and cursed himself for being a fool and not making his move on Emily sooner.

Using a switch to keep the gelding motivated, Tom diverted around the extended Byrne family's hotel at the Six Mile. These were all Emily's relatives, of course, and although he had not formally met them, they knew of the developing relationship, and did not approve.

By late afternoon Tom was getting close to Parry's Lagoon. Unfortunately, by that stage, getting his mount to keep up anything more than a reluctant trot was becoming impossible.

There was, he decided, no option but to camp for the night, resting the horse and preparing for a big day. Searcy and his new mates, he decided, were unlikely to have set off after him just yet. It would have taken an hour or two to figure out that Tom had left town, and they would then have had to provision and prepare a patrol.

Still, taking no chances, Tom watered his horse in the stony bed of the fast-flowing Ord, then forced him into one last big effort, climbing a good-sized peak in the ranges, with a view along the track back towards Wyndham. On a flat shelf in the rock, he lit a small, miserable fire, and made a meal of hot tea and salt beef.

When he was done eating, the sun was low, with the stone hills glowing red all around him. Up high as he was, the sight made him pleased to be back in the bush. It was only this that gave him peace at last, a feeling that did not last for long.

A glance back along the track, laid out like a ribbon far below him, showed a pall of dust rising from five horsemen heading fast, south from Wyndham. Tom felt a prickle of apprehension. Could it be them?

Yes, it could, he decided. Searcy was a persistent bastard, and was probably on a tight schedule. These riders were travelling too light to be diggers or travellers.

'It's them alright,' Tom said to himself. 'Too close for bloody comfort.'

Aware that he was in for the chase of his life, he saddled the reluctant gelding and prepared to descend the hill in the half-dark.

# Chapter 50: Tom the Afghan

Within a mile, Tom knew that he was never going to outpace the police patrol. He wished he'd thought to steal a better horse before he left Wyndham, but from here there'd be no opportunity to upgrade before Turkey Creek.

His only chance now was to leave the road, and try to throw the trackers off the scent with a cross-country ride. Yet, he needed a creek to divert into, or a shelf of flat rock next to the track. Otherwise the trackers would clearly see his exit point. They would almost certainly have already followed his spoor to the abandoned night-camp of just half an hour earlier, for a good moon had risen.

Riding slowly now suited Tom's purpose of looking for an escape route. Even a fallen tree would help, but the side of the track remained featureless: just kerosene grass, stones and dry acacias. The police could only be a short distance behind now, and Tom knew that they would not stop while there was light to see.

There had been few times in Tom's life when he had doubted himself, but now he began to wonder if he would soon feel manacles on his wrists and ankles. That he'd be thrown aboard a steamer, hauled across the Gulf to Palmerston, with Alf Searcy crowing like a cock rooster over him.

Tom wished that he was back in Wyndham, taking Miss Emily Byrne out for supper, settling into the pub dining room with a good steak. It was all Alf Searcy's fault, that arrogant, jumped-up man.

Tom was filled with a building sense of indignation, when he saw a series of uncommonly tall rocks just off the track to the left. This was strange because he couldn't remember having ever seen them before. It also seemed that the rocks were lit with flickering light from a campfire.

With no real weapon to draw, he rode on, getting closer, peering at the scene. He still hadn't quite worked out what was going on when one of the rocks moved. Even more incredibly, the lower portion of it proved to have four legs. A long neck extended as if pulled by strings from a puppeteer, and the thing made a noise that broke the silence like thunder.

It was just one of several camels, Tom realised, aware that his pulse rate had gone nuts. Next he heard a gentle voice, not in English, but in the Persian tongue of the Afghan cameleers.

Tom recognised the man before the voice. It was Esau, well-known Hall's Creek identity, coffee maker extraordinaire, and best friend of midwife and store keeper Susan O'Neil.

'Bloody hell,' Tom cried. 'Is that you, Esau?'

Esau stood up from the fire. Behind him stood a tent of hides. His voice was deep, slow and smooth as silk as he addressed Tom with a military rank, as always, in deference to his leadership of the Thirteen. 'Captain Nugent. What are you doing here, and why such a hurry?'

Tom dismounted and led his horse over to the Afghan's camp. 'Jesus, you're a sight for sore eyes. I've got the wallopers in hot pursuit, and this gelding has no stamina. He's the weirdest thing – steps high like he's on show, and breaks out in a cold sweat when you push him.'

'How distant are the police?' asked Esau.

'Maybe just a mile or two, and I get the feeling they're not planning on throwing their swags out any time soon.'

Esau scratched his long beard in contemplation for a moment, then, 'Captain Nugent. If you don't mind, please unsaddle that horse and chase him off. I shall drive my camels up and down over the track to wipe your trail.' The Afghan walked to one of the enormous camel packs, now leaning against a small boab, rummaged through and removed a clean set of clothes. 'Wear these, while we pack away your saddle and the things you have on.'

After chasing off the horse, hiding his gear and dressing in pantaloons, tunic, robe and turban, Tom scarcely had time to smoke a pipe at the fireside before they heard the thunder of hooves. The police party came up, slowing to a walk and riding directly into the camp. Only the trackers held back, nosing around on the road for sign.

'Just a couple of Afghans,' complained one of the policemen.

'Hey, you two 'Ghans,' shouted another. 'Stand up straight when the law of the land rides into your camp.'

Tom, looking through the folds of cloth that partially covered his face, recognised Alf Searcy. He and Esau both did as they were told.

'Have you two seen a white man ride past?' asked Searcy.

'Yessah,' said Esau. 'If you please sah, I saw one white man ride past. In a big hurry, too. Just a little while ago.'

'What's wrong with your friend? Can't he talk?'

'Sorry sah, he cannot speak no English.'

'Salaam, salaam,' said Tom, keeping his face pointed low, and facing away from the moon.

'Right then,' said Searcy, 'we'll get on the road after our man.' He wheeled his horse and applied his spurs with a loud and showy shout of 'Yah.' The others followed, and the sound

247

of horses at the canter receded south towards Hall's Creek.

Tom and Esau laughed together so hard they almost fell over.

'Thanks mate,' Tom said. 'If it wasn't for you I'd probably be taking off cross-country, and on that poor neddy I wouldn't have lasted a mile before those trackers had me.' Like most rogue bushmen, he wasn't overly concerned about the white police, but trackers were another matter.

Tom slept with camel smell strong in his nostrils, and the next morning, after a good breakfast, he helped Esau load and balance the packs. When this was done, the Afghan ordered two camels to kneel with a mysterious command.

'Now climb aboard, Captain Nugent,' said Esau.

'I'm not so sure about this.'

'It's not hard, I promise you,' Esau replied. 'Hall's Creek is a long way on foot.'

Tom felt himself swaying as the camel rose, finding the sheer height uncomfortable. Yet, within a mile or two he was enjoying the ride. Esau smiled in approval.

Strangely, however, as they moved at a good clip towards the Denham River, a dusty brown shape emerged from the scrub and began to follow them at a distance of two chains or so.

'It's that damned gelding,' cried Tom. 'Can't get rid of him.'

And for the next three days, all the way to Hall's Creek, the gelding stuck to them like honey, coming up close and staying with the camels at their night camps on the Denham and the Bow.

'I'm starting to like that crazy horse,' said Tom. 'He's not much to ride any distance, but he never gives up.'

The only anxious moment was near Turkey Creek, when Searcy and his patrol came riding back the other way, obviously drawing a blank in Hall's Creek in their search for Tom. They reined in alongside the camels.

'Hey you,' shouted Searcy. 'Any sign of that white man you saw riding past the other night?'

'No sah,' said Esau. 'Never seen him again.'

The police party would have ridden on past, but then they spotted the gelding plodding along in the rear.

'Hey! That horse, where did he come from?'

Esau did not bat an eyelid. 'I don't know sah, he started following us yesterday.'

There was much examination of brands and discussion between the constabulary. Soon forgotten, Tom and Esau rode on. Within an hour, the gelding reappeared behind them, taking his place up behind the last of the camels.

Esau and Tom parted just before Hall's Creek. Saddling up the gelding, and packing his own clothes back into his swag, Tom remained in the Afghan's robes so as to appear incognito around the town.

'I'll get them back to you shortly, and I can't ever thank you enough.'

'My pleasure, Captain Nugent. It was the least a friend could do.'

Unwilling to ride, for an Afghan on a horse would have been an unusual sight, Tom led the gelding through the outer diggings, avoiding stores and grog shanties. Esau had told him how the rest of the Thirteen, along with Jake and the girls, had moved to a new claim out of town, but he still wanted to see the old place.

When he finally trudged into Rosie's Flat, he expected the mine to be busy with industrious Chinese, like most of their claims. He did find the place alive with Asiatic diggers, but few seemed to be working. Most were celebrating, singing and dancing. Even more strangely, there were white guards standing around with rifles. Tom guessed they had been hired to protect the claim, and that meant only one thing.

Tom sidled up to one of these guards. 'What's going on here?' he asked.

The man looked at him sideways. 'You speak well for a 'Ghan.'

Tom pulled his head covering low. There was something familiar about this man, and he didn't want to be recognised. 'Thank you sah. But what are these Celestials so worked up about?' Tom felt a lump in his throat. He almost didn't want to know. 'Why are they celebratin'?'

'They just stumbled on a "jeweller's shop" down that shaft. They've hired us to stop anyone who might want a slice of it.'

Tom swallowed, staring across at the shaft that he had started with his own hands and given so much in sweat and fingernails to deepen. A 'jewellers shop' was the diggers' name for a gold reef that has widened into a hollow, filled with slugs of solid gold.

'Jes—allah,' Tom breathed. 'How many ounces?'

'They dunno really. Not yet, but they reckon maybe three or four hundred.'

Tom stared, then laughed a little in the back of his throat. 'How did they find it?'

'They reckon there was two reefs, one below the other. The Ragged Thirteen was working the top one: a real thin leader, barely worth the trouble. The Chinese dug the shaft deeper and found a second reef. The bottom one is much richer.'

Tom had nothing more to say. Feeling hollow in the chest, he turned away. As soon as he was out of sight, he mounted the gelding. Esau had given him directions to the new claim and, if the gelding felt rested enough for the ride, he hoped to be there by midday.

# Chapter 51: To Hell with Hall's Creek

I've been thrown by horse, and gored by bull,
An' trampled by the same,
I've been bit by dogs and old Joe Blake,
Been rocked by storm and rain.

I've worn out boots, on the desert routes,
An' near drownded in the Wet,
But this last twelve month I found me match,
The toughest bastard yet.

Yes, I met my match in Hall's Creek town,
The bane of young and old,
The worstest cur I ever saw,
A mongrel thing called gold.

My mates and I, we dug a shaft,
We dug half way to hell,
Some other folks from across the sea,
found a fortune hidden well.

It don't seem fair, but that's just it,
we rode away and left,
Not knowing that our futures sat,
a little deeper down that cleft.

I'm going back, to cattle work,
Out on the furthest runs,
and leave this place to memory,
and other fools their ruin.

I'll do a hard day's work, for stockman's pay,
Forty shillings every week,
I'll gladly take on horse and bull,
And to hell with old Hall's Creek.

by Larrikin (With help from Fitz and Sandy Myrtle)


Tom rode up to the new claim, and he could see in a moment that news of the Chinese strike had reached the camp. Most of the gang were sitting, drinking rum around smoky fires. And how different was a day time rum-drinker's fire from a night time one!

Carmody and Tommy the Rag were packing the last of their things, the hostility the others nursed against them plain to see. All-in-all the mood was ugly, and only the sight of Tom, in Afghan clothes, riding a very tired horse into the camp, distracted them.

'What's this?' shouted Sandy Myrtle, lumbering to his feet. 'Who's so bad mannered as to ride up without so much as a cooee?'

Tom swung down from his horse, then swept the turban from his head. 'It's Tom Nugent, and I thought I'd find the

Ragged Thirteen here, not a bunch of beaten-down lags.'

The announcement buzzed through the air, and they all came around. Tom could scarcely stop chuckling as the kid from Borroloola hugged him around the legs and every one of the Thirteen wanted to shake his hand and clap him on the back. Someone took the gelding away to water and graze, and someone else brought a pannikin of rum. Jake and the girls arrived on the scene, and Tom thought that it was just like a birthday celebration.

'Oh it's us, alright,' said Sandy at last. 'But you're here just in time for the break-up.'

'Break-up? Why would that be?'

'Haven't you heard what the Celestials found in our old claim?' spat Fitz. 'Tommy here, an' Carmody, were supposed to stay there and look after the place, but they gave it up after a day.'

'I've heard alright, but why did you move here, if there weren't any gold?'

'Oh there was, at first, but it ran out fast enough — there's a few pounds hidden away, to account for your share.'

Tom drank his rum down, then insisted on a tour of the claims. Jack Woods showed him how the reef gold had lain at the top the rise, weathered and lying exposed.

Tom scratched his chin, 'Have you dug underneath at all?'

'Not much. No one was keen. We've mainly been panning the gullies these last few weeks.

'Well listen. There were two leaders at our old claim, with the poorest one on top. What if there's another one underneath, right here, just like the Chinese found.'

'I'm not digging another bloody shaft.' said Fitz.

'That's not what I mean, let's strip it off with shovels and barrows.'

Jake cut in. 'Ned Shaw has a horse drawn bucket. It'd be perfect for that.'

Carmody had his arms crossed in front of his chest. 'Sorry Tom, but I'm done.'

Even Jack Woods shook his head. 'No one has the stomach for digging no more, Tom. There's news of colour down in the Pilbara. I'm going to head that way.'

'What about you, Sandy?'

'I'll probably head back to the Centre. I heard whispers of a strike at Arltunga. Might head that way.'

Tom was thinking to himself. To entice Emily away from her school room he needed land. He had to make something of himself. He thought again of that block near the Overland Telegraph Line that could be had for a good price, but a few pounds was not enough. He needed a nest egg.

'Give my idea a try,' cried Tom. 'Let's dig for two more weeks, that's all. If it doesn't work out, then we just shake hands and ride our separate ways. Can we really afford to ride away from a second claim without knowing what's underneath?'

There was a dead silence at first, then Sandy was the first to speak. 'I s'pose not.'

The others grumbled in the affirmative.

'Alright, then,' said Tom. 'Let's drink today and be proud of how it feels to be the Ragged Thirteen. Tomorrow we start work.' He paused. 'And keep an eye out for those damned traps.' He placed the turban back on his head. 'If anyone asks, I'm just a poor Afghan cameleer.'


Scotty had been taking the occasional wild desert rose to Red Jack for months. Yet, he did not have time to ride out and search for them every day. Now that Tom was back, if there was even a breath of breeze the men worked right through. When Scotty's shift came around he laboured 'til dark without complaint.

Given a spare hour or two, however, he went searching for flowers. Finding them was getting harder, for the season was so dry that even beauty had trouble finding sustenance. No matter how dowdy or dried up the bloom, however, he still took it to Red Jack, and each time her face would light for those few magic moments. And Scotty would sit on the top rail and watch her work the horses.

One the third day after Tom came back, Scotty found a special flower near a bend in the Black Elvire. There was a tiny soak between two sides of a hard wall of rock, dampening the sandy soil. Ferns and tiny flowers grew in profusion. Amongst them was just one desert rose, almost perfect.

Now, Red Jack lifted the flower to her nose and her face lit up. Scotty felt his heart thump like hoofbeats in his chest. It was a special moment. The sun was just clipping the horizon behind the yards, and her hair glowed like fire. Mephistopheles was in the yards, a great black shape, muscled and graceful. Other horses waited also, ready to be broken by one of the best horse breakers the bush had ever seen.

'I thought I should tell you,' said Red Jack, 'that I'll be moving on soon. As soon as Larrikin's mare drops those twins, and that won't be long, I'll be ready.'

'We'll be finishing up as well.' Scotty said. He hesitated for a moment, then spilled his heart. 'When ye go, I wish tae go with you.'

Red Jack placed a hand on either side of Scotty's chin and kissed him delicately on the lips.

'No. I ride alone. That won't change.'

As she walked away from him, across the dusty yards, his vision blurred with pain. There had to be some way to change her mind.

# Chapter 52: The 'Orphan'

Two days to the new moon and the sky darkened quickly. A faint yellow glow on the western horizon was the last remnant of a warm dry-season day. Tom Nugent's eyes, however, were as good as a cat's in low light. Years of night watches on droving jobs, and desperate dusk-to-dawn rides had honed that sense to blade-sharpness.

Tom also knew the lay of the land around the Ragged Thirteen's old claim at Rosie's Flat. His current position, lying prone in an old trench near where Jake and the girls had camped, overlooked the Chinese diggings, without offering himself to view.

His eyes were fixed on the man he had spoken to a few days earlier: the guard with the rifle, protecting the Celestials and their rich new find. Ever since Tom had stopped to talk to that guard, something had bothered him. 'I know the bastard from somewhere,' he said to himself. Everything about the man: his face, his walk, and the way he handled his rifle, was familiar. Tom continued to watch while the Chinese miners finished up for the day, performing the last few chores by the light of slush lanterns.

The last miners came up from the shaft, and a barrow of rich ore was drawn up into the centre of the camp so it could not be pilfered. Tom was interested, but even more interested in the heavy lumps of pure gold that had come from the 'jeweller's shop' they'd found, deep down in the shaft.

'The Ragged Thirteen's gold,' said Tom quietly. 'The gold that should have been ours.'

The Thirteen had been digging, out at the new claim, with high hopes. Tom had stayed positive as they stripped load after load of spoil off the surface of the hill, running in a ribbon parallel with the direction of the first leader. But in his heart he knew that it was dead ground. There was no second vein of gold underneath. No miracle, and he had been wrong to talk the others into staying. Now he had to make things right for them.

Tom watched as one of the Celestials, a boss to judge from the swagger, counted a number of coins into the white man's hand, and bowed. The guard shouldered his rifle, and left the claim, walking along the track towards town, whistling as he went. At that moment, Tom remembered a name, and a drunken meeting some two or three years earlier.

Picking himself up, he dusted down his clothes, and set off in pursuit, leaving his gelding where he had tethered him, at the base of a black wattle tree. He followed on foot for half a mile, some hundred yards behind, until his man reached a sly grog shop run by an old cheat called Hobbs.

The place was near empty, and the guard pulled up a chair. Once seated, he shouted for rum. Old Hobbs himself skidded out with a bottle and glass, pouring it full. He was scarcely half way back to the bar before his customer demanded another.

'A man's not a bloody camel, ya know. He doesn't carry moisture in his damned hump!'

Tom waited until the man had downed the second rum before he stepped out of the shadows, adjusted his turban, and sat down at the table. The rum drinker's face darkened with annoyance.

'Scuse me, but I don't recall inviting such as you to sit down with me.'

'I know who you are,' said Tom. 'You're Jack Martin – the man they call the Orphan.'

The reaction to this was instant. In a fraction of a second the rifle that had been leaning against the table appeared, laying across the tabletop to point at Tom's gut. 'Who the hell might you be, then?'

Tom lifted off his turban, keeping it off for a moment or two before replacing it. 'My name's Tom Nugent.'

'Tom Nugent? The captain of the Ragged Thirteen? The poor bastards who used to work that claim I'm mindin' for the Celestials on?'

'You got it. You and me met up in Borroloola once.'

'I remember now, you were ridin' with Harry Readford.'

'And proud to do so,' said Tom.

The Orphan drained the last of his glass, then banged the table to get the barman's attention. 'More rum, and hurry it up.' Hobbs hurried over, and waited for a coin, which was slow in coming. The Orphan said loudly, 'Bein' an Afghan and all,' he winked, 'I take it you won't be drinking.'

'That's right,' smiled Tom. 'No rum for me.'

When Hobbs had gone the Orphan squinted slyly. 'I heard that the traps were out looking for you.'

Tom inclined his turbaned head. Two days had passed since word reached his ears that Alfred Searcy had sailed back to the NT. 'That's true, and I'd say that they're still looking for you too. I heard about the robbery on the Palmer River. Is that what you're planning here?'

'To be honest, they're paying me so well I'm not even think-ing that way.' The Orphan paused. 'So why did you follow me?'

'I've got a bit of a hankering to find out where the Celestials have stashed the gold from my claim.' Tom smiled. It was a well-known fact that they always took their gold home to China rather than cashing it in locally, mainly because it was worth more per ounce over there.

'Why would I tell you that? If I wanted to steal it, I'd take it myself, but as I said, things are good, and I'm keeping clear of the law in this state.'

'Just tell me where it is and I'll make it worth your while.'

'And what do I get out of it?'

'A one-sixteenth share, fair dinkum and risk free. You don't have to raise a finger.'

'I'm listening,' said the Orphan.

Half an hour later, both men, mounted now, rode into the Hall's Creek township. They steered clear of a prize fight going on between two bloodied and shirtless men before a yelling, betting crowd on the main strip. Leaving the horses tethered to public hitching posts they walked away from the gas-lit area, into the duller alleys of the town's little Chinatown.

Winding their way past smells of Asian cooking and gambling dens, they reached an intersection with an outdoor dance hall and pub on one corner. The two men took a table closest to the street, with the Orphan looking pointedly across at the opposite side.

'There're three types of Celestial on the diggings here,' said the Orphan. 'The Pekinese, Cantonese and a smaller group from Macao. The ones working your claim are from Canton, which is why they wear their hair in a bun and not a pig-tail. That's their Joss House, across the street.'

Tom looked. The diggings-style temple was built of poles, and clad with sawn timber, as substantial a building as most in the town. Chinese letters were painted in red above the open door.

'They bury the gold in the ground under the altar, and a courier takes it up to Wyndham and back to China every three or four weeks.'

'When's the next shipment?' asked Tom.

'Soon. Prob'ly the next few days, but I have to warn you, four or five of their best men sleep in there every night. They're young tong fighters, tough as nails, and they're armed.'

Without any warning, a band consisting of an accordion, a drum and fiddle started up, from near the stage behind the two men. They turned to see a dance act come out onto the stage. One of the dancers was a graceful Aboriginal girl, and the other a grown man no more than four feet tall. He was hamming it up, making a hash of the dance to make the crowd laugh.

From the Joss House across the road, a young Chinese man emerged, then another. Both were square-jawed, athletic types. They laughed at the act, then called for three more of their mates to come and watch, laughing amongst themselves.

'That's them,' said the Orphan in a low voice. 'They like the free entertainment.'

Tom wasn't listening. He was watching how the young Chinese men left the Joss House, moving closer, half way across the alley to get a better view of the act. After the dance was over, they turned and disappeared into the red Chinese lantern light of the interior.

Tom continued to sit, thinking hard, the seed of an idea germinating in his mind.

# Chapter 53: Dear Tom

My Dear Tom

I pray that this letter reaches you in whatever lonely extremity you have reached. I imagine that you are on the run and far from here. Please know that my thoughts and prayers have followed you every step of the way.

Yesterday the strangest thing happened. A woman who looked like her poor old hide had been pegged out in the sun for the last fifty years, pulled up outside my boarding house. She stopped her horse team in the middle of the road, smelling of strong spirits and swearing like a trooper at anyone who complained. She knocked on the door, introducing herself as 'Missus Dead Finish,' and told me that I could write to you by addressing my letters to Aazar the Afghan, care of Hall's Creek Post Office.

Oh Tom, isn't it a crime how happiness was snatched from us! Checking my crab pots is now a lonely task, and every stroke of the oar makes me think of you. It's strange how life twists and turns, and how sometimes the events of the past, that we think are far behind us, creep out of the shadows again to choke the fun out of life.

I pray that you are free, sound in mind and body, and that your circumstances are such that I might soon hope to see you again. For my part, little has changed, apart from three new students, the sons of a teamster, who prefer horseplay and mischief to arithmetic. These young imps are making my days a little harder than before. On the positive side, however, I'm getting much better at swinging a cane!

I won't carry on too much, until I'm sure that this letter has reached you, lest it is really being read by 'Aazar the Afghan' (in which case, hello, but can you please see if you can find my dear Tom and pass this on to him).

Your loving correspondent

Emily Byrne

Dearest Emily

Your letter was a mitey burst of fresh air in this lonely circumstance. Please forgive my little ruse, for I have played the part of an Afghan these last weeks to throw that dog Alfred Searcy off my scent. It seems to have worked, so far, as word lately reached my ears that he has sailed back to his post at Borroloola. Even so, my time here in the diggings will soon be done.

The good news is that it seems that my mates and I have located the gold we worked so hard to unearth. Not exactly in the manner we expected, but we've found it nonetheless. Something tells me that tonight is the night. All the stars seem to be lining themselfs up for great deeds like a string of packhorses in the sky.

At the same time, Larrikin's mare (remember I told you about her) is showing signs of getting ready to drop. It seems that she's having twins, which is rare and dangerous for horses as you would know. It's unlikely that both will survive, but we hope and pray that they might. She is getting very close to her time, and one of the boys is watching her every minute.

If all goes well I will probly hit the road tomorrow, back towards the Territory. If the Almighty smiles down on me in the business of tonight, I'll soon be settled on a cattle run of my own. I first saw it some two year ago and discreet enquiry tells me that it's still available, overlooked by the rich men who lust for holdings much more vast. I, for my part, just want somewhere I can be my own boss and raise cattle the way I wish. I'll take the boy with me, and prob'ly Blind Joe, if he wants to come, along with his women.

It's a block of some two hundred square miles, with its share of poor country, I'll admit. Yet around the winding creek you'll find acre after acre of Mitchell grass flats, glowing yellow in the sunshine. Oh what cattle I'll grow there. Searcy and his vindictive soul will never find me, as I'll register the lease under a different name (not Aazar the Afghan). My first big effort, after a set of solid yards and some fencing, will be to build a homestead fit for a queen.

It will have a cool verandah out the front, paved with slabs of river stone, a kitchen out the back, and spare bedrooms so we can welcome visitors in style. The sitting room will be big enough that we can push the lounge chairs back and hold dances for the nearby station people, maybe the odd race meeting in the Dry. The front yard we'll water from a hole in the creek, growing soft couch grass and shade trees. In time we could hang a swing from a heavy bough. I recall such from my own childhood days, back in Lochinvar, when my mother would push me to and fro.

Every year or two we'll drove a mob of fat store bullocks to Queensland. The cheques will come in and there'll be a spree in Palmerston, with new clothes. Just picture me (and somebody else I fervently do hope) strolling down Cavenagh Street like nobody's business.

When the block is registered in my name, I'll be writing to you again, and there will be heady matters for us to discuss. Yet, it all depends on this night. I've gathered my most loyal mates: Larrikin, Sandy, Wonoka Jack and Fitz. Also I have reckoned on giving Tommy the Rag and Carmody the chance to redeem themselves. This time tomorrow I believe that I will be a man of means, worthy of your hand if I may be so bold as to say so.

Next time you write, please address your letter to Tom Holmes, (a name I have used before, and a good one), care of Tennant Creek Telegraph Station. I'll think of you every mile on that long road back to the Territory, and look forward to the time when we can be together.

Your affectionate rowing companion,

Tom (Aazar the Afghan)

# Chapter 54: The Night they Robbed the Joss House

At four in the afternoon, Tom set his pocket watch to the same time as Sandy Myrtle's and sent the big man into town with Larrikin. Their saddle bags bulged with costumes that had been the subject of much discussion, with some important input from Jake's two girls. Larrikin had his dancing shoes tied by the laces to his saddle dees.

'You're the only man in the world I'd do this for, Tom,' Sandy said.

'I appreciate that,' said Tom. 'For without you two we wouldn't have a hope in hell of pulling this off.'

'I'm just a tad worried about my mare,' said Larrikin. 'Promise me someone will ride for Red Jack if she starts to foal. She's close, her teats are full and she's waxing …'

'That's a promise,' Jack Dalley piped up 'Don't worry about her. The boys an' me will be watching, and Scotty's got his nag saddled up ready – he'll have that red-haired witch here in a jiffy.'

Sandy and Larrikin rode off at a trot, and two hours passed before Tom, Fitz, Wonoka Jack, Carmody, and young Tommy the Rag chased up their steadiest packhorses and their own mounts. They dressed in dark shirts and dungarees, and strapped revolver pouches to their belts. All four of them had scarves ready to tie across their faces; 'Like Dan Kelly and Joe Byrne must've worn before they took to wearin' ironmongery,' as Tommy the Rag put it.

'Now, remember boys, we're not about to shoot anyone,' said Tom. 'We take what's due to us and that's it. Now come on, let's ride.'

They took the journey into Hall's Creek nice and slow, then wound their way down narrow tracks between the claims, keeping their mouths shut and trying not to attract attention.

But by God, thought Tom, it felt good to ride high in the saddle, wearing a good pair of boots, with a weapon at his hip and adrenalin flooding into his system. Sure, he had his Arab garb on top, complete with turban and cloak, but his regular bushman's clobber was underneath. The night was perfect for this kind of work — dark, with air cool as crystal and the stars riding high. The moon was so thin it looked like a snip of fencing wire.

Heading into town, they moved off the main track, cutting through scrub between a couple of worked-out gullies before reaching the alleyway that served as the diggings' Chinatown. Tom led a couple of pack horses. Fitz, Tommy the Rag, Carmody and Wonoka Jack came behind, talking and laughing and passing a bottle like men on a blow-out.

They reached the intersection alongside the Joss House. Tom dismounted, and the others followed suit. The Joss House was in full view, along with the open-air dance theatre across the road, where a noisy crowd occupied the tables, drinking and cat-calling, yelling for the next act to come out.

'We'll wait here,' Tom said. 'Try to look busy.' He set to work checking one of the horses' hoofs, swearing about the damn thing being lame, all for the benefit of anyone watching. After a minute or two he consulted his pocket watch and looked anxiously across at the dance stage. Still, nothing was happening.

'Hurry up, damn you Larrikin,' he muttered, and looked up to see his old mate Jack Martin, the 'Orphan,' pass along the street, giving him a subtle nod that surely meant that the gold was still there. That the 'job' was on. The adrenalin that buzzed inside Tom quickened his heartbeat.

Then, less than a minute after the appointed time, there was a burst of shouting and applause. The music started up, and Larrikin ran onto the stage, twirled once, then started to dance. Tom had forgotten how damn good he was. He started with a tap routine, then free danced in perfect time with the fiddle, accordion and banjo. How on earth a motherless child from the Norman River had learned to dance like that was one of life's mysteries.

The crowd clapped, but Tom was watching the Joss House. Soon, the first of the young tong guards came out the door so he could see the show, and as Larrikin's routine went on, the second emerged. The first called inside and the others joined them. All five were now watching Larrikin dance, but remained fixed against the wall near the door, making entry impossible. Still, Tom knew that it wouldn't be long now, the next part of the act was about to start. That would surely draw them away. He tore the Afghan turban from his head, and removed the cloak. He tied the scarf he had brought over his face, leaving only his eyes free. The others followed his example.

'Come on, Sandy,' Tom said, under his breath. 'Now!'

As if in response to the urging, and with an attention-seeking bellow, Sandy Myrtle, wearing nothing but a tiny skirt, his huge belly and man-breasts open to the crowd, wobbled onto the stage. The audience screamed with delight. How could every eye not be drawn to him? They shouted with delight, laughed until tears ran from their eyes. For Larrikin's every step and twirl, Sandy followed, writhing his hips, shaking his chest. The five tong guards laughed and clapped, moving halfway across the road to get a better view.

'Let's go get it boys,' said Tom, turning to his mates. 'Remember that the Orphan reckoned we'd find it under the altar. We've got a couple of minutes at best.'

Leaving Tommy the Rag in charge of the horses, Tom, Carmody, and Fitz ran around the dark side of the building, then slipped inside like three shadows. Each of them carried a pair of canvas saddle panniers. Carmody had a shovel, and Fitz a short-handled mattock. Wonoka Jack followed, also entering the Joss House, but his only task was to watch the tong guards from just inside the doorway.

The Joss House interior was lit by candles and smelled of incense. The altar was up towards the front, and all three of the men fell to their knees as if to pray, but instead pulled aside a floor covering, revealing the earth below.

Fitz started chipping away with the mattock, the iron head biting deep into the ground, while Carmody used the shovel to scoop away the spoil and chuck it willy nilly back on the temple floor.

They had penetrated only eight or ten inches when the mattock struck wood with a hollow thump.

'That's it,' hissed Tom.

They went at it with their hands, revealing the lid of a wooden crate. Tom took a grip at one end, and Carmody the other. Fitz also found purchase, and the three of them lifted it out.

'Bloody Christ it's heavy,' hissed Tom. His entire body was sweating, hands slick with clammy dust. Carmody slipped the shovel blade between the lid and body of the box, opening it to the accompaniment of a soft splinter of wood.

There was a groan from Fitz at the contents: calico bags of gold dust, soft and heavy as a policeman's cosh.

'Leave them,' whispered Tom. 'The dust isn't ours, but these damn lumps of gold … by rights they belong to us.' His fingers found them before his eyes. They were stored in larger bags, heavy and irregular. 'Hurry boys, they'll be getting weary of

Sandy in a minute ... and he'll be getting weary of them.'

They tore open the canvas panniers, and shoved gold in, trying to keep a balance as best they could. Now there was only the sound of three breathing men and the occasional hiss of a candle. They blocked out the laughter and music from outside, concentrating on the work of taking the gold.

'Hurry you bastards,' hissed Wonoka Jack from his post near the doorway. 'I think they're about to come back.'

Tom scrabbled in the box one last time. 'We've got it all, lads. Let's fly.' He was last out the door, bolting past the guards, who had mercifully turned to watch the show again. He and the others worked with nervous fingers to strap the heavy panniers to the pack horses. Then came the first shout of alarm. He turned to see the Chinese guards running into the Joss House, exclaiming loudly, audible even over the sound of music.

On the other side of the road, one of the hecklers had pushed Sandy Myrtle too far. Red in the face, the big man was shouting down at a bloke sitting at a table near the stage, brandishing a giant fist, threatening to punch his 'stupid head off his shoulders.'

'Go, now lads,' shouted Tom, swinging onto his horse. He turned to see one of the guards emerge from the Joss House, stopping to aim and fire a revolver. Being in front of the blast, the discharge was beyond loud, and the weapon flashed a tongue of flame. As for where the bullet landed Tom had no idea. When next he looked, the five tong guards were in hot pursuit, and other Chinese were melting out of shopfronts and alleys up ahead, forming what seemed to be an impenetrable barrier.

The gang were mounted, however, and they charged for the end of the alley, scattering men, dogs, and a donkey that had come from nowhere. More commotion came from behind, and Tom turned to see that it was the half-naked Sandy, just ahead of Larrikin, galloping hell-for-leather to join them.

There were more gunshots, but so much dust was being

raised, and the column was charging down so fast, that they must have had little hope of a target.

'Stay with me,' cried Tom, setting his sights on the gully across the road. Once they were into the scrub, he would back these ragged mates of his against anybody.

# Chapter 55: A Tale of Two Foals

An hour before midnight, Scotty rode off to fetch Red Jack. By the time he returned with her, Larrikin's mare was agitated and sweating, milk seeping from her teats. The red-haired woman washed her hands and examined her.

'They're sitting well, I reckon,' she said, 'and the contractions are strong. Let's see if we can bring the poor things out alive. You blokes could make a bed of dry grass for when she wants to lay down, and someone please fetch another lantern or two.'

In a flurry of activity, the members of the Ragged Thirteen who weren't out on the raid, cut dry grass from around the gully, and packed it down to make a bed. When it was done, Red Jack wrapped the strands of the mare's tail with clean rags, to keep it out of the way. She was already opening up, and out came a steady trickle of fluid.

'Right boys, her waters are breaking,' said Red Jack. 'Our girl means business. This a special thing, I hope you fellas know, for a horse or a woman doesn't make any difference.' Then, 'Where's that damned Larrikin, why would he have gone out when his mare was about to drop her foal?' Jack Woods was about to answer, but she turned and glared at him. 'Actually, given that half the camp is missing, I don't want to know.'

Red Jack gentled the already tiring mare down, legs splayed out at first, though she constantly altered position in an attempt to ease the spasms. The whole crew, black and white, settled down to watch, helping where they could. There was nothing they wanted more than to see this end well. Out in the darkness, the other horses were vocal and agitated, as if they knew what was happening, talking to the mare with their whinnies and nickers.

'Wouldna' be grand if auld Tom an' Larrikin were back fer this moment eh,' said Bob Anderson. 'No doubt it's been a long time comin'.'

The mare turned herself upright, still on the ground, with her legs folded under her. There was another rush of brown fluid, then a bubble of clear tissue appeared, followed by a foot. The mare was pushing in waves, with a heavy grunt each time. A second foot appeared, then stopped and seemed to come no further, pulsing in and out with each spasm of the mare's great muscles.

'I have to hurry things up,' said Red Jack. 'It's taking too long.'

And while she kneeled behind the mare, delving inside, adding her own grunts of effort to those of the mare, there was the sound of rushing hooves. Into camp rode Tom, and five of the others, pack horses following. They pulled the horses up, with Blind Joe and a couple of the boys running to grasp bridles and steady them down.

Tom and Larrikin led the way in on foot. Seeing what was happening, they said nothing, made no fuss. Just gathered around to watch wordlessly. One or two of the others clapped them on the shoulders gently to mark their return.

Even the horses out there in the darkness fell silent as Red Jack used her hands to assist. The two feet were soon followed by two long legs, a snout, then an immense bag of tissue and fluid, squeezing out in a rush. Even as they watched, that shapeless thing in the lantern light became a living foal, struggling onto his sternum and wriggling his way free of the sack that had contained him, breathing air on his own account.

'Chestnut,' opined Bob Anderson.

'Sorrel maybe,' said George Brown. 'But it's hard to tell just yet.'

Red Jack was still at work, her hands again delving inside the mare, gently aiding, smoothing the way, and pulling a little where she could. The second bag was smaller than the first, erupting out from the mare, falling shapelessly on the straw. That second foal lay uncommonly still.

'Of all the rotten luck,' cried Red Jack 'The little one ain't breathing.'

Men who had not prayed in twenty years were fumbling for long-forgotten words, calling for the bright stars above to be their witness as they swore to be better men if only God would spare that helpless little creature.

Red Jack's face was lined with worry as she broke the sack herself and manipulated the foal's head to drain the fluid, stroking and shaking in an effort to clear its windpipe and nasal passages. Then, in a moment that no one there would ever forget, Red Jack closed the left nostril of that undersized bundle with her left thumb and forefinger, and gently breathed into the other.

Most of them had seen this done before, but not in such a way. With the healthier twin already trying to wriggle towards his dam, the sight of the red-haired woman blowing life into the second tiny animal was almost mystical. The magic happened. They all saw the little foal jerk her hind leg. Red Jack laid her down. It was obvious to all that the little foal was breathing now, kicking at the tissue that still constrained her lower limbs.

Red Jack turned, face shining in the lantern light. 'It worked. My blessed soul it worked. The poor little mite is breathing.

They are both alive … this one's on the small side, but bloody perfect.'

The second foal was a patchwork of black, brown and white, a combination known as skewbald, her dark eyes taking in everything around her for the first time as she broke free of the last of the sack that had surrounded her for so many months.

Larrikin went up close on his hands and knees, like a man in a trance, tears spilling down his cheek. Some of the others might have wondered what this moment meant for a man who'd never known a mother or father.

The mare was resting, but turning weakly, summoning the energy to bring out the placenta, but trying to look at her twins at the same time.

'Bless me if those two aren't the most beautiful things I've ever seen,' said Tom. No one there could have disagreed.

Within a quarter hour the stronger of the two foals was trying to stand, falling comically over in his eagerness. The men laughed and tut-tutted and tried to think up names for them both. The smaller foal took almost an hour to find her feet, but once she was up she was even steadier than her twin. Long before dawn, both were able to find a teat, and the rum bottle was being passed from man to man.

Red Jack refused. 'I don't need it. I've had my fill of something better tonight.'

'You sure have,' said Larrikin. 'I know these two foals are yours now. But I count myself a lucky man just to have seen what you done tonight, and I'll go to my grave thankful for it.'

Now that the foals were out of danger Tom called the gang together. 'Forget sleep. Roll your swags and get ready to leave. We've got every Cantonese for twenty miles around on our tails. They won't follow us out here tonight, it's too dark, but they'll have a tracker on our trail by dawn.'

# Chapter 56: The Break-up

With dawn not far off, Tom sent Blind Joe on a good night horse to a peak about a mile away, to watch for any signs of pursuit. Then, while camp was struck, horses saddled and packs loaded, Tom and Larrikin divided the gold into sixteen fair parcels.

Jack Martin, 'The Orphan,' rode in for his share, whooping with delight when he saw the glint of gold. 'You blokes,' he warned, 'aren't out of this yet. You've got those tongs stirred up and no mistake, and they're mobilising every Celestial for miles around.'

'Thanks for the advice,' said Tom. 'And good luck to you.' The Orphan rode off into the night, whistling a tune as he went.

Within the hour, the eastern half of the sky was saffron yellow, and the birds chattering and singing in the scrub. The men were ready, their mounts saddled and packed. One by one they took their gold and stowed it deep in saddle bags or rolled into swags.

Only Red Jack refused her portion. 'I've got these two foals, they're worth more than gold. Dole it out between the rest of them.'

And as if they knew that words needed to be said before

they rode off, the Ragged Thirteen, along with Jake and his sisters, formed up in a rough circle, shuffling feet and smoking pipes.

'Well I suppose this is the break-up,' Tom said. 'It's been an honour and privilege to be mates with you bastards.'

They didn't know what to do, so they clapped and hollered, all aware that this was the end of something special. When the cheering stopped they formed a rough line to take their leave of Tom, one by one.

Sandy Myrtle was first, huge and humble. Touched with the sadness of the moment. 'I'm proud to have ridden with you, mate.'

Tom took a massive fist in his own. 'Likewise, Sandy. Where are you headed?'

'Back to the Centre. Little place called Arltunga.' He waved one arm at Jimmy Woodford, who was standing lankily beside him. 'Jimmy's riding with me.'

'Good luck with the mining then. I thought you'd have had enough?'

Sandy shook his head. 'No more grubbin' for gold for this feller. You're looking at a storekeeper from here on.'

'You too, Jimmy?' asked Tom.

'Nah, I'm not the storekeeper type. I'll find somefin' to do.'

'Good on you both,' said Tom. 'And all the luck in the world.'

Scotty came next, big and handsome, his hat in his hands. 'Guidbye, Tom. An' may fortune foller yew around, all yer days.'

'I'll miss your cookin', mate,' said Tom. 'You're a born cook. Are you going to stick with Red Jack?'

'I will, fer a bit. She'll 'ave to tarry while t'ose little neddies grow a tad, but then she swears she must ride alone. Most likely I'll be there 'til Larrikin rides back fer his mare.'

'Well,' said Tom. 'She's a force of nature, that woman. There aren't no point arguin' with her.'

Young Jake was waiting for his turn, shaking Tom's hand

like a grown man. 'I can't thank you enough Tom. Me and the girls'll head for Broome now. I hear they've found some pearling grounds, and the bay's alive with luggers. Thanks to you, I've got enough of a stake to set up as a chandler.'

'You've thought about this, haven't you?'

'I have – and I've an uncle down in Perth who's in that line of work and can be me supplier. I've already written to him.'

Carmody and Jack Dalley, along with Wonoka Jack and his brother George, were planning on riding together as far as the Katherine. 'At least I can hold my head high, having redeemed meself,' said Carmody. 'And I've you to thank for that, Tom.'

'You're alright Carmody. There'll always be a place at my fire for you – as long as you don't bring that damned brother-in-law of yours – Maori Jack.'

They both laughed fit to bust, but when Carmody went off to finish readying his horse, he turned quickly away so the others didn't see the tear in his eye.

'And you two?' Tom asked of the Brown brothers.

'Dunno,' said George. 'Hopefully we'll pick up some work on the Katherine.'

'But we'll never forget these days,' added Jack.

Bob Anderson came next. His lips were turned down at the corners. 'I lairned it all from you, Tom, best of all how to love this country. Now, I want acres of me own – and we passed some braw lands, on the Queensland side a' the Territory.'

'We'll compare notes one day,' said Tom. 'When we're genteel old farts on some verandah, getting drunk an' telling bullshit.' He caught sight of Tommy the Rag, who was the only one really crying, tears streaming down his face. 'Hey Tommy, are you going to come over here and shake me hand or not?'

The young feller, with his stockwhip looped around his shoulders ready to ride, wiped his face, walked over and shook hands.

'Cheer up Tommy,' said Tom. 'It's not the end of the world.

Plenty of places to see, and things to do.'

Tommy shrugged his shoulders. 'All alone it don't seem like any fun. Can't we all just split up then meet up again, some-where?'

'Sorry mate, but one of the tricks of life it to know when to start things, and when to finish them. We've had a good run, but it's time for the next round.'

'You can ride with me, Tommy,' said New England Jack. 'I've only seen a bit of Western Australia so far. I hear tell of more goldfields.' He grinned wickedly. 'There'll be cattle to steal and beef to sell – all the fun we can handle.'

Tommy smiled through a new batch of tears. 'Thanks mate. I'll ride with you happily, for as long as you'll have me.'

Larrikin and Fitz were planning on sticking together, and both seemed energised. 'We're thinking that we might ride for a few days,' said Larrikin, 'then find a likely looking station … maybe Rosewood or Nicholson. We'll work cattle by day and piss it up against a wall at night.'

'Larrikin doesn't want to go too far away,' added Fitz. 'He'll come back for his mare when the foals are weaned.'

'Makes sense,' said Tom. 'Might have some stock work for you meself, one day, if all goes to plan.'

The sun arrived over the horizon, sending sharp rays of light on the deep red ground. A crow cawed from a nearby tree.

Red Jack and Scotty left first, carrying each of the two foals over their saddles, for they were too small to walk any distance. Tom wanted to make sure that they had a good start, and re-solved to give them at least an hour.

'Let's slip the bottle round one last time, before we go,' called Tom, and they passed the rum from hand to hand. The last dram slid down Carmody's throat, just as Blind Joe rode in at the gallop. It was rare to see him rattled, but his eyes were wide.

He didn't have to say a thing. They all heard a sound, more like roar. A hundred, maybe two hundred Cantonese on the march. They came over the rise some half a mile away, carrying shovels, and pick axes, even one or two shotguns.

'Looks like it's time to go,' said Tom.

'What if they catch us?' said little Ellen, mounted on her pony next to Jake.

'Catch us?' laughed Tom. 'Why with us mounted, and them afoot? We might be going our separate ways, but we're still the damned Ragged Thirteen, from now until the day we die. Farewell, good mates,' he called, and one by one they touched spurs to their horses' flanks, and rode away.

# Chapter 57: Banka Banka

On the long ride to the Territory border, Tom Nugent had plenty of time to think. After months of hard labour on the goldfields, and those life-changing months in Wyndham as a prisoner and free man, it felt good to be back in the saddle, riding past red cliffs, dramatic river gorges, and plains of waving speargrass taller than the horses.

Tom did not ride alone. A little way ahead rode Blind Joe, and behind him, Joe's two women and one picaninny, all on the one horse. The boy from Borroloola was old enough to ride on his own now.

Tom liked it when the boy rode alongside and asked questions like, where did the clouds come from? Why did the trees know how to grow the right way up? Where did the Queen live? He was a sturdy kid, and bright as a pin.

When they reached the Territory border Tom set up camp, then led the boy down to the banks of the Negri. 'It's time, and past time, that I gave you a name,' he said.

'I already got a name.'

'You need a whitefeller name. I want you to grow up with some learnin' and able to fit in where you have to. I'm fixing things to have some land of my own, and you'll be a part of it too.' Tom reached down to where the clear water ran in a glassy sheet over the stones. He lifted a handful, and smoothed it onto the child's hair.

'This aren't a proper, churchy kind of christenin', but from now on,' Tom said, glancing at Blind Joe and his women. 'This young fellow will be called George. Not just that, but I'm changing names too.' He pointed to the east. 'As soon as I cross the Territory border I'm no longer Tom Nugent, but Tom Holmes. That should keep those wallopers off my tracks for a while.'

Blind Joe thought that Tom putting water on the boy's head was a great joke, and laughed until his wives led him back to the campfire.

Tom's traverse of the Murranji Track was easier than it had been for Searcy and O'Donohue, for the endless thickets of bullwaddy and lancewood held no fears for him. On the third day they found a 'dropped' bullock. Tom brought it down with one shot from his Snider rifle, and the five of them ate beef until they could hardly move, drying the rest over a smoky fire, with the dingos prowling out in the darkness, waiting for the bones.

At the Tennant Creek Telegraph Station, Tom refused to tarry, but turned his little party north. He had a map, deep in his saddlebags, and consulted it, along with a compass. After half a day's ride, the frenetic pace slowed, and Tom began to look with interest at every tree, every gully, and particularly the creeks and part-dried lagoons.

He took careful note of the location of every field of Mitchell and Flinders grass, each stand of cypress, of proud woollybutts or salmon gum, and every hillside soak. They camped at broad waterholes, and at dusk Tom took out an old catgut line. He used a hook baited with dried beef or frogs to bring in catfish and black bream.

They saw bare footprints here and there, and plenty of old cooking fires or abandoned wurlies around the waterholes, but no people. Not yet. Tom looked with interest. He was not a rich man, who could afford to push the people who belonged here out, and bring in his own white workforce. He'd need goodwill to get the locals on board with his pastoral enterprise, and he knew well that the Australian Aborigine was the world's best natural stockman.

'This good country,' said Blind Joe, picking the last morsels from a catfish skeleton, still with ash from the fire clinging to its head and tail.

Finally, three days after they arrived in the area. Tom selected a flat and dry section with access to the creek, and good pasture for horses. It was close to the main north-south track, and central to other sections of the run. There wasn't much water, but enough for horses, household necessities, and a vegetable garden.

'This is it,' he told his little band. 'This here is where we stop, and make new lives.'

Blind Joe thought it was funny how Tom spent the rest of the afternoon pacing out little squares, here and there, back and forth. 'That's the sittin' room,' Tom announced, 'big enough for a regular party. And here will be the kitchen, right at the back of the house, made of good stone from that hillock yonder.'

'What you goin' call this place, boss?' asked Blind Joe.

'I'm going to call it Banka Banka,' Tom said, after the little creek that wound around below the homestead site.

Tom left his new family in camp, and rode like the wind to Palmerston. He was careful of being spotted, even by old friends; camping alone, out of town, keeping his hat low, and crossing the road if he saw a policeman.

First he called on one of the less reputable gold dealers. Then, a wad of cash in his pocket, he visited the Government Lands Office, where he paid a filing fee, and the first five years' lease, registering the block as Banka Banka Station in the name of Tom Holmes.

The next morning, before leaving town, he stopped to write a letter, scarcely able to contain his excitement.

Dear Miss Byrne

Sorry for the long passage of time since I last wrote, but towns and post offices have been scarce as chicken's teeth for a while. My lack of words don't speak for any lack of good wishes.

There's big news. I've done it, anyway. A place of me own, all legal and registered in my name. (Well, pretty close to my own name, anyhow). It's called Banka Banka Station. It's dry country, but with dams built, and yards, it'll carry more than enough stock to keep me busy, and bring in some money.

I'm riding back today with three new packhorses and enough nails to start bilding you the homestead you can be proud of. I'm hoping you will come and marry me and share this life. Please answer back with your thorts.

Yours Afectionatly

Tom

Back at Banka Banka, Tom laboured like a dog on the homestead. He built a saw pit, enticing a couple of muscled local Warlpiri lads, who came in looking for flour and tobacco, to work for him. As he suspected, they stayed only a week or two, but that was enough to get a pile of timber sawn. Tom laid termite mound floors, and compacted them 'til they were as hard as granite. He waited a month, then rode to the Telegraph Station looking for mail. There was nothing. He wrote again, and posted it before he left.

Dear Miss Byrne

I guess my last letter must not have reached you. I enclose twenty pounds in cash for you to take the steamer over if you'll please say you'll marry me. The Banka Banka homestead ain't too much yet, but it'll be a mansion by the time I'm done. It's a sight, for sure.

I started out with no cattle at all, but a few hundred cleanskins have mysteriously appeared, and now carry my brand. There's wealth for men with the strength to build it, in this country.

Please write back, soon if you can. Better still come along yourself.

Tom

Tom rode into the Telegraph Station to post the new letter, then hurried back to the half-finished homestead.

## Chapter 58. Epilogue

What happened to these legends? These larrikins who rode, robbed and drank rum together? Many of the facts have been lost, but these, as far as can be ascertained, from historical records, grave sites, and information from family members, were the fates of the Ragged Thirteen.

Alexander McDonald, better known as Sandy Myrtle, rode back to Central Australia, where a new rush, first for gemstones, then gold, was underway at Arltunga, fifty miles east of the town of Stuart, now Alice Springs. He built a pub there, amongst the ghost gums and spinifex. He called it the Glencoe Arms. This was a life Sandy enjoyed, plenty of rum and company, sitting on a stool up behind the bar, pouring beers and yarning with travellers and diggers. Fighters and troublemakers found themselves out on the street, and few dared argue. By then Sandy weighed twenty-eight stone in his boots.

Legend has it that he got so fat, his workers had to lift him up into a buggy when he went to visit a station he part-owned, out in the scrub.

A young Arrernte woman called Korulya used to do odd jobs around the pub, and Sandy allowed her to sit inside out of the heat. Slowly he fell in love with her. When their daughter came along they called her Myrtle, after Sandy's nickname, and the station he had managed back in his youth.

Late in life Sandy was cared for by his sister, Annie, in South Australia. He died at Miss Lawrence's Private Hospital in Adelaide, on the 4th of May, 1919.

Jimmy Woodford rode with Sandy back to the Red Centre. For many years he earned beer and tucker money collecting meteorites and selling them. Later, it seems, he ended up in Queensland, but the trail goes cold after that.

Bob Anderson, the man who, according to family lore, the Ragged Thirteen called the 'foot runner,' arrived in Normanton, Queensland, where he purchased a bullock team. He learned his trade the hard way, carrying stores between Croydon, Georgetown and Cloncurry, while he looked around for options. He married at around this time, and fathered sixteen children, not all of whom lived to adulthood.

Seizing an opportunity, Bob set up Tobeymorey Station, on the Territory/Queensland border. He also ran the Urandangi Store in the early 1900s. He was killed in a fall from his horse on the 19th of January, 1923. A memorial stands on the site where his body was found, though his grave is at the Urandangi cemetery. Bob left hundreds of descendants, many of them hard bush characters who helped forge the Queensland and NT pastoral industries.

'Larrikin' and 'Fitz' went back to stock work, droving and ringing across Northern Australia. They most likely lie in remote graves, lovingly made by their mates on the track. There are thousands of graves like this; men (and women too), buried far from loved ones, hospitals and proper fenced graveyards. Many have rotted away or sunk into the red sands or black soils of the inland.

Jack Dalley settled near Cloncurry, droving when the mood took him. His sons were all drovers, and served in World War One with distinction. He was knocked over by a car in the late

1920s, in Ramsay Street, Cloncurry, but recovered quickly. He was over seventy when he died.

'Wonoka' Jack and George Brown found work at Katherine, sawing timber in a pit, for hotelier Barney Murphy. When this work was finished they headed for a new goldfield not far from the town, out on Maude Creek. Jack grew ill, possibly from a condition related to tapeworms, and was forced to return to South Australia, where he died.

Jim Carmody, was also at the Katherine, and it was the river itself that was his undoing. After a long bout of fever, he went fishing one morning in 1889, and failed to return. His body was retrieved from the water a few hours later. Some theories ran that he fell in, became entangled in his own catgut line, and drowned. Others supposed that he had been seized by a cramp while sitting on a log over the water.

Maori Jack Reid ran a hotel with Henrietta in Marble Bar, worked as a carrier and tried his hand at mining, while selling grog on the sly. He died on the island of St. Aignan, in June 1907.

Red Jack rode off without Hugh Campbell, the man they called Scotty, as soon as her twin foals were old enough to do the hard miles. Scotty wandered for a while, looking for Red Jack, but she was always a step ahead; not just a myth, but an obsession. He cooked on Flora Valley Station for a while, but later became very ill, with a condition that stopped him from sweating. He headed back home to Scotland, where he died, still a young man.

'New England' Jack Woods continued to follow the gold, and butcher stolen beef. Tommy the Rag was presumably his partner for at least some of his adventures. This 1936 article in the Western Mail describes Jack's movements:

> From there (Hall's Creek) Jack followed all the rushes through the Nor'-West: Murchison, Coolgardie and outlying fields. There was frequently a strong suspicion

*as to the source of his meat supply, but nothing wrong
was ever proved against him. He was a true bush law-
yer, and openly boasted that he preferred a crooked deal
to a straight one. There was more thrill, he said, in the
former. But money was only a medium to get drink –
which was his great weakness.*

Jack Woods eventually returned to New England, and lived out the rest of his days with family. Of Tommy the Rag I can find no record.

Alfred Searcy found the strain of policing larrikins like the Ragged Thirteen, and the genuine lawlessness of the north, too much for his health, and he returned to Adelaide in 1890. He was unemployed for six years, then took over his brother's job as a clerk with the South Australian parliament. He wrote several books; some fact, some fiction, that still make good reading today. He never mentioned being out-smarted by the Ragged Thirteen. He did, however, relate the time that he and O'Donohue had marched some of the gang into Roper Bar station. He also grumbled that some ruffians had chased off their horses on the way into Borroloola.

And what about Tom Nugent?

No letter from Emily Byrne ever came, yet he would not be alone for long. On a cattle drive he met Alice Nampin, a Garrwa woman who would be his companion for the rest of his life. They had at least two children, Maudie and Mysie.

Even today, prejudice runs deep, but despite a history lit-tered with unforgivable instances of kidnap, slavery and rape, there were also many loving, long-lived relationships between white and black that stood the test the time, and left children who were strong, proud, and resilient. The offspring of such couples were not so often taken by authorities – they lived in rough bush homesteads with their white fathers and Indigenous mothers. Many grew up on horseback, working cattle, and were the backbone of the NT pastoral industry for four generations.

The little boy from Borroloola, George, was a natural rider and stockman. In the early 1900s, Tom was able to expand, purchasing Buchanan Downs Station. In an admirable show of trust, for the time, it was managed by George for many years. Surely he was one of the earliest Aboriginal managers of a cattle station. As Tom explained in a 1907 interview with the Australian Star newspaper:

> In 1884 I came across a tiny little black toddler, just able to crawl on all fours. He was a few months old, and had apparently been lost. When I came across him he was making for a waterhole. I took him home and reared him on mare's milk, and he is the man now in charge of Buchanan Downs.

In 1900, Jack Woods came to visit, and stayed for a few months. According to Bill Linklater, who left the most accurate account of the Ragged Thirteen, and was working on Banka Banka at the time, if anyone talked about the old Ragged Thirteen days, Tom would say, 'Why bring that up? It's ancient history.'

Life on Banka Banka Station, meantime, was good. In the same article as the above, Tom goes on to say:

> We have a piano at Banka Banka but (with a smile) we have no one to play it. We have a gramophone too, and of course we are all good at playing that. There is hardly a thing a man could wish for that is not there. We've got all the meat we want; I grow plenty of vegetables, while fish, such as the black bream and jewey abound in the fresh water. Other necessaries we get from Port Darwin, 700 miles away. We send to Anthony Horderns for clothing and boots.

Down on Banka Banka Creek, there was a waterhole where Tom liked to sit in the evenings and read. In his last days he liked poems that stirred up memories of his youth best of all. Will Ogilvie was his favourite wordsmith, and Tom would sip from his rum bottle, read a line or two and savour it while he watched the red sun glow red and the rainbow bee-eaters flick their wings over the water.

In 1911, however, Tom grew sick from dropsy (oedema), and he died on the seventh of August of that year at the Tennant Creek Telegraph Station. He was sixty-three. His grave still stands there today, in the scrub nearby.

Of all the pioneering Australians I've researched, I like Tom, the 'captain' of the Ragged Thirteen the most. He had his own code, and it wasn't the same as ours, but he was loyal, wise, funny and strong. He was a better man than most of those who looked down on him and the wild, special life he led.

Finally, what happened to Red Jack?

She rode on, from town to town, with her black stallion Mephistopheles, her string of horses and her memories. No one understood her, no one could contain her. As far as I know she rode and broke horses until she grew too old and frail to stay in the saddle.

We'll let the story rest there.

# Author's Note

I'd like to thank all the readers on Stories of Oz who shared the experience of creating this novel, by reading and commenting on the weekly instalments. Your encouragement and enthusiasm meant a lot to me.

I particularly enjoyed making contact with descendants of some of the Thirteen, notably those of Tom Nugent and Bob Anderson. Thanks for your oral history stories, and assistance with family trees. I appreciate your tolerance for any errors in my attempt to bring your forebears to life.

My factual sources for the story were many, including Birth, Death and Marriage records, along with newspaper clippings from that fabulous online resource, Trove. *A True Account of the Ragged Thirteen*, a handwritten manuscript by William Linklater, held by the NT Library, was my most important source, followed by *The Ragged Thirteen* by Judy Robinson. Ernestine Hill wrote several articles on the Ragged Thirteen. They were based heavily on Linklater's recollections, but were useful nonetheless. Alfred Searcy's books, particularly *By Flood and Field* were invaluable sources.

Red Jack and the Ragged Thirteen were real people, but their stories remain cloaked in myth. Few of their contemporaries could agree on the names of the lesser members of the gang, let alone exactly what happened. The main elements of this story were once told around camp fires across the north in the great tradition of the Aussie yarn. Facts were embellished and altered along the way.

I'd like to say a word or two about the depiction of Indigenous characters in this story. They played a much bigger part than I portrayed here. Most of the Thirteen had relationships with Aboriginal women. Few records remain; in most cases not even names. I would have liked to delve deeper, but there was no information, and I did not feel that these were my stories to tell.

I avoided using the more racist terms in currency at the time, though the Thirteen would almost certainly have used some of the more bigoted words. For anything that remains in the text that might be considered offensive, I apologise.

Thanks to the unflagging support of my father, Robert Barron, who makes the Stories of Oz venture possible. And to my wife Catriona, and sons Daly and James, your contribution is more important than you know. To the rest of my family, friends, author friends, online friends, and every reader who has ever taken a chance on one of my stories, thanks so much; you are appreciated.

Greg Barron
Eungai Creek
June 2019

More *from the same*
author at:
ozbookstore.com

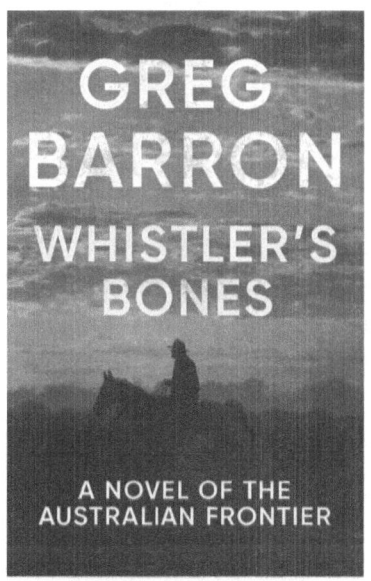

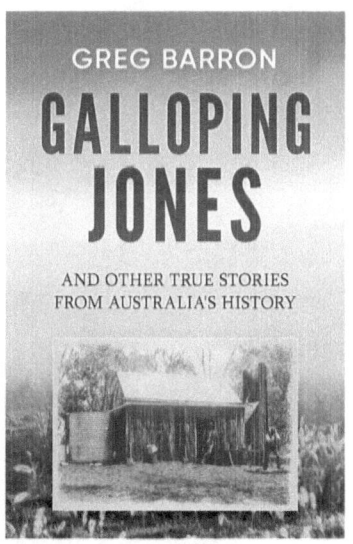

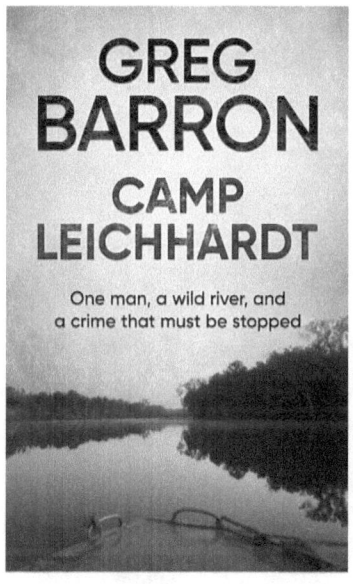

www.ingramcontent.com/pod-product-compliance
Lightning Source LLC
Chambersburg PA
CBHW030630110726
47901CB00002B/394